The Children of Sisyphus

Orlando Patterson

with an introduction by Victor Chang
University of the West Indies

Longman

Longman Group UK Limited
Longman House, Burnt Mill, Harlow,
Essex CM20 2JE, England
and Associated Companies throughout the World

First published by Hutchinson New Authors Limited 1964
First published in Longman Drumbeat 1982
First published in Longman Caribbean Writers 1986
Reprinted 1989

Produced by Longman Group (FE) Ltd
Printed in Hong Kong

ISBN 0-582-78571-5

To Mother and Jeanne

'I said that the world was absurd but I was too hasty. This world in itself is not reasonable, that is all that can be said. But what is absurd is the confrontation of the irrational and the wild longing for clarity whose call echoes in the human heart. The absurd depends as much on man as on the world. For the moment it is all that links them together. It binds them one to the other as only hatred can weld two creatures together. This is all I can discern clearly in this measureless universe where my adventure takes place.'

from *The Myth of Sisyphus* by Albert Camus
(Hamish Hamilton, London, 1955)

'And the daughter of Zion is left as a cottage in a vineyard, as a lodge in a garden of cucumbers, as a besieged city . . .

'Come down and sit in the dust, O virgin daughter of Babylon, sit on the ground; there is no throne, O daughter of the Chaldeans: for thou shalt no more be called tender and delicate . . .'

Isaiah, Ch. 1 and 47

Introduction

About the author
HORACE Orlando Patterson was born on 5 June 1940, not far from Frome in Westmoreland, Jamaica, but left there at age two, going with his mother briefly to Falmouth, then to Kingston where they lived until he was about five. After this his mother again moved, this time to Lionel Town in Clarendon, and a year and a half later to May Pen where he attended elementary school until he left for Kingston College (high school) in January 1953.

At Kingston College Patterson was part of an experimental accelerated programme so that he was sitting the Higher Schools' Certificate examinations (now Advanced GCE) by 1958, doing so well in the examinations as a whole — and particularly in History which was his first love — that he narrowly missed being awarded the Jamaica Centenary Scholarship for boys that year, winning instead a Jamaica Government Exhibition to the University of the West Indies. He taught briefly at Excelsior High School before entering the university in October of 1959, fully intending to read History. He was directed instead by the university into the newly-formed Faculty of Social Sciences to read for the Bachelor's degree in Economics, though he became more involved with Sociology in his second year.

He graduated in June 1962 and went to do his Ph.D at the London School of Economics on a Commonwealth Scholarship. In his first year there, he completed and revised the novel that was to become *The Children of Sisyphus*. It was published in April 1964 and after this he concentrated on his academic work, as well as writing several articles and papers for the New Left Review on whose editorial board he sat. He finished his dissertation in 1965 on the Sociology of Slavery — later to be a book — working simultaneously on a second novel, *An Absence of Ruins*. Both books were to be published in 1967 within weeks of each other. In 1965 after the completion of the dissertation, he was offered an appointment to the Faculty of the London School of Economics.

In 1965 Patterson married Nerys Wyn Thomas, and briefly visited Jamaica in 1966, deciding to return in 1967 to the Mona campus of the University of the West Indies to teach. He left after two and a half years because of 'the political situation,' because he found it difficult to write in Jamaica and because the intellectual ferment which had existed for a little while in 1966 was dissipating. He accepted a position at Harvard University where he is currently Professor of Sociology.

The author of several academic books which are standard reading in the field, such as *The Sociology of Slavery: An Analysis of the Origins, Development and Structure of Negro Slave Society in Jamaica* (1967), *Slavery and Social Death: A Comparative Study* (1982), described as 'a major and important work . . . among the landmarks in the study of slavery,' Patterson has so far published three novels: *The Children of Sisyphus* (1964), *An Absence of Ruins* (1967), and *Die the Long Day* (1972). For him his academic work and his fiction are equally important and he plans to devote more time to fiction as he gets older because 'it's the sort of thing one gets better at . . . as you grow older.' In the same interview with Mervyn Morris in July 1980, Patterson revealed that he had completed a fourth novel which he was revising and was a third of the way through a fifth novel. For the moment, however, *Children of Sisyphus* is considered his most successful novel.

Background

In many ways, Patterson's early background and upbringing prepared him for the writing of his first novel. At elementary school, he read 'voraciously' and he recalls vividly how excited he was the first day the Jamaica Library Service opened a branch in May Pen, and what an extraordinary and thrilling experience it was to borrow books. Frequently he was the only reader there, borrowing mainly novels.

He started writing short stories while he was at Kingston College, mainly for *The Daily Gleaner* and *The Star* newspapers, 'short whodunits with surprise endings' for which he was paid up to two guineas. At university, he continued writing short stories, joined the Scribblers' Group and was President of the Literary Society. At this time he also wrote a radio play 'The Do-Good Woman' which was broadcast by the Jamaica Broadcasting Corporation, and it was someone at the JBC who told him that they were interested in adaptations. While the genesis and creation of any work of art is a complex one, we can, in Patterson's case, trace at least three major strands woven into his first novel. The first of these came from an adaptation of a bible story about a woman who was a prostitute. This idea was dropped but then he thought about the situation applied to a Jamaican urban working class woman. In the middle of his second year of university, he started the draft chapters of *Children of Sisyphus*.

A second impulse came from Patterson's own, and the University's, interest in the Rastafarians which resulted in the publication in 1960 of *The Rastafarian Movement in Kingston, Jamaica* by Smith, Augier and Nettleford which recommended, among other things, that 'the Government of Jamaica sends a mission to African countries to arrange for immigration of Jamaicans;' that 'preparations for the mission should be discussed immediately with representatives of the Ras Tafari brethren;' that 'the general public should recognise that the great majority of Ras Tafari brethren are peaceful citizens, and that the police should cease to persecute Ras Tafari brethren.' (p.38) Patterson knew West Kingston very well having lived for about a year in Jones Town in his last year of high school. Towards the end of his second year of university, too, his interest in Sociology led him to visit Back-O-Wall to talk to the Rastafarians. Also, the summer after his graduation, he worked as a research assistant, studying prostitution and recreational patterns of the working class. In his own words, 'I was all over the red-light district and western Kingston.'

A third strand of influence in the novel was supplied by Patterson's eclectic reading. He had started reading a lot of philosophy from his Kingston College days, discovered Camus while browsing in the library, and became very interested in him and the *Myth of Sisyphus*. He read it, he says, obsessively 'over and over, almost like a bible' so that he knew whole chunks of it by heart. Thus, the idea of the dungle being symbolic of a kind of Sisyphean concept, ie. that the common man's struggle to better himself is hopeless and futile, became a central metaphor in his book. Patterson says he never started to consciously write about the Sisyphean experience, using West Kingston as a setting. Still, his interest in the plight of the poor and his refusal to see them as an undifferentiated mass but rather as 'distinct, individual human beings each with his or her own special set of cares, hopes, aspirations' (*Daily News Magazine*, 21 November 1976, p.8) resulted in a novel of great social realism.

Patterson's depiction of the deprived and destitute urban working class in the Kingston of the late fifties — the novel is set some time in 1959 before the granting of Independence — was something of a landmark. His novel, he says 'took the Rastafarians and the urban slums seriously, long before it became fashionable to be concerned about them'. (*Daily News Magazine*, 21 November 1976, p.8)

The only two books which had previously shared some of his concerns were Alfred H. Mendes' *Black Fauns* (1935), and Roger Mais' *Brother Man* (1954). The Trinidadian Mendes was writing about an urban yard situation, rather than the slums, and depicted none of the filth, squalor, and degradation of the dungle, nor were his characters seen as hopeless. Mais, too, while setting his novel in the poorer sections of Kingston, did not confront the brutish realities which Patterson did, and his Rasta hero is elevated to the status of a Christ figure, while the harshness of the poverty and pain is transmuted and deflected by that novel's poetic quality.

Setting

Patterson's Dungle is harsh and uncompromising. He transmits the literal and metaphorical meanings of the original source of the core word 'dungle' which is 'dung hill' and depicts a world in which dung — human and other — is constantly present. At the same time, associations which arise from the word 'dungle' such as 'jungle' and 'dump' are ever present. His characters live a kind of wild-animal existence, "a wolf-pack at war" (p.9), savage, predatory and clawing out a kind of survival, amidst overwhelming odds. They are also the detritus, the remnants, the castaways of modern urban society. The novel opens with the garbage men dumping their garbage loads near the Dungle, significantly located between the city dump and the cementery.

Dungle and Back-O-Wall no longer exist today as depicted in the novel but have been replaced by a sanitised Tivoli Gardens. However, Patterson's depiction of the area is charged with such energy, forcefulness and authenticity, that it remains imprinted on our memory, an assault on our senses:

> The mean, derelict smell of human waste mingled with the more aristocratic stink of the factory chimneys. Towards the right of the highway several meagre cows strayed in a dry, scorching common. And on the left were the shacks: dreadful, nasty little structures — a cluster of cardboard, barrel sides, old cod-fish boxes, flattened tar drums and timber scraps.
>
> (p.7)

Characterization

It is in this setting, vividly and starkly evoked, that Patterson places his sad collection of humanity: Dinah the prostitute who has lived there for fifteen years and who now seek to escape from it with tragic results, and Cyrus the unsuccessful Rasta fisherman whom she supports by her prostitution. There is also the random collection of Rastafarian brethren headed by Brother Solomon, a defrocked Anglican priest who constantly oscillates between his ganja-induced world of dream and vision, and the sordid reality of the dungle, and who is Patterson's mouthpiece for much of the philosophising in the novel. There are three other women: Mary who dreams of escape from the dungle through the future achievements of her 'brown' daughter, Rossetta; Mabel who is a kind of reflection of Dinah in her attempt to escape. and the old woman Rachael who is invested with much of the gloomy fatalism of the novel. It is she who says 'Nobody can leave the Dungle for good. Once yu born in it the/World was the Dungle. The Dungle was the World.' (pp.165-6). And again 'Massah God know why 'Im put we down ya. 'Im say is ya we mus' stay. Wha' de use yu try an' run?' (p.164)

Outside of the dungle too, Patterson supplies us with sharp satirical sketches of characters such as Mrs Watkins in her Mona Heights house with her pretentious friends; Seymore Nathaniel Montsaviour (clearly Alexander Bustamante, then the leader of the party in power in Jamaica); and the civil servants acidly etched as sitting "with towels around their necks and glasses of ice-water in their hands." (p.81) Patterson's portrait of Shepherd John, the Revivalist leader, and his flock of servile women though very lightly sketched and therefore not providing any sense of their complexity is nevertheless sharp and pointed, and transmits quite clearly the belief that Revivalism has no solution for the problems of the poor.

Style and language

The central controlling image of Patterson's book and its title is derived from his reading of Albert Camus' *The Myth of Sisyphus* which proposes that it is legitimate and necessary to question whether life has a meaning. Behind Camus' version of the story lies the Greek myth of Sisyphus, who was punished by the gods in the afterlife for having offended them. He had to roll an enormous rock up a slope, and when it reached the top, the rock rolled down to the bottom and Sisyphus' task began at the beginning again. This 'futile and hopeless labour' was thought to be the most dreadful punishment. (Camus p.107) For Camus, the figure of Sisyphus came to represent the existential belief in the futility of man's effort to better himself, the recognition that all of life is Absurd. Sisyphus, then, because his 'whole being is exerted towards accomplishing nothing' (Camus p.108) is the Absurd hero, and is seen as demonstrating the notion that it is the struggle to survive that invests man with worth and stature. As Camus says, 'the struggle itself towards the heights is enough to fill a man's heart.' (p.111) As it is with Sisyphus, so with his children. The myth thus embodies the themes of frustration, futility and non-achievement in the novel.

Patterson uses both Dinah and Solomon to express varying aspects of this Sisyphean philosophy and at times the fiction gets too heavily freighted with it. Thus Solomon articulates his sense of the absurdity of life:

> But with your inner striving, brother, there is the complete comedy, for when the mirage vanish you have not just the agony of your own thirst still unquenched but the added agony of knowing that the mirage was always unreal. Hear me, Brother, to seek after God, to seek for some meaning, some essence, is unreality twice times over. (p.186)

> To perceive the truth of existence is to perceive an unutterable tragedy. (p.47)

Patterson's attempt to make Dinah articulate a sense of the Absurd is also difficult to accept as credible:

> The arid patch was a moment in a vast eternity. The patch itself was nothing, but the moment was real. She had discovered something. It was immense, too big for her to understand, but she knew her soul comprehended it. The more she realized the unreality of the barren patch, the more it receded into the vast eternal nothingness, unseen but implied by itself, so much more was she impressed with the certainty of the moment, with the conviction that only it was real. (p.143)

For Patterson "life has its own inherent course and gives its own inherent meaning" and so even in the most abysmal conditions, man has to continue his struggle to endure — the struggle is all. In this context then, Dinah's attempt to escape from the dungle is doomed though heroic. Her vision of happiness and escape is shown to be vain and fleeting, and she is nearly torn to pieces by the savage congregation of Shepherd John which thinks she has killed him. In her dying agony she heads back to the Dungle and ironically encounters the garbage man, Sammy, with whom the novel opens, thereby completing the circle with the implication that she has indeed become garbage. It is in the somewhat crude vision of Dinah crawling up the mound of garbage, with one breast almost completely ripped off that Patterson explicitly evokes the image of Sisyphus toiling up the slope with his rock. Mary's dream that her 'sweet, sweet brainy brown daughter' will go to high school and university and then marry 'a rich Englishmen, an' she goin' come back here fo' me an' tek me fe go an' live wid her in her palace' (p.73) is seen as an illusory and futile. Indeed the opposite is true, for Rossetta has no hesitation about leaving her mother when she sees it is to her advantage to do so.

In the end Patterson's irony obliterates all including Cyrus' optimistic but futile last words: 'Tomorrow we shall meet again in Paradise.' (p.190) In view of Solomon's revelation that he had concocted the lie about the Emperor's ships coming to repatriate the Rastafarian brethren, the ending is the final absurdity. His irony extends beyond the dungle as well. It reaches out to engulf political parties, organised religion, Revivalism, the middle class, the civil service, the police, the social worker, the jargon-spouting university student.

The novel is very much a young man's book, showing the virtues and the faults of a young writer. It has narrative drive, it is vital and exuberant and continuously exciting, and it depicts vividly a locale and a set of characters never before encountered in literature. But it is not — as Colin Rickards claims — 'ranking far and away above the best of them']i.e. Naipaul, Selvon, Hearne, and

Lamming] (Review, *Sunday Gleaner*, 5 April 1964, p.4) While he does some very nice things such as the symbolic use of the dungle, dodder (a strangling, parasitic plant that kills its host), cacti and sargasso to suggest menace and entrapment, and while his main character, Dinah is a believable creation, Patterson is too often guilty of strained metaphor, inflated writing, tonal unevenness and awkward plot manipulation. As Mervyn Morris noted in his review 'Disciplined self-criticism, cutting, rewriting could surely have made this a much finer book.' (*Public Opinion*, 24 April 1964, p.13) In fact, Patterson has admitted that all he revised, once the book was accepted for publication, was the first chapter. This would account for sentences like 'a numbing, palpitating ambivalence surged madly within her . . . she twisted with agony in the intense negation of her being.' (p.16); or 'The knowledge of what she thought so abhorred her consciousness that she always drove it to oblivion.' (p.77) What, too, are we to make of sentences like 'The sea was as calm as a nanny, and just as grey' (p.66) or 'The night was as plaintive as a weeping negress' (p.48) or 'The stars were numerous and daring, hanging close above like eyes of happy ghosts.' (p.94)?

It is incredible, too that Dinah who was brought up in the country does not know how to crack an egg or how to cook it, and yet can use a vacuum cleaner with no difficulty. The reader has difficulty in figuring whether it is Mabel's obeah curse that brings Dinah back to the dungle or some pre-ordained fate. The scene at the Ministry of Labour seems entirely gratuitous and does not advance the plot, and we get the strong feeling in the final pages that Patterson is merely manipulating his characters rather than that they are acting from some internal logic.

Part of Patterson's achievement in the book is his accurate rendering of the range of the Jamaican speech continuum, from the deepest Creole to standard Jamaican. He has a good ear for the working class speech patterns and duplicates with painstaking accuracy the 'tracing' that forms so much a part of the Jamaica oral tradition, as well as the range of colourful swear words and obscenities. He captures equally well the politician trying to talk

Creole and not quite making it, and the over-earnest university student coming to proselytise among the Rastas, the varying speech idioms of the Brethren, their religious rituals, their jokes, their swearing.

Patterson evokes, too, the physical reality of everyday life by his references to the now disappeared 'Chi-Chi' bus, to domestic items such as the 'yabah,' the chamber-pot or 'chimmie', food items such as cod-fish and flour, ackee and curry goat, and his vignettes of low life read like dramatic set pieces, whether it is a brawl on West Queen Street, a Revival meeting, a 'tracing-off' in a backyard in Jones Town, or a political demonstration.

There is no doubt of the authenticity of this novel, nor of its author's compassion for the tortured, doomed souls which abound in the work. Despite this, however, there is a nagging sense that this is a kind of 'thesis' novel, that Patterson has a point he wants to prove, and that he consequently manipulates his characters and his plot just to demonstrate that point. The result is that we are distanced from these characters and their predicament, and while we may be interested in their plight, we do not, in the end, particularly care for them. There can be no denying, however, that Patterson's first novel remains an impressive achievement both for its vitality and sheer originality.

Victor L. Chang,
English Department,
University of the West Indies,
Mona, Jamaica.

Suggested additional reading
Patterson, H. Orlando. *An Absence of Ruins*. London: Hutchinson, 1967. *The Sociology of Slavery*. London: McGibbon & Kee, 1967. *Die The Long Day*. New York: William Morrow, 1972.

"Rethinking Black History," *Sunday Gleaner*, 20 August, 1972, p.7.

" 'Every Nigger is a Star' is Silly and Potentially Harmful," *Jamaica Daily News Magazine*, Sunday, 21 November, 1976, pp.2,8. *Slavery & Social Death: A Comparative Study*. London: Harvard University Press, 1982.

Anon. Review of *Children of Sisyphus*. *Times Library Supplement*, 2 April, 1964, p.269.

Camus, Albert. *The Myth of Sisyphus*. Harmondsworth: Penguin, 1975.

Coulthard, G.R. Review of *Children of Sisyphus*. *Caribbean Quarterly*, 10.1 (March 1964), pp.69-71.

Grimal, Pierre, ed. *Larousse World Mythology*. New York: Hamlyn Books, 1973.

James, Louis. "Rastafari at Home and Abroad," *New Left Review*, 25 (May-June 1964), pp.74-76.

Jones, Bridget. "Some French Influences in the fiction of Orlando Patterson," *Savacou*, 11/12 (September 1975), pp.27-38.

Jones, Bridget, "Orlando Patterson" in Daryl Dance, ed. *Fifty West Indian Writers* to be published by Greenwood Press in 1986.

Owens, Joseph. *Dread: The Rastafarians of Jamaica*. Kingston, Jamaica: Sangster's Book Stores Ltd., 1976.

Norris, Katrin. *Jamaica: The Search For An Identity:* London: OUP, 1969.

Morris, Mervyn. "The Dungle Observed," *Public Opinion*, 24 April 1964, pp.7,13.

Panton, George. "Not For the Squeamish," *Sunday Gleaner*, 29 March, 1964, p.4.

Ramchand, Kenneth. *The West Indian Novel & Its Background*. London: Faber, 1970, pp.129-131.

Rickards, Colin. "Brilliant First Novel," *Sunday Gleaner*, 5 April, 1964, p.4.

Smith, M.G. Augier, Roy & Nettleford, Rex. *The Rastafari Movement in Kingston, Jamaica*. I.S.E.R., 1960.

Wahl, Jean. *Essays in Existentialism*. London: Routledge & Kegan Paul, 1969.

Walcott, Derek. "A New Jamaican Novelist," *Sunday Guardian* (Trinidad), 17 May, 1964.

I

'OH, WHAT a life, what a worthless, lousy, dirty life,' one
of them cursed beneath his breath, staring at the tick
that was sucking the life from the hoary grey ear of
the donkey that pulled the cart. He stuck the handle of the whip
between his foot and the long rubber boot which he wore and
scratched himself angrily. He glanced lazily behind him as if to
ensure that the other two carts were still following, then he
spat on the ground and continued his scrutiny of the tick.

The three garbage-men sat upon the wooden seats of their
carts, quietly grunting the fears of their thoughts over the
boisterous black heads of the teeming, blazing city. Their wide
black faces, the bars of their brows, a dreary portrait of restrained
anxiety. They sat up there, necks droopily outstretched, eyes
half awake, askance, mouths permanently half open in some
strange, prolonged astonishment, they sat up there like condemned men being hauled by the asses to a fate unknown,
unthinkable.

They were like men possessed, up there above the city,
wretched and lost. Abandoned to a fate which seemed to terrify
them, partly because they were perpetually plagued with doubts
of its existence, partly because they felt that if indeed it did exist,
then in some bizarre way they already knew what it was. Perhaps,
the dismal blankness of their faces seemed to say, perhaps it was
nothing more than the workings of the moment. Just them, the
garbage-men, them and the empty terror of the uneventful,
everlasting now. The street called the Spanish Town Road.
Sketches of a long and narrow pandemonium. But colourful.

Never forget the colour. Of their faces, of their hands, of their ragged skirts, of their naked, gleaming torsos bleeding with sweats of scalding chocolate, of their buttocks peeping out. Black and brown and hardened, impure touches of white. Churned with the steel-grey of the majestic factory chimneys. Trucks, cars, bicycles, big chi-chi white buses and the wheels of urchins. Avoiding each other only by the satanic power of some unseen hand. Battalions of handcart-men pushing their rectangular burdens with the large, stained baskets of the higgler, perched largely, defiantly, up front, a massive plaid handkerchief of red and white tied elaborately on her head, and he behind pushing, pushing, everlastingly pushing with that mournfully gay movement of his legs, one foot forward, then the other, then the other, now down upon the piece of tyre that was his brakes. For at times he must stop. They are too many, the faces of the city. He must stop and return the vile sweetness of their curses. And on again, in and out, then left, then right, pushing, pushing, always pushing.

Some were the faces of the hawkers. They were everywhere. Selling, pleading, begging, cursing, spitting, thieving, with their multitude of trinkets. It is not hard to hear but difficult to understand the ghastly squeak of their voices.

'Ear-rings, sister; pretty gold ear-rings? Well, what about dis one, pretty silver bangle?'

'Good-luck charm! Get rid o' all your worries before they get rid o' you!'

'Best bargain in town,' the noise roars from the loudspeaker of the little Syrian store, 'my goodness gracious, my gracious goodness!'

'Two-an'-six a dozen, lady——

'Two shillin', then, nice lady—all right, one-an'-six——

'Don't go, please; all right, take it, then, take it fo' shillin'——

'Lady! Lady! Dog! . . .'

And the groceries of the Chinamen with the dank, musty interior: stench of flour and stale cod-fish and sugar in crocus bags. And the drugstores full, always full, filling in the prescriptions of the obeah-men, the oils and the herbs and powders of hope.

It was all in the moment, every thing, every movement, every feeling of the city was embedded in their fate as they trudged along with the burden of their garbage. The tough, silent meagre little dogs; the uproar and clammy tang of the nearby market, stale, freakish smells of yams and fish and meat. The clanging of the pans, the pots and mugs and grey aluminium dishes being sold in the stalls on the pavement which they now passed. All was instilled in the dreary consciousness of the garbage-men, the three garbage-men, marking the tenacious trail of the mute, relentless asses. Seeming to pass, yet for ever present. As fierce as the blazing heat of the morning sun. As cruel and indifferent as the vacant, black faces of the babies clinging to the naked breasts of their pregant mothers whose swollen bellies continue to cast moving shadows of gloom on the murky streaks of the gutter by the pavement below them. As meaningless as the garbage stacked up behind them.

The garbage-man in the middle suddenly swore aloud. It was a low guttural sound which seemed to come from the depths of him. He did not know exactly why, but he felt particularly stink that morning. Stink and sour all over. Last night he had another quarrel with his missis about going to that blasted revivalist church with her. Ever since she had gone and joined up with that mad group of zealots the two of them had been at war. Jumping and screaming and spinning in the air like a damn' mongoose with fire under its tail. Not a hell of that for him. And he didn't like that parson man who called himself the Shepherd either, he didn't trust him at all. He didn't like the way he kept looking at the young women members as they caught the spirit under the pretence that he was searching for the chosen one.

But it was not just his missis and her church that was making him swear. Nor was it the fact that every now and then he felt some remorse at having gone to a whore a little after she had left for church. In any case, he didn't consider Dinah a whore. She was so different from the rest. Not a bit like the others you picked up on Harbour Street. She was really somebody to go to when too many worries start to pour down on your head. She had character, that Dinah. And she wasn't a whore, even if she lived in the Dungle with one of those Rastafarians, even if other men bought her body every night.

No, it was just the Monday morning that was getting him down. Jesus Christ, how he hated Monday-morning time! It had something about it that positively made him want to vomit. All those weary men pulling themselves out to work with their pick-axes and shovels, their hammers and saws. He hated the sight of those stiff khaki drills with the sharp-starch-pressed threads sticking out all parts of their behinds. He hated the noise and the bustle. He hated the sight of their faces. He hated, he hated; great Lucifer, how he hated! . . .

The garbage-man up front continued to contemplate the tick. From somewhere far away behind him he thought he heard Sammy swearing. Ordinarily he would have cursed too in sympathy, but his attention had suddenly been arrested by an unusual sight. The tick, he thought he saw it move on the ear of the donkey. Yes, he was sure he had seen it move. But that was strange, though. Ten years he was looking at ticks sucking donkey-blood and this morning it was the first time he ever saw one moving. It was some kind of a sign. Sure as God it was. . . .

The garbage-man on the third cart was tall and extremely thin. He hunched his shoulders and constantly sought to hide his head between them. A street-cleaner. A garbage-man. It had been six months now. But he had not ceased to wonder since that first morning he took the job how he managed to continue. The lowliness of his position weighed down upon him like a boulder. Every moment was a desperate step uphill, every movement of his shovel in the filth was a despairing surge of will, every glance of their eyes a terrifying punch of humiliation. He could only seek to forget by grasping frantically upon every incident, every object that would mercifully hide him from the consciousness of the moment. So the rebellious uproar of the higgler would be the peasant laughter of his mother, the bark of the hawker would be the command of one of his many fathers, the playing of the children would be the vehicle to the past of his childhood.

He had to forget. He would tell himself that he would not face them again. It was all a façade, anyway. All a meaningless, ghastly façade. And so it didn't matter what he convinced himself to believe. They weren't there. Those things. Those creatures of the Dungle. No, they weren't human. If anyone told him that they were human like himself he would tell them that they lied. Those eyes peering at him. Deep and dark red and hungry for what he carried. And for his own blood, too, he was sure. No, he had to forget. Only by forgetting could he possibly bear the burden of the moment. . . .

The carts had begun to pass a saloon and dance centre which was hidden from the road by a bamboo fence on top of which was a large poster that read:

LULU AND SASSY'S BLUES HIDE-OUT

KINGSTON'S FAVOURITE NIGHT SPOT
OPEN EVERY DAY AND NIGHT INCLUDING SUNDAYS
MUSIC BY COUNT ANTONIUS THE WIZARD THAT WIZARD
CURRIED GOAT AND RICE FOR SALE—2/6. ALL WELCOME.

The thundering rhythm of an amplified sound-system speaker roared somewhere inside. Suddenly there was a crash. The little door burst open and two women clenched with the heat of their rage to each other fell outside on the pavement, rolled over together several times and finally settled in front of the garbage-cart in the lead. The donkey jerked to a stop, watched the wrestling women for a second, then nonchalantly began to munch a sheet of newspaper it saw nearby. The garbage-man's eyes nearly popped out of his head as he looked over the front of the cart and noticed that one of the women was stark naked. Only the underwear of the other remained. Several men with glasses of rum in their hands ran out after them, laughing.

The two women scratched and bit and tore each other's flesh till the blood gushed down their skins. The woman with the underwear got on top of the other, held her by the hair and battered her head on the asphalt. Each time she smashed the other's head she screamed: 'You dirty black bitch, you; trying to tek me man from me! You nasty niggering dog, you!'

The battered nude barked and bellowed and scratched the other in her face, screaming back: 'Ah never trouble you man, you damn' liar. Who would want a ugly runt like dat?'

'Call me man ugly! Call me man ugly!' She pommelled the other across her face. 'At least it better fe live with him than fe pregnant fo' a dirty Yankee sailor!'

'Hey cut it out! Oonoo little nastiness, cut it out!' the garbage-man in the middle shouted. The three half-drunk men managed

5

to pull the women from each other and pushed them back inside, where they continued the fight.

Their voices died with the distance. Mechanically, the three donkeys turned off the Spanish Town Road, down the Industrial Terrace. The three garbage-men knew the road as well as the donkeys. So well that they could close their eyes and tell every inch of ground they passed on. At the side of the road a deliberately burst hydrant would be spouting water and they could hear the voices of the women as they scraped the water out of the little pool before it, no longer alert for the police who had long given up any hope they might once have had of preventing them from bursting it.

On the left side of the road would be the miserable little huts of Back-O-Wall, slutty and grimy with the tiny little peepholes beneath the old zinc ceilings. Through them half-naked children too hungry to play, and shrivelled, atrophic old men with their black gums, too weak to move, would be peering. And there would be the younger ones, seedy and slow with long hands and drooping shoulders lounging on the sidewalk, glaring up at them from beneath their foreheads, with the whitish yellow of their eyes, all waiting, waiting for the night to fall.

Then farther down, right there beside the hollow patch where they dumped the carcasses of the dogs and the pigs, there would be the thick, thorny acacia trees and the cacti and tangled shrubs that made up the little bush which separated the terrace from the city's cemetery. Running in between the bush were the dodders, the *love-bush*—bright tangerine, healthy, juicy, as they sucked the life from the thorny trees and stunted shrubs. And the factories which you began to see as you approached the end of the terrace were bright too, teeming with activity. Tall, aloof, enclosed structures, towering above the little jungle of huts and carcasses and garbage.

The men held on more tightly to their reins as the carts bungled over the railway line running across the terrace almost at the end. They waited for a Shell Company vehicle to pass by then went on to the dual highway of the Marcus Garvey Drive. All of them went in the direction of the city until they came to a crossing. There Sammy, the garbage-man in the middle, turned and went in the opposite direction to the place where

6

they dumped the disinfected food. They parted without a word, the other two men continuing in the same direction with the same vacuous, remote stare on their faces.

Now in the vicinity of the Dungle, Sammy felt more than ever like cursing. Once more he became frightened by the thought of encountering them again. The cart moved slowly forward. The mean, derelict smell of human waste mingled with the more aristocratic stink of the factory chimneys. Towards the right of the highway several meagre cows strayed in a dry, scorching common. And on the left were the shacks: dreadful, nasty little structures—a cluster of cardboard, barrel sides, old cod-fish boxes, flattened tar drums and timber scraps. A few, the more luxurious, consisted of the carcasses of old cars. Before one of the huts that faced the road a man and a woman were just about to clash and at the moment she was holding her breasts to Massah God, invoking him to help her kill the dirty bitch. The man was laughing and swearing at her, pointing to her large, inflated belly and shouting that it was only newspaper that was there.

'All day long me see you wid pregnant stomach, year in, year out, an' when time fe baby come me can't see no baby. All you 'ave stuff up inside there is newspaper. Is shame you shame that you can't 'ave baby like other woman!'

'Help me, lawd, help me!' she screamed. 'Protec' me baby while ah kill de bitch!'

She sprung forward, but too hastily. A roll of old newspaper fell from beneath her ragged skirt. There was a roar of laughter as the man grabbed the newspaper and held it in the air, holding his nose at the same time. Screaming hysterically that she could have a baby too, that she was having a baby, only it was taking a little time to come, she started looking frantically about for a brick. The garbage-man hurried along before the incident reached its climax.

Another hundred yards. He was getting nearer. They would be on him at any moment now. He shuddered, then stopped the cart. A fairly tall, well-built Rastafarian cultist came out of the little shop beside him and walked up to the cart. Sammy watched him with unwilling awe as he approached. He began to feel afraid. What was it? What was it this man had that he dreaded so much, that everybody else feared so much? The unaffected gracefulness of his walk, the calmness, the slowness? His beard? Like Moses he used to read about. His eyes which saw everything but did not seem to see? Everybody feared him. Everybody respected him. Only the most privileged of the cultists dared to address him as Brother Solomon; to everybody else he was Mr. Solomon. Yet, as far as the garbage-man knew he never did anything bad for anybody to fear him. He never cut up anybody, he never murdered anybody. For all he knew he had not even the distinction of having spat at an American tourist. Still, everybody feared and respected him.

As Brother Solomon came up to him, the garbage-man took up two pieces of cod-fish and a small bag of flour which had largely managed to evade the disinfectant. He handed them to the Rastafarian, cowering under his silent, awesome stare as he took the shilling handed him in return. Then he hurried on, lashing the donkey angrily.

Another fifty yards. Any moment now he would begin to see them. Yes, yes. Already there was one of them. Ragged thing. Black skin, scaly with exposure. Hair peeling off. Eyes yellow-brown and dark, deep and sallow, piercing. Bang-belly, bang-belly. One, two, three of them creeping from out of their little darknesses. Sagging, top-heavy head with the hair on it like black-pepper grains, peeling, peeling, peeling. And the mouths, raw and dripping with dark, rotten teeth.

The garbage-man eyed them nervously, angrily, and lashed the donkey even harder. As he drove on they seemed to smell him out and came out of their mangy little holes. Bang-belly, bang-belly. One, two, three, four . . . Behind him. Beside him. From in front of him. One by one. Two by two. Ants upon a spasm of cold. He hated the sallowness of their eyes. He hated those dirty black beards. The unkempt locks of the cultists never failed to frighten him, for they always reminded him of a picture of Satan he had once seen in a Seventh Day Adventists' book for children. Those old ones crawling, crawling like crabs on a sandhead. They made his blood run cold. And the young ones with their bellies and their mouths. They were going to eat him up when they couldn't find anything in the cart. Those ugly, inhuman little bitches you see there. And the dogs beside them.

In an effort to forget them, the garbage-man began scanning

the huts to see if he could get a glimpse of Dinah. He seemed to have seen everyone except her. There was Moneyman, the scuffler and beggar whom everyone said was rich. There was 'Big White Chief' who swore to God that he was white, that his mother was white, his father was white, his entire ancestry was white and that he was made to look black only because of some sin one of his forefathers had committed in England. There was Mary too, sitting on a stool in front of her hut, swooning as always over her daughter. And coming towards him was Rachael, that cynical old bitch. Nobody knew where she got her money from, but she lived better than most people in the Dungle. Always singing that stupid, mournful song of hers. She waved at him. He spat on the other side of the cart and did not answer.

Eventually he reached the part of the Dungle that was not inhabited. The gathering herd had grown into a mob behind him. It was a wide open field of debris which undulated from the driveway to the nearby sea. He drove the cart up the little patch that led from the road, stopped about a chain in and pulled off the canvas that covered the debris in the cart.

As he threw off the canvas, a swarm of flies flew up in the air and then came back down upon the debris again. Immediately they swarmed in upon him. He dug his shovel into the muck and flung it out, unmindful of which of them it fell on.

It was a free-for-all. A mad, raging, screaming, laughing, angry, hungry scramble. A wolf-pack at war. Men and women and children and beasts all joined in snatching and grabbing and biting one another for any new prize they found in the garbage. Old Cassandra screamed with delight as a rotten bit of cod-fish fell upon her face. A youth plucked the beard of another and kicked him in the pit of his stomach for snatching his piece of bread and stuffing it down before he had time to get it back. 'Long-mouth Clara', too weak with consumption to enter the scramble, looked hungrily at the luscious piece of disinfected mackerel that a ragged old beard held and, catching his eyes for a moment, she pointed suggestively to the clump of sargasso beside the beach. And Brother Nathaniel, standing a little way off, looked towards his heaven, Ethopia, held his right hand righteously towards the sky and invoked the wrath of the black god Selassie on the white man for bringing down such misery on his people. It was his way of getting the others to give him some of their scrapings.

Gradually the turmoil died down as the garbage was ransacked of every ounce of value. The two women that remained behind were impatiently trying to separate the flour upon which disinfectant had fallen from that portion upon which there was none by the simple process of smelling it out. But the public sanitary inspectors seemed to have done a good job, for they were having little success. One of them, however, suddenly had the bright idea that 'what no poison, fatten' and, snatching up one of the large bags, promptly strolled off with it. The other did not take long to see the wisdom of her argument and soon all that was left of the flour was gone.

The garbage-man eyed them curiously as they walked away. He swore, this time loudly. The donkey pricked up its sensitive ears at the sound of the familiar words and received an angry lash on its behind. It galloped off and the crows that stood a little way off, impatient and bewildered, swarmed down upon the scene to devour what the strange intruders had left for them.

When he had almost reached the road the garbage-man, under some strange impulse, looked back at the scene he had just left. Something about it frightened him. There was, he imagined, a freakish, infernal beauty in the oddly graceful way the mounds of filth undulated towards the unseen shore, in the way the sea murmured and sighed and lashed the shore at intervals with the breaking crack of a crocodile's tail, in the way the crystal blueness of the frightfully near horizon rose sheer from behind the debris as if in flight from the menace of the sea. Great Lucifer, what fantastic havoc was the sea playing under the cover of the towering filth? Everything seemed to flee from it. The whole atmosphere was a moment of frozen flight. And there was with the flight, yet seeming to be left behind, a wide, vacuous, lingering, yet perpetual beauty.

Everything fled, that is, except the crows. Christ, Almighty God, the crows! The crafty, crab-like way they moved. Like groups of fallen angels defiling what seemed no more capable of defilement, intensifying all the macabre beauty of the scene.

The garbage-man shuddered slightly, spat behind the cart and looked in front of him. Then with a heavy sigh he flung the whip in the cart and allowed the donkey to lead the way while he rested his elbows on his knees and cushioned his heavy black jaws between his palms. Vacantly, he continued to glue his eyes upon the grey space between the two long ears of the donkey.

2

He would be there. He would be waiting for her. Do, Massah God, make him keep his promise. At the corner of Fifth Street and Lindsay Avenue in Denham Town he had said. He would be there. He had to be there.

Slowly, cautiously, she stepped from the road on to the little track that led into the Dungle. The more she thought of it, the more she found it hard to believe that he would turn up. Why would a Special Constable want to keep a whore as a woman, anyway? He had just promised to keep her so as to get the best out of her last night. But why would he want to do that? She always satisfied her men. He would be there waiting for her. He had to be there.

But she had to hurry. Cyrus would be home soon from his fishing. It would be hell when he found out she had left him. She tried to convince herself that she didn't care a damn. But deep down she knew she felt some strange hesitation. That pained her most of all. For the past fifteen years she had been living in the stinking filth around her and now she had her chance she was hesitating. It was Cyrus she was afraid of. It was Cyrus she was afraid of. It was . . . oh, such a lie. There was something else. Something was holding her back. No, it was Cyrus she was afraid of. Something else, inside of her, deep down inside of her.

Ambition. She knew she had ambition. They said if you lived in the Dungle long enough there wouldn't be any ambition left in you. But she had lived there fifteen years and she knew she still had ambition. If there was one thing Man-man had taught her it was that.

'Notten, notten in dis worl' like ambition,' he used to say to her, licking the last drop of rum from the bottle and slumping over on the table. That's why she couldn't leave him. He was old and twisted and withery. So like a dry-weather breadfruit. But he had ambition. The woman who had taken her from her mother in the country as a domestic under the guise of adopting her had kicked her out when she complained to her what her husband was doing with her at nights. And it was Man-man who had picked her up off the streets and carried her home and given her ambition.

And it was Cyrus that she was afraid of. There was nothing else keeping her back. In a funny kind of way she feared Cyrus. That was why she lived with him. He appealed to her instinct of self-preservation. When she was with him she had to please him. At any moment he would charge upon her and destroy her. So she had to please him. She had to love him.

It was so from the first time she met him. It was a round two weeks she hadn't bathed. She didn't get much customers the night before and Rachael, with her usual frankness, had suggested that maybe she smelled too much. Men might be a pack of bitchy pigs, but there was a limit. She cursed the old bitch properly, smelled herself a little later and decided that she really needed a bath. She hated bathing. It wasn't the men who passed and stared, they could have stared till their eyes dropped out, she couldn't care. Nor was it the water so much. It was just the damn' waste of time the whole thing appeared to be.

Dusk had fallen. A diabolic silence fell upon the place. She took off her clothes and went into the water, cursing softly as it chilled her nakedness. She waded about for some time and to her own surprise found that she was beginning to like it.

It was not until he had thrown down the net on the black shore and she heard the swish of the water that she turned and saw him. She stared at him, half annoyed, but did not move. 'Wha' de hell yu want? Yu never see naked woman yet?'

He stood his ground. Tall and black and strong. He stared silently at her, as if calculating something. She recalled that he was some kind of a fisherman or went out sometimes with the other fishermen to help them. Apparently he had just come in from the sea, for he was still naked except for the little knitted trunk he wore, the top of which fell down to the very pit of his stomach exposing him almost completely.

'Ah troublin' you, sister? Wha' yu worryin' 'bout, woman?'

Silence again. And the upright nakedness of their bodies staring at each other. Darkness came down and made them two black statues in between the shadows. Quickly though. In August time darkness come down quick-quick.

But though she tried to neglect him she couldn't. His presence troubled her in an odd way. Every now and then she looked up from the water at him. He was always there, standing and staring exactly as he had been. Same place. She was beginning to be afraid of him. It was such a strange fear. And when at last he began to walk towards her it grew slowly like a passion. As he drew near to her the fear tightened, then it gripped her like the jaws of an alligator. She made as if to scream. He stopped.

'Why yu goin' on like if yu don' know me?' His voice was low, fierce.

'I know yu, but not fe talk to, why yu don' leave me?' She began to feel ashamed at the way she trembled. Something about him forced her to submission. She hated the feeling, but felt compelled to it. But what the hell was it? She had courted thieves and drunkards and murderers, not to mention the narcotic sailors. She had been raped, mauled, plundered and knifed. She was a woman who had lived life. She had been proud of her experiences with a fierce kind of pride. She passed through hard life. She was a big woman. She washed her panty and buttered her bread. So what the hell was this she felt now?

He walked a step nearer to her. She saw his beard held up proudly. He breathed deeply and his broad nostrils widened and contracted whenever he took an extra large breath. His eyes were dark, glazed and bright, like lakes in moonlight jungle. He was coming closer.

'Woman, ah never know yu did 'ave such a good body. Rastafari did mek yu fo' me.'

'Jus' clear off, yu hear!' she managed to stammer. 'Ah not 'avin' anything fi do wid you, Rastas. Oonoo treat you woman too bad. Oonoo seem to t'ink dat woman did only mek to

serve an slave fo you an dis is one woman wha no make fo'
dat.'

'Is not me say so. Is God Rastafari say so: "An' the rib which
the Lawd God had taken from man, made him a woman an'
brought her unto man"——'

'Move off! Leave me alone wid yu scriptures; don' bring down
no worries 'pon me head, yu hear; me 'ave enough a'ready.'

'An' hear I, woman, Adam said, "Dis is now bone of my
bones, yes, an' flesh of my flesh"—Adam was a black man, yu
did know dat, sister? A black man was de firs' to inhabit dis
earth——'

'Leave me, leave me!' She was beginning to panic. She didn't
believe in what the Rastafarians preached, but she was afraid of
it. Right now she had some vague suspicion that he was casting
some kind of spell upon her.

'An' is like Adam, my black ancestor say: "She shall be
call woman, for she was takeneth out of me".' He paused,
placed his hand upon his chest proudly, and uttered, 'An' I is
Adam.'

'Move off!' She was afraid even to scream. It was incredible.
She couldn't understand the spell he cast over her. He had put
a terrible piece of obeah upon her, sure as God. Yes. The words
he just spoke cast a spell on her.

'Those is de words o' de 'oly scriptures, written by de 'oly
one, de God Rastafari, whose only son is de one an' only Haile
Selassie, King of Kings, Lord of Lords, de conquering Lion of
de tribe of Judah. Yu wan' more proof dan that?'

He stared through her with a kind of mocking condescension
still exalted by the utterance of the name of the Holy Emperor.
Then something strange began to happen to her. She had been
facing him all this while naked and unashamed. But now as
he glared at her a sense of shame gradually overwhelmed her.
She couldn't understand why her hands should come so
suddenly to her breasts, why she should stoop so. The action
was so alien to her being, so stupid and childish, she could have
kicked herself. But she still cowered before him. She decided
she had to run and make a dash for her clothes. He waded
quickly across the inlet and intercepted her.

Where they stood the sargasso completely surrounded
them. The sea beside her was a wide sneaky door. In the distance

across the harbour were the mountains of St. Catherine, a dark fading purple.

'Let me go, let me go!' she cried, wondering why she did not scream.

'Don' lie to yuself, woman,' he said haughtily, 'lie to anybody, him could be a king, but don' lie to yuself, for when yu do dat yu lie to yu God.'

'Wha' yu mean by dat?'

'Ah mean yu don' want to leave. Yu want it.'

'Want . . . want what?'

'De 'oly juice.' He approached her slowly. She did not move. She did not dare to. She could not.

'Therefore shall a man leave his mother and father, an' shall cleave unto his wife,' he said, half mockingly, half seriously, 'an' they shall be one flesh.'

He paused. There was the silence, there was the darkness and there was hardly a movement as his shadow loomed towards her. She sunk into his grip. His mouth swallowed hers and in agony she bit him on his lip till it bled. Relishing in the pain, he tightened his embrace. She warmed to him against her will and sucked the saltness that flowed from his lips.

Suddenly he snatched her away from him. He held her at arm's length, his eyes gleaming fiercely and viciously. She felt to scream; she felt to cry with joy. She felt to run; she felt to sink into his flesh. He flung her from him and she fell upon the black moist sand. With a delicious rebellion against her will she turned over on her back and lay prostrate beneath him.

Quickly, with a restrained excitement, he disposed of the little net trunk. A numbing, palpitating ambivalence surged madly within her. Against her will she panicked. Yet all along she had wanted to panic, to scream, and it had only been against her will that she had not. She twisted with agony in the intense negation of her being. Even now as she panicked she thought she realized that she panicked not so much against him but against her own panicking. If she didn't have him now, now, against the double ambivalence of her will, it would be death. She got up and made as if to flee. She wanted to escape, and she wanted to escape only so that he could hold her back, so that she could hate him more and further terrify herself in her desire for him.

She was halfway up when he pounded upon her. He pawed her across her shoulders and spun her round. He sank to the ground upon her. He ravished her. Long and cruelly and sweetly till the purple mountains had dissolved into complete nothingness and the sargasso a black mass hovering over them, he raped her, he mauled her, he gushed her being with complete rapture.

And when they had done, and still naked, he had carried her to his hut nearby the sea there to live with him, he had thought comfortingly, An' they were both naked, the man an' 'is wife, an' they were not ashamed . . .

But all that going to end now. Six years of it was enough. She had been good and faithful to him as far as it was possible for a whore to be good and faithful. She had had a pickney for him. She was through. Too much of one thing good for nothing. Tonight, tonight. And she was sure now that it was he that made her hesitate. She was afraid of him. It was simply the thought of what he would do to her if he ever found her after she left that made her feel so hesitant now. There could be nothing else because she had ambition. Man-man did teach her that. She wasn't like those other people who sold their souls to the Dungle. Christ Almighty, she knew some of them who had the means to better themselves, who got more pay than many in Denham Town or Jones Town and who still didn't leave the stinking place. The place set a spell on them. It work obeah on them. Well, she wasn't like the rest. She knew she had ambition.

She walked cautiously so few people could see her. However, she was so taken up with avoiding others that she made the terrible mistake of taking her eyes too long from the ground. As she passed behind Mary's hut her foot suddenly sunk into something soft. She looked down and swore. Why the hell couldn't she have seen it in time. And it was so blasted stink. But after all, though, why the rass-clate when Mary wanted to ease herself she had to do it right in her backyard and not go like everybody else down to the seaside. That lazy bitch. All she knew to do was to brood over that mulatto daughter of hers. She wiped off the filth with some old newspaper and moved on.

A few paces later she was passing Brother Solomon's hut. It was one of the better of the lot, the walls being made out of refrigerator boxes and the ceiling from well-flattened asphalt drums. A slight shudder passed through her as she went by the hut. Cyrus's was immediately behind, almost touching on it. Cyrus had an almost childlike devotion for Brother Solomon and had even moved his hut from beside the sea to the back of Brother Solomon's. Maybe he thought some of the strange powers of Brother Solomon would fall out on him. All sorts of rumours were spread about Brother Solomon which as much irritated her as it increased her fear of him.

Some said that he was a prophet, a reincarnation of the famous Marcus Garvey, that champion of the negro race who had felt the vile wrath of the white man for his just and wise teaching. Others, like old Zacharry, claimed that Haile Selassie had embodied his spirit in him so that he may watch their ways and guide them in the paths of righteousness until he was ready to lead them out of their bondage in Babylon back to Ethiopia. A Moses, a black Moses, Brother Zacharry would so often declare. And just as often Brother Brisco would correct him. Another Moses he was, yes. But it was quite unnecessary to describe Brother Solomon as a black Moses. For was not the first Moses black? Was it not only the white man who had corrupted the scriptures and claimed that he was white? And there were others who were convinced that he was a mystic, whatever that meant. They said that he had strange writings on his walls which summed up all the wisdom of the white man and which he could use at his command. Several people, including Cyrus, who had once had the privilege of entering the portals of his hut, had indeed claimed to have seen the strange writings on the wall and the mystic signs. And Dinah herself could admit to hearing queer noises coming from his room at nights and even more dreadful was the strong, pungent fragrance of incense which stifled her and which Cyrus always forced her to bask herself in with the hope that it would purify her and give him some of Brother Solomon's powers.

But it was the way he looked at her which Dinah feared most. When his big black eyes rested upon you they seemed to pierce every little crevice inside of you. She was sure that if she saw him now he would sense immediately what she was going to do. And after that she would have been paralysed. She would not dare to go.

But he was not at home and with a sigh of relief she hurried inside the shack. She bent down before the thing which they slept on, some strips of board resting on two large boxes at either end. On it were some old clothes resting on newspapers finally covered by a sheet made of several crocus bags sewn together. She took up the crocus-bag sheet and tried to hide the box beneath the bed while she went to the sea to wash off the filth. She had to dig away a part of the floor so that the box would fit underneath the bed. A stinking stench of stale dung and debris stung her nostrils and she had to move away her head until she became used to it.

When she had washed her feet she walked a little farther down the coast to an old jetty the Shell Company had abandoned and which the men now used for tying their boats on. She strained her eyes, but was unable to make out anything at sea. Good. It would be some time before Cyrus was back and she would be far away by then. Again the lull inside of her. The hesitation. But she knew that it was only Cyrus she was afraid of. Cause she had ambition. . . .

They had picked him up out of the gutter where he had fallen during the night. He had burst an artery and the foaming red blood with white spots was all over the pavement. He had a bottle of rum in one hand and the other was pointing to the door of the Government Savings Bank. He should have been manager there one day, Man-man. . . .

But no matter how much she was afraid of Cyrus he wasn't going to keep her back.

She walked a few paces up the fence of the Light and Power station that bordered on the Dungle until she could spot the common across the Marcus Garvey Drive. She saw her son Nicholas playing cricket with the other boys. That was good too. The little nuisance wouldn't be there to molest her. Christ, how she was glad to be getting rid of him! She never saw the reason why she should have to be burdened with the care of another human being when she could hardly take care of herself. But she realized how hard she was. She wished for a moment that she could feel sorry for him. Oh, but it was such a farce. She knew deep down that the very fact that she wished she could feel sorry for him was indicative of her true feeling. It was cruel the way she was going to leave her pickney. But she had to be cruel. If she was going to leave the Dungle she had to be merciless. For it had its charms. The Dungle was an obeah-man and it would cast its spell on you as it did with almost everybody that lived there. But not her. It was so easy to be merciless.

So she went back to the hut. She took out the little box and began to pack her few belongings. She had to hurry. A feeling of apprehension was creeping upon her. Fast-fast. Two dresses. When she left she left and nothing was going to keep her back. One panty, plus the one she had on. Dungle spell or no Dungle spell. A pair of pedal-pushers, indispensable to her profession. Cyrus or no Cyrus, make him do what he want. A bra, a pair of rubber slippers. And she didn't care a rass about Nicholas. As a matter of fact now she thought about it she hated the little shit. She hated him. She hated him.

She changed into the better of the two dresses and placed the dirty one in the box. Then as she stooped to put on her underwear a stroke of terror ran through her. The canvas door was pulled away without warning and a shadow loomed at the doorway. She drew up the underwear, not daring to look who it was, and at the same time tried to kick the box beneath the bed. A creaky voice broke behind her. With a sigh of relief she turned round to face the old woman who was staring curiously at her.

'Oh, yu sucking ol' bitch; why de blasted 'ell yu don' mek people private, eh?'

The old hag didn't bother to answer. From her expression she didn't seem even to have heard Dinah. Her large withered face, beneath which you could see the skull marks clear and precise, was held placidly forward. Her ragged clothes, patchy and smelly, hung loosely upon her lean, spare frame. When people cursed her, which they did often, they never failed to tell her that she was so striking meagre you couldn't tell her back from her belly. The only thing that moved were her bony jaws as she sung, exposing ugly, greyish-brown gums. The words cackled out slowly, drawlingly, as if each would be her last.

> ' 'Aven't no father, 'aven't no mother,
> I jus' a poor gal, ready to die,
> Sen' fo' de parson, tell 'im to run,
> 'Cause I jus' a poor gal, ready to die.'

Dinah's anger faded. She knew she could trust the old bitch, no matter how stupid she might go on at times. Furthermore, it was no use trying to hide anything from her. Sooner or later she would know anyway. She just had a way with other people's business. She even regarded it as a kind of privilege being a sort of overlord of the Dungle by virtue of her long establishment there.

'Wha' de bombo-clate yu wan', Rachael? Ah don' 'ave not'ing fe give yu.'

'Oh get off, ah ever beg yu anything yet?' the old woman replied with good-humoured sauciness, staring inquisitively at the box which Dinah was making no effort to hide. At length her two small beady eyes moved from the box to Dinah and watched her as she combed her hair. Then they moved back to the box, then back to Dinah again, each time the suspicious gleam in them increasing.

'Is whe' yu goin', Dinah gal?'

'Same place me always go when me leave here. Don' ask me nonsense.'

The little dry hag looked again at the box and Dinah, her lips falling slightly apart, her glance sidelong and crooked. Then she began to shake her head slowly.

'First time me ever see whorin' sta't at dis hour o' de mawnin'.'

'Then where de rass yu t'ink me goin', then?'

'Dat is what me would 'a' like fe know.'

'But see here me God. Woman, yu don' t'ink yu jus' a little too stinkin' fast, no? Don't wha' I do is my business?'

Rachael stood quiet for some time. Then she went over to the little box with Dinah's clothes. Dinah was on the point of pushing her away when she checked herself. Somehow she didn't think it mattered now who knew she was leaving as long as she got out. Rachael continued to peer at the clothes for some time. Then she closed the box and shook her head solemnly.

'Yu satisfy now?' Dinah asked her.

' 'Ow yu manage to leave, Dinah? Who yu goin' live wid?'

'A man, Rachael.' She turned to face the old hag, having a sudden desire to torture her.

'A man wid a good steady job who love me body because it still young an' have flesh on it want me fe come an' live wid him; fe turn him wife, him missis, so dat ah won' 'ave fe spen' me old days rottin' and stinkin' away on a load of shit.'

She laughed at the old woman with a soft, tickling pleasure.

'Which man goin' tek yu? Which man from outside want a whore from de Dungle?'

'Yu really wan' fe know? Ah will tell yu. Is a Special Constable. While 'im should be on 'im job prosecutin' me 'im fall fo' me. Now 'im wan' me fe live with 'im all de time. Yu know wha' dis mean, ol' fowl? Yu know wha' dis mean?'

'Maybe me too ol' fe know; why yu don' tell me?' The old woman's voice had a sarcastic ring.

'It mean me dream come true. All me ambition. I always wan' fe live in a room wid good solid wall round me an' a floor under me foot an' ceilin' over me 'ead. Ah always wan' fe eat good good food like wha' ah see in de picture advertisement. I wan' fe give up me life of whoredom an' live like normal woman.'

There was a long pause after she finished speaking. Then suddenly the air was pierced with laughter. It was a high-pitched, mocking, scandalous scream which rang almost a mile away. The old hag bellowed. She laughed until her weak frame gave way and she fell upon the dry filth below her. Dinah stared at her, anger gradually rising within her.

'What sweet goat goin' hurt him belly,' she said threateningly.

Eventually the old woman was able to control herself and almost in an instant the mirth was gone. Suddenly she became blank and rigid with a sneering flicker crossing her lips every now and then.

'Laugh,' Dinah said. 'Laugh yu head off. When yu fine out dat ah really gone an' leave dis stinking dirty place we goin' see is who 'ave de las' laugh.'

'So yu think dat whorin' too good fo' yu now, eh, Dinah gal?'

'Who de 'ell say anyt'ing like dat? Yu see me look like a idiot? Ah say is a damn' hard life an' yu can't deny dat. Ah say ah wan' fe leave de stinkin' dirty place. Yu t'ink dat ah wan' to be like yu an' live me whole life in dis rass place? Yu t'ink ah wan' to be not'in' else but a whorin' crow-bait?'

'Listen, Dinah, ah not tryin' fe discourage you but yu t'ink ah did'n' try to? Yu t'ink is one or two time ah did leave dis place an' did 'ave to come back. An' why? Why? 'Cause ah had was to come back. When Massah God mek yu an' put yu in ya 'im mean dat is right here yu goin' stay. I 'member when dis place was a swamp, Dinah, dat time me was a gal an' de flesh still 'pon me body an' ah could still catch de fattes' Yankee sailor-man 'pon Hanover Street. Dat was when me an' me man use to live 'cross there in Back-O-Wall. An' I 'member de firs' time de donkey-cart start to carry de shit an' dump it right here 'pon de swampland; dat time Kingston did only 'ave pit-toilet. An' I remember de last cart dat dump de last load o' shit here, dat was when de place start get respectable, for from dat time is only garbage dem dump here. I use to watch dem day by day till de place come hard so dat we could walk 'pon it like we doin' now. Me was one o' de firs' person to walk 'pon dis land o' shit here, gal. An' when de dirty police dem raid de squatters dem in Back-O-Wall when Backra ready fe buil' 'im factory, me was de firs' person fe hit 'pon de idea fe come an' live ya. Yu can't run a man from off of shit, dat is wha' ah say. Dem laugh after me firs'. But when later ah see dem comin' over one by one, two by two, as de police drop dem baton 'pon dem backside an' burn dem out, I 'ad de las' laugh. An' ah will always 'ave de las' laugh.'

She ended with an air of triumph, cocking her little dried-up head in a sneering half-glance at Dinah.

'Is wha' de bombo-clate yu wan' fe tell me? Dat since because me been livin' here from me is fifteen year ol' me must continue livin' 'pon it all me life?'

'Is not wha' yu wan' fe do, me gal, is wha' yu 'ave fe do.'

She spoke with an air of wisdom and mock authority. Dinah felt herself becoming slightly uncomfortable.

'Listen to me, yu bloody 'ead look like it runnin' water. Jus' mine yu own business an' leave me out. Ah didn't ask fe yu advice. I strikin' well know what ah doin'.'

'All right, Dinah, gal, live an' learn, live an' learn. Ah suppose is a good feelin' to try, anyway. Ah won' discourage yu any more. But jus' one little t'ing, wha' 'bout Cyrus an' yu pickney, yu no care about dem any more?'

'I stop worryin' 'bout other people now. Is time ah look 'bout meself; yu jus' stop foolin' 'roun' me; yu beginnin' fe soun' like dat rass social welfare woman who come here on Sunday evenin' time.'

'Cyrus was a good man to yu, gal.'

'Oh, why yu don't move off? Good? Ah suppose compare wid de other men in de place 'im is good. But no civilize man outside o' dis stinkin' place would make dem woman go out at night fe whore so as to support dem.'

' 'Im couldn' help it, Dinah; yu know 'ow 'im try 'ard fe get work; seven year now 'im tryin' fe get employment an' not one straight week 'im ever work.'

'Dat is his hard luck. I'm leavin'.'

'Mine yu mek 'im get cross like Mabel man, yu know. Yu see 'ow 'im swearin' fe kill her anytime 'im see her. Careful, yu know, Dinah; me would'n' like to see dem bury yu.'

'Ah really hate Mabel, every day we use to fight, 'member? But from de time she run 'way from de Dungle I admire her. The woman 'ave guts an' ambition if not'in' else.'

'So is policeman yu go an' tek up. Christ Almighty, gal, yu playin' wid fire, yu know! Yu should know 'ow de Rastafarian dem hate policeman an' call dem not'in' but *Babylon*.'

'Ah know,' Dinah said, as she finished combing her hair and threw the comb into the box, 'but ah could'n' care one rass-hole.'

'Dinah?' There was a slightly serious ring in her voice which made Dinah turn and stare at her.

'Wha'?'

'Yu really wan' fe leave de Dungle?'

'Wha' yu mean? Wha' yu mean?' Dinah was beginning to really lose her temper.

'Jus' wha' me say. Yu really t'ink yu want fe leave de Dungle?'

'But what a fresh, stupid stinkin' ol' piss-pot yu is, eh. Yu don' t'ink me know me own mind. Because yu never 'ad no will to leave you'self yu can't see 'ow me could, yu stupid ol' jackass. Dat is why yu always fail to leave de place. Yu never really 'ave de will to leave, yu never really want to leave, you never 'ave one scrap of ambition, yu worthless, dirty ol' crow-bait yu. But yu listen to me, I not like yu, yu hear. I 'ave ambition, I 'ave ambition. I not like yu. So jus' shut yu damn' trap an' clear off!'

She straightened herself angrily. It was time to leave. She placed the box under her arm and made for the little canvas door. But as she was about to go through the door she couldn't help feeling sorry for the old woman. She shouldn't have spoken to her this way; after all, it would be the last time and she really didn't mind the old bitch. She turned round and glanced at the old woman. Rachael stood calmly looking at her. She had a faint mysterious smile on her face, as if recalling some vague memory.

'I gone, Rachael,' she said, almost with compassion.

'Walk good,' the old woman replied vacantly, 'don' mek cart mash yu.'

3

Twilight come down quick-quick. A vast red splash across the grey, calm sea. As the deceptive peace of night fell upon the place, little mysterious kerosine glows began to twinkle from within the shanty hovels, coops and sheds, clustered together like little flocks of wet crows. And the flags of the great Emperor hovering above them, gold and red and green all shading now for oneness, rising every now and then in the wake of the evening breeze, then falling limply, drooped, the little flags of glory.

The little spots in the golden splash grew larger till the vague outlines of small canoes could be seen, then the black skin of the naked fishermen. There were four of them, tall men, strong men. They all wore beards and kept their long hair uncombed till it dignified their shoulders in wiry, woolly braids. As they reached the shore they headed for the little notch of dark blue water. It was an indent perfectly suited for tying their boats, as it was not only near to the shore, but took the form of a sudden drop, so that they could step out of their canoes right on the edge, which was no more than ankle-deep. It was a dangerous little hole which they called the rat-trap, and the water that settled there was warm and seductive, coming from the bowels of the nearby power station.

Cyrus stepped out on the black silty shore. It had been a bad day. But his face, if it betrayed weariness, showed little disappointment. He was too used to bad days to make it bother him. He would go to his hut and eat the food his woman had prepared for him. Perhaps if he had the mind for it, or the energy, he would make use of her before the sailors did. Oh, mighty God of Ras, it pained him so much to know that his woman went whoring to help support him. But what to do. It was prophecy. They were the children of Israel suffering for the misdeeds of their fathers. But the day of departure would soon come. The Holy Emperor had sent his prophet already to lead them out of this land of bondage. It was just a matter of time.

But until the time came it was suffering and more suffering. It was damnation and injustice at the hands of the white over-lords and their brown lackeys. They would have to suffer at the hands of Babylon and it would be a sin to try to evade it. It would be blasphemy in the sight of God Rastafaria, who must have had just cause for punishing them. So when he allowed his woman to follow the paths of wickedness and the ways of whoredom he was actually doing what was right. He might even receive some recompense in Ethiopia for his penitent submissive-ness. But, oh, Selassie, oh, Holy Emperor, who leads against the foe, it was such a terrible suffering, how terrible is thy wrath.

He helped the other men out with their nets and walked towards his hut. As he passed one of the dirty little shanties held upright on either side by two sticks on which the red, green and gold flag of Ethiopia waved, the tinkling of money caught his ear. Money-man was checking up the money he had managed to scuffle that day. He must have made a lot, for Cyrus remembered him going out dressed up as an old cripple in the morning.

'Peace an' love me god-brother,' Cyrus greeted, pushing his head into the little oblong door. ''Ow de scufflin' today?'

'Love again, me Brother, but de Lawd say mind thou thy own business an' thy own business will mind thee well,' was the curt reply.

Money-man, even to his best friends, never played the fool when it came to matters dealing with his money. He never shared what he earned with the other brethren, and many despaired of him, saying that he was too mean and selfish to be a true Rastafarian. But Money-man, or 'A Certain Jew', as some preferred to call him, always pleaded that he was saving up his passage to go to Ethiopia. He wasn't putting all his hopes on the delegation, as the other cultists did, for the wickedness of the white man was such that they would put everything in

27

the way of the delegation to prevent them from succeeding. A more laudable reason for being mean could not be found. But many of the cultists still remained to be convinced of his sincerity.

Cyrus laughed and walked away. Money-man was still his good friend despite what they might say about him. He reached his hut and hurried inside, for he was beginning to feel hungry. No one was there. He looked towards the box in the corner where Dinah always left his food in case she had to leave before he arrived. There was nothing. But that was funny. He was sure she had a little money when he left this morning.

Getting angry, he walked outside and looked at the three sooty stones on the ground beside the hut which they used as a stove to cook on. The ashes were cold and it was clear that no fire had been caught there that day. He saw his son walking with a group of boys a little way off and called him.

'Nicholas, whe' yu mother?'

'Don' know. Me was playin' in de common an' when me come she gone.'

'She don' say whe' she gone?'

'No. An' it look like she gone fo' good too. She tek her clothes an' ever'thing wid her.'

'Wha' yu say!' Cyrus ran inside to verify the boy's statement. Then he dashed back outside. His features became contorted with a kind of painful stupidity. His dark brown eyes gleamed fire. He plucked his beard; he swore by the name of the Holy Emperor till even Brother Nathaniel had to wake from his evening slumber.

'God bli'me! God! Rastafaria! Babylon let loose!' he screamed, rushing towards Mary's hut.

'Whe' Dinah gone? Whe' Dinah gone?' he roared.

'Hush! Yu wakin' up me baby, yu wakin' up de little angel,' she said.

'Baby? Which blasted baby yu talkin' 'bout? Tell me, woman, tell me quick before me wrath fall 'pon yu, whe' me woman gone, whe' Dinah is?'

'She is a baby to me. Don't care how big she get she is still my baby, my——'

'Oh, your bombo-hole woman! Damn an' blas' yu stinkin' soul to hell! Don' mek me wring yu rass neck, tell me whe' me woman!'

'But 'ow me mus' know? Is de firs' me hearin' now dat Dinah not here. Jus' leave me out. Lawd, now look wha' yu mek 'appen.' She ran towards the bed and held the girl in her arms. 'Baby, baby, not even a little sleep yu can get, eh, sleep, me pretty, sleep, me baby.'

It would be useless talking to Mary, so he dashed towards the 1939 Ford carcass where Rachael lived. The old woman was roasting a piece of cod-fish for her supper. He held her roughly by her arm and spun her round. She yelled with pain and pulled away her hand.

'Wha' de backside wrong wid yu? Is mad puss piss yu drink or wha'!'

'Whe' she is? Whe' she gone? Don' tell me yu don' know or else ah wring off yu stinkin' neck.'

'Wring it off! Wring it off!' she dared him boldly. 'Is long time I been waitin' fo' somebody to do dat fo' me.'

Cyrus released her, but still glared at her menacingly.

'So yu not tellin' me whe' she is, yu bleedin' ol' 'og, yu not tellin' me.'

Rachael's beady little eyes narrowed on him. Then they softened with a condescending kind of pity. A pity which she felt only she had a right to give.

'Sorry, Cyrus, don' know whe' she is. But don' worry, she will come back. She will come back.'

Bitterly, he spun round to face the little crowd that his shouting had attracted. They were mostly women and their children, ragged and half naked, staring at him idly.

'Yu all lying to me! Yu know whe' she is! But Babylon shall fall. Ah goin' to find her. An' when ah find her, as there is a black god, ah goin' to kill her. Ah goin' to murder her an' teach her de place o' woman-kind. Ah goin' to teach her not to follow de ways o' Babylon.'

'Ahh me god-brother, glory be. Babylon seem to set a plague on de mind o' we woman dem. Dem jus' seem to be walking out on we into de land o' Babylon one by one.'

It was Crocus, a short, stocky man, who, though not yet a true cultist, was a strong sympathizer. He had wicked black eyes that were always moist and gleaming. As he came towards Cyrus, rocking on his bandy legs, he felt he had every right to sympathize with him since Mabel, his own woman, had left

29

him not too long ago. A few yards away from Cyrus he held his hand ceremoniously towards the east and shouted:

'De black god of we, de true Children of Israel, descendants of de black King Solomon an' de black Queen Sheba, they shall burn up de white dogs an' de brown traitors fo' pollutin' we woman wid dem evil ways.'

'Whe' she gone? Why she leave? She don' know is here she belong until we ready to return,' Cyrus pleaded aloud to himself.

'Is a conspiracy! Is de white men dem conspiring 'gainst we an' we woman. Dem know that de time is near when we shall leave dis 'ell, dis land of bondage. Dem know dat not'in' dem do can stop we, so dem tryin' fe kill we out before we leave. Firs' dem start to tell we 'bout birth control an' all kind o' tripe dat we mus' practice if we is to improve we lot. An' when we find out dem scheme dem tryin' dis new one now. Dem tryin' fe get 'way we woman dem from we. Is a plot, birth control and all dem other stunt is a plot fe kill de negro race!'

'Ah mus' find her, Crocus. De time fo' departure is drawin' near. The delegation them soon write and sen' the date. Ah did want to carry her to Ethiopia with me as me queen. Whe' she is? Whe' she gone?'

His anger started to boil up in him again. He would find her. Now-now. He marched to his hut and put on his black drill pants and his green, gold and red shirt. Taking up his staff, he dashed outside. He turned towards the Marcus Garvey Drive when suddenly he heard a sharp commanding voice calling his name.

Instantly he turned round. He stared for one long moment at the figure standing at the doorway. His anger melted. His face smoothed into an almost submissive countenance.

'What ails thee, Brother. Has the wickedness of Babylon infected you?' Brother Solomon's voice was the same calm lowness.

Cyrus jumped to attention. He stuck his forefinger out and drew up his forearm ceremoniously until the side of his palm rested on his right breast.

'Peace an' love, glory, Brother Solomon.'

There was a long, piercing glance. Brother Solomon was thinking. He always seemed to be thinking.

'Come inside an' make me give you some words of wisdom, Brother, you seem to need it.'

Cyrus found it difficult to believe. He would be going into that room again. That strange mysterious room that had all the knowledge of the world in it. Slowly, hesitantly, he walked towards the door, he walked up the little step, the only one in the Dungle, since Brother Solomon's hut was the only one with a floor. Then, with extreme deference, his head bowed unconsciously, he entered. He closed the door behind him.

The room was clean and neat. There was a large bed with a clean floral sheet upon it. Above it was a hanger holding a black suit and a white shirt starched and pressed. There was a chair in one corner and a table in the next. On the table stood a large frame with the picture of the Holy Emperor on it. Below the picture were written the familiar words which, though Cyrus could not read, he was able to identify as *The Prince of Peace*. In another corner was a tall pole with the flag of Ethiopia hanging from it. Right below the window, which looked out into his own hut, Cyrus saw another table. It had three long narrow legs and on it was an oddly shaped lamp. Around the lamp were three candles, one red, one gold, the other green. In front of them was a queer-looking container with a burnt, brownish substance in it.

But it was the writings on the wall that interested Cyrus most. Those mysterious scribblings. If only he could read he would leave the room a wise man. If only he could read. Suddenly he heard Brother Solomon.

'We must not forget the holy ritual, Brother Cyrus.'

Cyrus jumped to attention again, holding his arm in the ritual position. They both repeated the cult's version of the Ethiopian national anthem:

> 'Ethiopia, the land of fathers,
> The land where all gods love to be;
> As the swift bees to hive sudden gather
> Thy children are gathered to thee
> With our red, gold and green floatin' o'er us,
> With the Emperor to shield us from wrong,
> With our God and our Father before us,
> We hail thee with shout and with song.'

There was a respectful pause. Then Brother Solomon sat down on the side of his bed. As Cyrus sat in the chair, after Brother Solomon beckoned him to it, their eyes met, but immediately Cyrus looked away. No, he could never stare into those sage, searching orbs. His eyes shifted back to the scribblings on the wall until he heard Brother Solomon say, 'Tell me now, Brother, what ails thee.'

Cyrus explained humbly what had happened. Brother Solomon listened to him with a kind, paternal patience and when he was through said: 'I understand how you feel, Brother. The passions of the world and the body is strong an' all you can do is fight it. But if this woman choose to leave you and go and adopt the ways of Babylon let her. You're big and strong and handsome and the juice of life still run like a stream through you; you can find another mate easy-easy.'

'Ah still can't fo'get her so easy, Brother Solomon. Me spirit did go for her bad-bad. Ah was a good man to her as far as it was possible to be good in dis hell we livin' in now. Ah did tell her dat when de Holy Emperor sen' fo' we ah would carry her to heaven wid me as me queen; but she leave it all. She gone to live in de ways o' Babylon. Gone an' leave her own pickney fe starve an' suffer.'

'Come, cheer up, Brother, if she is really a good woman she will see her mistake soon; she will realize that as long as we here we make to suffer an' no matter what we do, an' no matter where we run, we can never escape the fact that we living in hell an' we have our burden to bear. We're the children of Israel suffering for the sins of our forefathers, me Brother, but the time will soon come when we will be redeemed.'

Cyrus listened to every word carefully. This was gospel, the living tidings of a great prophet, the greatest since the incredible Marcus Garvey. Garvey, that first man to proclaim black nationalism: 'Africa for the Africans—at home and abroad! One God, One Aim, One Destiny!' Those were the preachings of the great black prophet. And Brother Solomon was no less great a man. So now, with a zeal, if not entirely naive, was not lacking in a kind of child-like faith, he enquired of the knowledgeable man in front of him, 'Brother Solomon, tell me . . . how . . . how long more we goin' 'ave to wait?'

He asked the question almost in a whisper, for somehow he

felt he should not have asked it in the first place. The Great King in the east would send for them and deliver them out of bondage when he saw fit and only when he saw fit. But Brother Solomon was not severe. He understood his brother man too much for that.

'I should say to you, be patient, me Brother, and leave it at that. But you will still not be satisfied in your heart even if you told me you was. I'll tell you what I know, Brother. The delegates we sent to the Holy Emperor to make final arrangements for our return just write us. Their answer show promise. They said that they don't speak to the Holy Emperor yet, but that arrangement is being made by his holy servants on our behalf. So when we hear from them the next time we will hear the good news and know just when we'll be leaving this land of Babylon.'

'Lawd, Brother Solomon, how me goin' to pray and pray fo' de day to come.'

'Don' be too much on a hurry, me Brother. Remember you have to suffer you lot before you leave. Don' think that things going to be any easier until that day come.'

'Yes, Brother Solomon, ah still goin' to go on bearin' de pangs of hell till we ready fe leave.'

He hesitatated an instant. He wanted to say something but did not know quite how to come out with it. But Brother Solomon read his thoughts.

'You want to say something, Brother; go on, don' be afraid.'

'Brother . . . Brother Solomon, I . . . I did hear say that you 'ave so much knowledge dat . . . dat you 'ave a way o' relieving you'self of de pangs of dis worl' an' . . . an' actually put you'self in heaven . . . is . . . is true, Brother?'

Cyrus breathed heavily after he had asked the question. He did not know how he had brought himself to ask it, though he had wanted to for quite some time now. He had heard these strange rumours about his hero. And he felt, if anyone, he had a right to know if it was really true. Brother Solomon stared through him for a long time. Then a sad, painful smile broke across his face. He came out of his reverie and looked at Cyrus.

'Me Brother, is hard to explain these mysteries, but as a Brethren you know the simple truth that man is God. The white man in him trickery create another God. Him say that

33

that God live in the sky and him call up there heaven; then he say that when we dead we will go to heaven if we do good. Of course this is the horrible trick he use to pacify us in this life while he rob us of all that belong to us an' live off the fat of the land himself. He tell us all kind o' nonsense about blessed are the poor for they shall inherit the Kingdom of Heaven. What Kingdom? The one in the sky, of course. But we know that the true God is Rastafari. We know that Rastafari mean the Holy Emperor who leads against the foe. And we know that the greatest embodiment of that holy master is found in the person of the Holy Emperor.'

'King of Kings, Lord of Lord, the Conquering Lion of the Tribe of Judah, selah!' Cyrus added reverently.

'Yes, me Brother. But there is another thing that they hide from us. The most important of all. And that is that man is God. The spirit of Rastafari is invested in every one of us. Is just for we to find it. This, this, Brother, is the wickedest sin that the white man commit on himself and us and that the brown allies now perpetuate. For when they enslave us in this land of Babylon after taking us from the sweet heaven of Africa they not only enslave we body but also we mind. An' even now we still enslaved, but is a different kind of slavery, a more subtle kind——'

'Beg pardon, Brother Solomon,' Cyrus butted in, 'but ah want to tek in everything you say; wha' you mean by subtle?'

'Good question. When I say subtle, me Brother, I mean cunning, crafty. You hear about the serpent in the Bible; well, the serpent is the symbol of the white imperialist, me Brother. An' that is where most of him strength lay; him is a schemer, like Brer Anancy, you remember Brer Anancy, little an' runty an' cry-cry an' smart. Him have all the cunning of Anancy and all the strength of Brer Fox. So, as I was saying, the white man now enslave us not so much in the crude form him used to do one time but now him use other tactics to keep up with the times. So now him whip is poverty and his claim to superior culture and the Slave Driver is the dirty black lackeys who lap up his myths and the Slave Master is the filthy white capitalist from abroad. Development! Economic development, that is the new Sermon on the Mount, Brother. Hear it well. It enslave the white man long time. It enslave the brown lackeys and the black traitors long time. And it keep us in perpetual damnation, Brother. It's our sweat that made England. It's our poverty it smothering over now. An' what this all mean, Brother? It mean that the God that is within you is locked up in the filthiness of poverty. There is hardly any escape. For you so anxious to get out of the trap of poverty that you ready to sell you soul to the new Sermon on the Mount. Out of the frying-pan of poverty into the fire of white corruption. To find you soul you have to break away all the stink and muck that surround you without falling into the trap. And it hard, me Brother, it hard. You have to be a man of high will, you have to read all the books of the great mystics of the East and if you try, if you try an' try an' try, you might succeed some day, some night. But when you go to Ethiopia you save you'self all that trouble, me Brother, for then the white man's chains will be off an' you will find the God within you, the God that you really is, without a effort. Without a single effort, me Brother.'

'Of a truth, Brother Solomon, of a truth,' Cyrus said softly when Brother Solomon had finished speaking. The latter by this time had got from the edge of the bed, stooped to the ground and moved away the mat. Then he scraped away some dust, lifted a little handle and opened a small, carefully concealed trapdoor. Nailed to the bottom of one corner of the door was a little box. Gently, he put his hands through it and took out a few pieces of the dry, crisp substance that looked like parched leaves. Carefully, he replaced the door and the mat over it. Then he went to the table on which the three candles stood and took from behind the little jar a long chillum pipe. He stuffed in the dried leaves and lit it. With a trance-like gaze he puffed the holy herb. After a few puffs he handed it to Cyrus.

'Peace an' love,' he said gravely. 'Peace an' love, me Brother, puff ye the holy herb of God and obey the holy scriptures, for, as it is written, "the dove came in to him in the evening; and lo, in her mouth was an olive leaf plucked off".'

'Of a truth!' Cyrus exclaimed with soft ecstasy, 'of a truth, "the sorrows of hell compass me, in my distress I call upon the Lord, there went smoke up out of his nostrils, and fire out of his mouth devoured: and it was the holy herb of wisdom".'

'Peace an' love, me Brother. We do not beg, we do not steal, we depend upon the grace of Rastafari for livelihood, we know that he will look after His own, and, most of all, that the holy weed which we smoke guards us from all sickness and gives us wisdom, love and understanding.'

'Of a truth, of a truth,' Cyrus uttered, now almost transcended. 'But the oppressors of Babylon in their wickedness has banned the holy herb, has taint it with the name of marihuana and say that it cause us to do badness. Oh, Brother Solomon, when shall Babylon fall, when shall the oppressors suffer at the hands of the conquering Lion of the Tribe of Judah for their wickedness? When?'

'Pity the white man, Brother. His own mind shall destroy him. He make of the things of the world his god. And that god is now become a monster. I wouldn't be surprised if when the white man smoke the holy herb it make him do evil things. For one, the herb was made only for the black children of Israel to relieve them of their punishment and to give them wisdom and courage. But, then again, it is the attitude which the white man take to the holy herb that make it so detrimental to him. For him smoke it believing that it really going to do him evil and that is enough to make it do him evil.'

'Brother Solomon, you speak wid all the wisdom of the ancient Solomon.'

Brother Solomon did not answer. Instead, both men stared in abstraction towards the east. Both had their secret hopes. Then, pacified, and with a meditative air, Cyrus got up. It was time for him to leave. He had indeed been honoured and he felt he should not abuse it.

'T'ank you for you words of wisdom, Brother Solomon; ah don' know what ah would ah mek ah meself if you was'n' here to guide me path,' he said as he got up and walked towards the door. But Brother Solomon was not listening. He had fallen into a deep-deep reverie and had lost himself into the distant nothingness of the seeming blue above him.

4

PANTING, she rushed up to the corner. It was the one to which he had directed her, she was sure. There was the bar with one of its doors broken off, there was the gully, and there was the half-lunatic beggar whom he said always hankered about the place. But where was he? God Almighty, suppose he didn't turn up? Suppose he had made a jackass out of her? She had given him her body for the past two nights with the understanding that he would be taking her to live with him soon. Suppose it had all been a mean, dirty trick. To think that she, a seasoned whore as she, would fall for something like that.

She was tired. It was about two miles she had walked and with the box under her arms. She went over to the bridge that ran across the gully and sat on the concrete railing. A pimp walked past her and sized her up in one long, intense stare. But she kept her eyes on the bar door, thinking that maybe he was inside and would appear at any moment. Two minutes. Three minutes. The pimp walked by her again from the opposite direction. A few yards from her he stopped. Slyly, he approached.

'Business bad?' he half questioned, half suggested.

'Clear off,' she ordered, not looking at him.

'I know a good lot, gal. Pure Yankee sailor; jus' come off ship; pocket loaded; them all fat like ticks.'

'Haul you blasted ass; don' bother me!'

'Is wha' de hell you goin' on with,' he said fiercely, walking off. 'All you stinkin', rass whore goin' on as if you so blasted independent them las' days.'

More anxious than ever, she got up and walked under the street-lamp, stood there for a while, then walked back a few yards in the direction of the bar door. Suddenly she heard a voice calling her. It came from the side of the bar, on the little lane.

'Ah did'n' see you till a while ago,' he said. He was a broad man, fairly tall. He had that funny complexion which was neither black nor brown but seemed like a mixture of clay and ground charcoal. A real St. Elizabeth red negro he was. But she didn't mind.

'Ah been waitin' meself for a few minutes. I must 'a' pass de corner when you wasn't lookin'.'

'Yes,' he said, then he held her by the arm and led her down the lane, turned into an alley a few hundred yards down, then up another street. There was silence between them for some time as they walked. She thought nothing of it. It appeared as if he didn't. They only moved on briskly, sometimes stumbling over bits of garbage, sometimes slipping in the innumerable gutters that crossed the street. He didn't try to help her when on more than one occasion she almost fell. But she thought nothing of it. It appeared as if he didn't. They only walked briskly on. On to the clean, good house he had prepared for her; on to the sweetness she had prepared for him.

But as they came out upon another main road he looked down upon her and said briefly:

'Ah still can't understan' why you did'n' wan' to mek me come fo' you at you' yard.'

She took some time before she answered, noticing that his voice was too mild for his body, or his uniform. The silence had an embarrassment about it she did not like.

'Ah done tell you already that ah live too far to did ask you to come for me; furthermore, ah didn't wan' the people them in me yard to know me business.'

The guttural sound he made did nothing to cover up his disbelief. But he said nothing more about it. They walked the rest of the distance in silence.

A mile later they reached his room. It was one of three at the back of a larger house on a street somewhere in Jones Town. The place was quiet when they entered except for the slightly raised voice of a woman, spoken in an American accent.

They went straight to his room and closed the door behind them.

At last. At last she would be living like a human being. She would have four walls round her at nights; she would have a bed to sleep on even when she was not whoring. When she was not whoring? She had even forgotten that that too was past. Could she dare believe? The very thought aroused a strange sensation in her. Of a life-server walking unmolested through a prison gate. Strange, though. She was overwhelmed. Yet the intensity of her realization drove through her a pang of unreality. She was out. She had arrived. She was proud of her success. Happy in it. Conscious of it. Yet the very moment she became conscious of her joy seemed to have been the moment in which a perplexing uneasiness of something falling back was touched off. It was easy, however, to convince herself that this was merely the mystery of happiness. So she relished in it. And when he said, 'You like the place, no?', she could reply quickly, 'Yes, ah don' mind it,' even trying, unwittingly, to impress herself with the fact that she had to give him the impression that the room wasn't so vastly different from the one she had just left.

She caught his eyes. They were hungry. But what did she care? He deserved everything she could give him. Slowly, he came over to where she stood by the bed. His hands went out and trickled down her back, then to her bottom, and there they rested. She could see him waking with desire. She would play with him. She knew her trade. The sailors had all acclaimed her the best whore on Harbour Street. She knew it, and the fact had always swelled her with a resentful pride. Her body had thrilled him like that of no other woman. He had told her so that first night when she had tempted him off his duty to the little brothel where she operated. It would be paradise being able to do that every night, he had exclaimed. And she had smiled at him and his mild voice. She was hardly fond of him. There could be nothing like that between them. Each had something to offer. They both needed.

So now, as he tried to embrace her, she nimbly slipped out of his embrace and fell upon her stomach on the bed. Her feet were as far apart as the tight dress she wore would permit. She set her hips at an angle that tormented him. Clumsily, blunderingly, he tried to move upon her. Again she slipped him, this time rolling over on her back. By now two or three buttons towards the pit of her stomach were pulled, revealing her black underwear. He was fevering with irritation and desire. He winced. She experienced a slight sense of pleasing hate.

With a more determined effort he made for her. She was ready for him. She fell to the ground as he grasped her and he tumbled down upon her. In a jiffy she was up and laughing at him. Clay-red with anger, he got up.

'Listen!' he stuttered angrily, 'is wha' 'appen? Why you don' wan' display?'

She held her side and laughed yet more. The rest of the buttons pulled under the strain as she leaned her back to laugh. The flesh upon her was taut yet gleaming with a black suppleness. He, suddenly grasped her to him. He stripped her. She gave her body so completely to him that he had to hold her up. He was confused for her. He lifted her and threw her upon the bed. It was short, hasty, unsatisfying.

When he had pushed her aside to make space for himself and had rolled over and gone to sleep she could not help turning over and looking at him. She sat up in the bed, took one of his cigarettes and lit it. From the golden hue of the beams of sunlight that stole through the window she knew that the afternoon was dying.

5

TONIGHT. Tonight, dear God Rastafari. Tonight he would succeed. It had to be. He just felt it. Fool. Oh, such a fool. Didn't he have the same feeling every night? How could he live on hope so much. But hope he must. He knew well that it was the only thing worth hoping for. Go on he must. And tonight. He just felt it. The strange urge was there inside of him. He could feel that he would experience it. Ah me, my God, he sighed. God. God. God. I know I'm God. But to feel him in me. To experience me.

He locked the door of the miserable little shop. All quiet in the Dungle now. Even the other-worldly little lighted kerosine lamps and bottles were going out one by one. Rachael was now just humming her song. He could hear Old Zacharry's groan and his relieving chant. Groan on, miserable old man. Chant on, chant on.

> 'Oh, you sen' us off de sea-coast,
>   But de yoke is off when ah die,
>   An' back I'll come to haunt you
>   In that great bye an' bye.'

He walked upon the soft filth, which was now damp with dew, to his hut. Haunting sensation of pungent ambivalence, the jasmines. He went inside and carefully locked the door behind him. He lit the lamp. Then he moved away the mat and took out the ganja. He stuffed it in his chillum and put it down on the bed. Then he lit the candles. Green and red and gold.

His heart swelled as he saw the candles burning. A sigh sank down within him. 'My country,' he whispered. 'Oh, my country, my heart weeps for thee.' But will it always weep? Will it always burn? Some night will he not find some peace? Will that great moment never come? Even for a second. Even for the minutest fraction of a second. I, God Rastafari. Let I be I. Oh me, my God. For once, for once. Let me find my Ethiopia right here. He went to the picture of the Holy Emperor. He knelt. He prayed. 'Oh, Rastafari. Oh, Holy Master who leads against the foe. Once more I try. Once more I try to realize your spirit that is within me. If I cannot go to Zion in body then surely by experiencing thee I shall be there in spirit . . .' He paused. The words dried up at his throat. What more could he say? What else could he say that he didn't say every night, that he did not beg for every night? 'Help me, God Rastafari, for the sake of the Holy Son the Mighty Selassie, help me . . . help . . .' Again his voice trailed out. He remained kneeling for a few long moments. Then he got up, lit the incense and lay upon his back on the bed.

He took up the chillum pipe, lit it, and began to smoke. Slowly, slowly, the earth sank down below him. All sense of touch numbs down to vacancy. Eyes close untightly. A darkness blacker than the night seeps down. Gradually consciousness melts away into nothingness. As if on a cloud soaring past the stars, past all the gloomy depths of the dark, vast sky. Then there is lightness. A swirling, dreamy, ethereal lightness that carries away into the deep recesses of a remote, heart-stilling godness. Now . . . It would happen now. You feel a soul-stirring quiver somewhere deep within you. With a sharp shock your heart stops. Your blood gushes forward, warm, eager, fervent. Then with an engulfing thrill it too stops, suddenly, a latent crater. You lose yourself into the absolute rhapsody of it. Dissolve. Melt away. Be no more. You become a living soul. An ecstasy. Then you wait. You wait and wait and wait. For still you have not yet reached. You can almost experience it, you have almost become it. But something holds you back. What? Forget. Forget. Forget the stinking, bestial world. It is only things. Only things. But how can you? There she is. My God, no! Where in the deepest depths of this ethereal blankness can you hide. Run, run. But she still comes. The astral hunter chases.

She is crying when you last saw her. Ragged and dirty and

filthy. Both her wiry breasts are out and the naked twins each suck away the last dram of nourishment in her. Or is there any left? Look at the way they suck and suck and bite. Hear the way they scream and see the skin around their bang bellies stretch. And the five little ones behind her. Five gritty, tough, barren little steps and she their maker with two more. You see them? Five little crutches turned upside down with a thing like a football sagging a little above the crutch and resting on top, covered over with a leathery-like thing that resembles skin. You must not listen. Don't!

'Lawd, Mr. Solomon . . . ah goin' dead now . . . ah in fe it bad-bad now.'

'What 'appen, Keturah; wipe your nose, you look awful.'

'Lawd, Mr. Solomon, you remember that me did get a job as washer at this boarding house me did tell you bout?'

'Yes, what happen?'

'Well, today, jus' as me sta't to wash de clothes them, mindin' me own business, mind you, not troublin' nobody but meself . . .'

Today. Today, always today. If he could only see tomorrow. But try again. Make the eternity that is tomorrow today. He pulled hard upon the holy weed. Again the soaring sweetness. Again the feeling of joyful melting away. Of drawing closer. No time except the growing now. Closer. The chairs, the walls, the everything dissolve into the growing now. Closer. He would experience it. Yes. For sure now. Tonight it would be. And in. And in . . .

'So what happen while you sit there minding you own business?'

'Me dear Mr. Solomon, a woman no jus' pass an' see me an' look 'pon me long an' proper like me is puss over dog 'pon mango tree. "Me see you a'ready," she say, "is wha' yu doin' in dis part o' Kingston?", so me ask her if is any o' her business an' same time she say, "Ah 'member whe' ah see you now, you come from de Dungle, you is a Dungle pickney, ah can smell it 'pon you, wha' yu ah do in good people place? . . ." '

The incense poured into his nostrils. He drew deeper upon the holy herb. Again it sparked his blood with fire. Restlessly he shifted upon the bed. He turned upon his side, but he became too conscious of the beating of his heart. So he resettled on his back and stared through the little window at the heavens. The

43

heavens declare the glory of God. Maybe the holy scriptures of Rastafari would help him to succeed. But it would be so difficult distinguishing the good parts from those with which the white man had tampered. He allowed his mind to fall upon any passage that came to it. 'Blessed are they that mourn, for they shall be comforted . . . blessed are the poor for . . .'

'Now me is a poor beggar, Mr. Solomon. Me no trouble anybody. Why would a woman who me don' know jus' pick 'pon me like dat? When me never pay her no mind she lef' me an' say she goin' tell de missis. An' she go an' do jus' dat so dat her frien' can get me job. Lawd, Mr. Solomon, me is jus' a poor beggar woman wid seven pickney.'

'And what happen after she went and tell the missis?'

'The missis come out same time an' ask me if is true dat me come from Dungle, an' when me tell her yes she fire me same time an' never even give me a penny 'cause she say me lie to her an' dat she could'n' keep somebody dat come from a den o' thieves and cultists like de Dungle. Lawd, Mr. Solomon, is why she had to fire me dis big-big Monday mornin'? Is wha' wrong me do? De only sin me ever commit is when me find meself in a de Dungle, an', Mr. Solomon, me no responsible fo' dat. Lawd, Mr. Solomon, me is jus' a poor beggar wid seven starvin' pickney, is wha' me goin' do?'

'Tell me, what you give the pickney them since morning?'

'Since mawnin', Mr. Solomon? Not since yesterday them or me eat anything, sar. Hungry tearing out me guts till ah feel fe bawl out loud, but is me pickney dem ah worryin' 'bout, Mr. Solomon.'

'Look, take this piece o' salt-fish and flour, go and give them something to eat.' He took out the piece of fish and the little bag of flour Sammy had sold him and gave it to her. Her beady, yellow eyes gaped greedily out of their two meagre, withering holes.

'Lawd, Mr. Solomon, God bless you, sar, God bless you.' She almost snatched it from him, and looking at it for some time as if to convince herself that it was real, she hustled out of the little shop repeating: 'God bless you soul, Mr. Solomon. God bless you soul. . . .'

He turned upon the bed and pondered her blessing. He wondered why he had given her the cod-fish and flour. He could

44

hardly afford it, he knew. But then there were the holy words. 'It is better to give than to receive.' The words rested on his mind for a few moments. He gradually came to feel that there was something suspicious about them. This do good and good will be done to thou attitude always chilled him with slight embarrassment. It smacked too much of Babylon.

He got off the bed, walked towards the lamp and turned it up a little. His eyes fell upon the *Sic Vitae* which he had written out in large black letters on the wall. He ran unconsciously through the first half of the sonnet.

> *Like to the falling of a star,*
> *Or as the flights of eagles are—*
> *Or like the fresh spring's gaudy hue,*
> *Or silver drops of morning dew ;*
> *Or like a wind that chafes the flood*
> *Or bubbles which on water stood :*
> *Even such a man, whose borrowed light*
> *Is straight called in and paid to night . . .*

Ever since he had been defrocked from the Church of England on the grounds of insanity and had joined up with the Rasta-farians, he had felt uneasy about the third line of the sonnet and had even made several unsuccessful attempts at changing it. But the sonnet as a whole had never failed to fascinate him. Perhaps largely because it never failed to bring back memories of his youth. It was just two weeks after he had gone to theo-logical college that he had come across it while getting ac-quainted with the library in a little volume of metaphysical poetry. He could still see the little brown book, he could still smell the antiquity of its pages. That little book was to become his saviour during the three years he remained at the wretched college. Three years with all those hypocrites. Studying their catechism, praying to their gods and quarrelling with their whores.

The week before he came she had seduced him. Perhaps it was then that it had begun, the disillusionment. Parson's wife. Great Parson. Wonderful Parson who had taken him off the streets after his mother had died and left him an orphan. Parson who had taught him and cared for him and loved him. And his

45

wife, she had been sacred to him. So calm and commanding in her person. She was kind to him, but he respected her so much that he was almost afraid of her. Then the week before he had left for college, just a little after Parson had gone to Kingston to look about the new church bell, she had called him into her room. It was large, clean and dignified. He never knew before that a bedroom could emit dignity, but from the first time he had gone in there that was the only word he could use to describe it. The smell of the old furniture and the books, and the strange powder in the long metal container with the quaint design, the long, folding curtains and the white sheet. All weighed him down with dignity. And she, always so serene, in the middle of it all. Parson's wife. Stout and pure and white and gentle and kind.

She was lying on the bed with her housecoat on. No, she was not sick, she replied to his anxious enquiry, telling him to sit down beside her. She spoke to him. From the beginning he could detect a difference in her manner. Instead of the usual soft, kind but commanding tone, her voice had now become low, at times hoarse and confiding.

'You must be a good boy at college,' she said, and smiled.

'I will be. I'll never forget all that you and Parson have done for me, all that you've taught me.'

'Oh, you're only saying that now; wait until you go to Kingston and meet all those pretty girls, you'll forget everything about me.'

He flushed with surprise at her words.

'No, I never could forget you, you both made me what I am.'

'Maybe Parson, but not me. As soon as you see some pretty little girl you'll forget everything about me.'

He couldn't understand her. A dreadful thought suddenly passed through his mind, but he quickly got rid of it. He would pray to God that night for having for one moment misinterpreted the good woman in that manner. She came up closer to him on the bed. He thought he felt her shaking. He would pray even harder tonight.

She talked about all sorts of things. He couldn't believe it at first. Why shouldn't she be happy? What was wrong with Parson? And she kept coming closer and closer to him. She was warm and stout, Parson's wife. The nearness of her body began to frighten him. He wanted to run, but he was petrified in her nearness. He noticed her hand pulling away the front of her housecoat. It fell away. He consumed the whiteness of her flesh. His initial reaction was that of revulsion. Complete revulsion. But the intensity of his revulsion formed the very basis of a compelling fascination. He felt her hands on him and against his own will he responded almost to the point of violence. He would hurt her. He could only justify his actions then if he hurt her with all the passion of his self-killing revulsion. He knew to God that he could only face himself again if he was conscious of the fact that in that instant there was the need to crucify her. She felt the tormenting paradox of his soul and gave in to it hungrily. He lost himself.

And only when he lost himself in that little brown book could he forget. The terrible feelings he got in the mornings. The aimlessness, the futility. What was the point? Where was he coming from? Where was he? Where was he going? What was the point? What was the point of even asking what was the point? It got so that if he asked himself the question one more time he knew he would have done something terrible. These were the naive beginnings of his quest.

He had written out Henry King's *Sic Vitae* from the little brown book. He never felt he really understood the sonnet even after discussing it with one of the teachers who didn't seem to have thought much of it. Maybe it wasn't that he didn't understand. Deep down he felt that he must have intuited its true significance but its articulation evaded him. There was a tone of tragic finality about it which both horrified and fascinated him. He sensed that it sought to say something vital, to deny something, but it struck him that the very attempt at expression defeated the essence of the denial, a denial which was itself the denial of all things real, of all essence.

'Negation negates itself,' he used to murmur to himself whenever he completed reading the sonnet, never failing to revel in the esoteric absurdity of his own paradox. Yet he was sure that in the wisdom of what was communicated, whatever it was, there was a kind of tragedy. Perhaps he should have sought no further. All that was being expressed was that to be wise is to be tragic. To perceive the truth of existence is to perceive an unutterable tragedy.

He walked over to the little window and looked outside. The night was as plaintive as a weeping negress. All bitter-sweet with jasmines. Touched down with whimpering dogs and howling cats and frogs unseen. Dew chilled the sad, dark leaves of the sargasso, now numb and glued together with the slippery shades in shrouding and amorphous forms, unmoving. Frightfully gentle, everything. The sea a black serenity and the glows from the lamps of the little shanties, now innocent as death, chilled with a lardish frigidity.

But then! With a deceptive suddenness the tide had changed. Funny he had not heard it before, but now he had become conscious of the heavy breathing of Cyrus. He could hear old Zacharry's chant again as wistful and remote as the distant wail of the screech-owl; and at last he could hear the sea, black and snaky, as it crawled surreptitiously forward through the façade of stillness, then backward, forward, then backward, in its eternal vigil.

6

THE morning sun came in upon her through the wooden bars of the little green jalousie window. She jumped up and flung the sheet off her. She looked about for her underwear, then she yawned and stretched and with her hands circling her feet and her cheek resting on her knees she stared at the novelty of the whitewashed wall.

She had got up earlier on when Alphanso was preparing to leave for work. He had told her then about the people in the yard and how fast they were. He allowed her to continue sleeping since he would be having breakfast at the station that morning. Poor Alphanso. She wished she had liked him even a little. She took solace in the fact that at least she wasn't sure that she despised him.

She looked about the little room and a faint smile broke across her face. She felt proud and possessive in the knowledge that what she saw partly belonged to her. The bed with its soft, straw mattress; the wire-meshed safe with food and plates that could actually drop and break; the table with the two sturdy chairs around it, so inviting and cosy that she could hardly restrain the temptation to sit down in one of them and run her hand across the smooth surface of the table. And what was that thing with the mirror standing on it? She had seen it one or two times before in some of the better rooms her customers had taken her to. It was so modern and beautiful, how did they get the wood to come so smooth and polished? she marvelled. And in one corner resting on a wooden box she saw the little oil stove. That she knew, for she had seen one before in Mr. Solomon's shop which he used to make his meals on.

Quickly she slipped into her dress and buttoned it down the front. She walked over to the oil stove and lit it. She got an unbelievable delight simply out of striking the match, pushing up the top and lighting the wick. There was a feeling of domesticity about the whole process which she had never experienced before, and which, she convinced herself, filled some long-lasting gap in herself.

But having lit the stove she felt she should do something with it. In any event, she was hungry. So she went over to the safe, opened the little door and peeped inside. The fresh smell of food filled her nostrils with a sweet, saliva-dripping fragrance. There was a half-loaf of hard-doe bread, ripe bananas and green ones too, cod-fish, cocao, butter and eggs on one shelf. The one below held the plates and cutlery, and below that were the 'hard' food, yams and sweet potatoes, a few more stems of green bananas, plantains, a large green breadfruit and resting snugly in one corner was a yabah pot filled with soaking mackerel.

Never in her life had she seen such a collection of good food. It was not the habit to store food where she was bred. When you wanted it you went and bought it and if there was no money, well, you did the next-best thing, you went and dug it up from the filth of the garbage-cart.

But look here. Look what she saw. Food. Food to last almost a week. Fresh food. Good food. Not rotting. It was almost unbelievable. For a moment she thought it almost a waste of money to spend so much on food all at once. But she soon came to realize that she was looking at life still with the eyes of the Dungle woman. She must get rid of it. She must dig out those eyes with a heavy spade and put in new ones. Ones that belonged to people who really lived. Civilized people.

She suddenly thought of the civilized people outside. She looked up from the little safe and gazed towards the door. Soon she would be going out there. They would be looking at her, scrutinizing her. A strange fear suddenly overcame her. Would they be able to spot her? Was there something different about her that would make them know at a glance that she was not one of them? That she was a Dungle gal. Christ Almighty, but what did it matter? She tried to reassure herself. But she failed. No matter how she tried to think otherwise she knew that it did matter what they thought. Not so much the substance of what they thought. Oh, they could go to hell with that. So what if they all bellowed out that she was a whore? There was nothing meaningful in words that could smear her. But what tortured her was the expectancy that they would think something. That in an instant she would be abandoned in the alien grasp of their scrutiny. That there would be the impact of their presence and the consciousness of that presence. If now she was afraid of them shouting aloud that she was a whore, her fear came not from the fact that she would experience shame, but from the fact that she would have known then that they had known all along. The moment she did not fear to face, it was simply the verification of the suspicion that all along she had been the object of their consciousness, their expectancy.

And there was herself to contend with. She had to convince herself somehow that there was a struggle within her. She had to make of the moment the reality that she was a changed creature. No longer animal. Now she must believe, now she must want to believe that she did in fact believe she was civilized, human. She had dug out her former eyes and ruthlessly stamped upon them. Now her vision of the world had changed. Yet, there was something in her make-believe struggle that made her flush slightly with embarrassment.

She decided that it would be better to worry about the people outside when the moment came. Right now she was hungry. Her eyes suddenly caught sight of the eggs. They were such curious objects. She had never ate one before, but she had seen pictures of them being fried on old placards advertising cooking oil, placards she used to dig up from the garbage-cart and hang in her hut before she started whoring. She sensed that it was a staple diet of civilized people. Above the oil stove a frying-pan was hanging. She lifted it to the stove and poured some oil in it. She watched it until the oil had almost begun to boil. Then she went for the eggs. She took two of them, for she could hardly imagine how one of those little things could do anything for her hunger. There was some uncertainty as to just what she should do next. Fry them, yes. But not with this thick shell, the oil would never get into it. Then she remembered vaguely that the egg on the placard had been cracked in two beside the frying-pan. Yes, she would have to break it. Gently she tapped the top of the egg on the floor. It crumpled and flattened, but nothing happened. Impatiently, she hit it harder. It became slimy, but whatever was inside refused to come out. She paused and wondered what could be the matter. Then she recalled that chickens came from eggs. The thought was neither helpful, nor comforting. Almost angrily, she hammered it on the floor. The shell caved in and her fingers sunk into the slushy contents seeping out to the floor. She cursed, went for the broom in the corner and wiped it up.

She did not exactly like what she saw inside the egg, for she had always possessed an aversion to slimy things. She could recall losing many customers for that very reason. Nor did she like what she smelled. She took up the other egg and was about to take it back to the safe when she suddenly checked herself. Her eyes. They were not the same. What would Alphanso say? What would the people outside say if they heard that she had never eaten an egg before, that she didn't even know how to prepare one? She had to bear it, she had to learn. She must be human.

She took up the egg, and, being more careful this time, she hit it with the fork she had taken from the safe drawer. It cracked gently and the fluid contents fell to the frying-pan. But immediately she dashed away with shock. All during this time she had forgotten about the oil in the pan on the fire. It had long passed boiling point and a funny odour was coming from it. When the egg fell upon it a great hissing, and sprinkling of hot oil burst upon her, stinging her all over her face and arms. More startled than hurt, she recoiled angrily. Then as she stared at the fuming pan, still screeching away, a slow bitter rage gradually warmed up within her. She didn't exactly know what she was angry at. Whether it was herself at her failure, or at the eggs and the pan and the stove and all the rest of it, all the rest of those blasted civilized things that were so alien to her, that almost seemed to snub her. And if there was one thing that nobody or anything ever did it was to snub Dinah. Her temper suddenly surged to a climax. She ran towards the shrieking, fuming stove and kicked the whole blasted thing over.

She was angry almost to the point of tears, but in this she

attained considerable satisfaction, though her persistent awareness of the fact annoyed her against herself. In a desperate surge of consciousness, she sat down on the bed, placed her elbows on her thighs and the side of her head on her wrist in a pretence at frustrated resignation. Fortunately for her the flame went out with the impact of her foot, so there was nothing she could do but wait until she had convinced herself that her temper had cooled down sufficiently for her to go and clean up the mess.

In another half-hour she was helping herself plentifully to the familiar sweetness of cod-fish and bread and cocao. Then breakfast was done and she found herself with a new worry. She had already dismissed the thought of the embarrassment she would encounter on going outside. She relished the belief that they now came back to her. Ordinarily she would have felt proud to walk out there and feel their curious stares on her. She somehow always liked people to stare at her. Nobody, she was sure, ever looked at another for long except there was something of envy or fear in them. The old Dinah was proud and haughty and never minded a little malice every now and then. But now, she must remember, she had new eyes, new worlds, in which to live. She had to adjust herself, for better or worse. There was the chamber-pot to take out to the latrine. Then after that there were the clothes to be washed. Alphanso had mentioned their names to her and what they were like, as well as giving her some idea of how she was to find her way about. But she still would have to fight the fact that in their scrutiny was proof that her presence satisfied some terrible expectancy in them. That they had been waiting for her. They had had her trapped in a place where she could never have defended herself.

Oh, damn and blast it all, why the hell was she worrying, anyway? a part of her suddenly rebelled. But it was put quickly in place. She had to worry about what they thought. It was now vital to her being that she was conscious of herself worrying. She must at all costs appear, not only to them but to herself, that she was concerned with the problem of being civilized. What with her new eyes.

She stooped by the side of the bed and took out the chamber-pot. As she walked to the door she peeped at herself in the mirror. It was the same Dinah she noticed, and she thought she felt some disappointment. How could she be such a fool as to think a night could change her? They would know. They were bound to know. A sudden fear seized hold of her. She felt like running back to the bed and hiding herself under the sheet. But then realization took hold of her. She flushed at her stupidity and her attempt to stifle the sudden consciousness of the moment, with the feeling that she had been suddenly imbued with a resentful boldness, only made her flush more with embarrassment.

Still, she pursued the façade of her assumed boldness. Who the hell was she afraid of, anyway? Not them, let them go to the blasted hell. So now she had convinced herself that she was really embarrassed. She had convinced herself that her sudden boldness was the defensive workings of her unconscious. And she had compelled herself to believe that the goose-pimples which now popped all over her sprung from a genuine fear of her impending encounter with the civilized, rather than the awareness of the fact that she flushed only at the artificiality of her whole emotional state, at her absurd attempt at assuring herself that she was in fact embarrassed. That she was. She was.

This being so, it was natural that when she pushed the door open and walked outside her boldness should seem immediately to melt away. In fact it did. And this shook her for a moment with real confusion. She could only sink in her own bewilderment as the façade was shattered. As her real being realized what it had all along, and, in that instant, pretended to be. For in a singularly real way she did dread her present experience. She was terrified, not of them, but of the awareness that they had been waiting for her, that she was now totally embedded in the sting of their expectancy. She could only try not to look at them.

It turned out that there was very little space between the set of three rooms at the back and the main house. The left side of the main house projected a little from the rest of the building and made up the kitchen and the latrine which Alphanso had told her she should use. A short little paved verandah ran alongside this projection and on it was an old rocking chair in which a fat but droopy old woman sat, holding an old condensed milk can in which she spat every few seconds. In front of the room to the left of hers was Mrs. Davis, who was at that moment bathing her grandson. She was just as Alphanso had described her, short and stocky and mean-looking, her head resting stumpily on her shoulders without the assistance of a neck, her mouth set squarely, as she washed the boy, who should have learned to wash himself ages ago, in that niggardly, jealously brooding manner of an overfond grandmother. Then to her right was a youth of around nineteen or twenty who was obviously the younger of Mr. Macpherson's sons, cleaning his father's motor-bike. A few yards away from him was the little kitchen which she was supposed to share with Mr. Mac, so everybody called him, Alphanso had said. Inside, Mr. Mac was cooking his and his sons' breakfast. Everyone except Mr. Mac stopped what they were doing to stare at her. Their prying, gaping eyes perforated her long and hard, shamelessly. In a moment she felt as if they had stripped her of all her being and was tearing it to pieces, searching into every last crevice of it, as if it was the muck the garbage-cart deposited at the Dungle. For the first time since she could remember, Mrs. Davis neglected her little sweet baby, not even noticing that he was mischievously wetting up the tail of her dress. Carlton, Mr. Mac's son, still kept rubbing the motor-bike but his mind was no longer on the job. Almost a minute passed and the woman in the armchair only spat once in her little can.

She dared to take a step forward. Their eyes moved with her, like the glowing orbs of a cat in the night trailing the path of a rat before it sprang. She took another step forward, then suddenly jumped back as she heard a scraping sweep coming from the roof of the main house above her. She looked up and saw a withered but tough-looking old man peering down at her. He held a broom in his hand with which he used to sweep off the leaves of the ackee tree that overhung the house. Time had forgotten him, it appeared, for although the numerous lines in his face betrayed his extreme old age, you could see a sinewy stubbornness in the way the skin held on tight to his frame. 'Is rum cure me so,' he was fond of saying, 'ah can't dead till ah wan' to for rum is me medicine, me fountain of youth.' And Alphanso had admitted that he had convinced many of the truth of what he said. She held the dark, sunken eyes of the old man for a long moment, then looked away for sheer embarrassment. There was nothing treacherous or wicked about them, but, still, there was a kind of mischief, that kind of don't care, malicious disregard which always seem to come with second childhood. With their stares still moving with her, she walked the rest of the distance to the latrine. She closed the door behind her. As her eyes caught the latrine bowl she came back to herself. Another luxury. Another mark of the civilized. Sure she had seen sewers before, but only in those fleeting moments behind cheap hotel rooms. Now it was hers. This was her home and she could use it any time she liked. She could have kissed the smooth marble frame of the bowl. But she restrained herself and instead gently poured the contents of the chamber-pot in and pulled the chain. Then, again, it was with deep-felt pleasure, like a young boy at Christmas marvelling at the ingenuity of his toys, that she heard the quick, cleansing flush, that she saw the water miraculously spring from the sides of the marble and then disappear.

When she opened the door and walked back outside she made sure not to meet any of their eyes but walked straight to her room. There she hesitated for a moment. Then she drew the washing tub from beneath the bed, dropped the bundle of dirty clothes in it and walked back outside. The tap was just behind the kitchen which she and Mr. Mac were to use and at a position which was also a few yards from the right side of the main house. She rested the tub on the board across the cistern and turned on the tap. The water pressure was low, so she had to wait for some time before it had sufficient water for her to start.

Suddenly from behind her came the sharp, high-pitched, domineering voice of a woman. Dinah turned her head slowly and out of the corner of her eye she could make out a fat, enormously busted woman dressed in a housecoat and slippers. She had a vindictive, rather malicious, look about her which made Dinah, in her present confused state of mind, almost feel as if she wanted to shudder. Her lips were thin and pointed in that truculent manner of censorious middle age which, if she were young, might have been mistaken for sauciness. Her little nose was short and stubby and the bridge too flat to hold up her rimless spectacles which found refuge on the very tip. She was obviously Old Granpa Mac's wife, though young enough to be his daughter.

The woman, relishing her sour-faced irascibility, went over to Mrs. Davis and made some complaint about her husband. Dinah couldn't hear most of what she said except when she blurted out aloud every now and then that she was the respectable secretary of her Anglican church, and couldn't afford to have the good name of her household ruined. Mrs. Davis continued to wash the boy as if she had not heard the other woman.

Mrs. Mac tucked her stumpy, short hands in the little pockets of her housecoat, screwed up her mouth, and strutted off. Dinah had been observing her every action, listening as best she could to everything. She could see that she wasn't going to like this woman. She had been amazed at the way in which Mrs. Davis took the censorship of her husband. Christ, what a hell of a fight would have broken out had it been her! But it suddenly struck her that perhaps Mrs. Davis hadn't fought back because she was . . . civilized. She didn't even think of doing the things she would have done, of responding the way she would have responded, because she was different from her, completely different. Unwittingly, she looked down at herself. Different? But why should she be different? She tried to get angry with herself but failed.

She turned off the tap and lifted the tub to a box nearby and began to scrub. Just then she heard something that made her start. It was the loud, scandalous laugh of a woman coming from the room whose door was at the side of the house not very far from her. For a moment she could not understand why the laugh had such a frightening effect on her. But on further thought she realized that it was the familiarity of it that had startled her. But where had she heard it before? No, it could not have been anyone she knew. None of her friends were that well off to be living in a room such as this. Still, the laughter haunted her.

By this time Mrs. Mac had already charged upon her next victim, her stepson, whom she chided sharply about not paying his rent. The man merely grumbled angrily beneath his breath but made no reply. After threatening to call in the bailiff she began walking in Dinah's direction.

Immediately Dinah stiffened. This woman terrified her in a way she had never experienced before. Not so much her person, but the sheer novelty of her. She thought for a moment that the woman represented one case of the peculiar effects of being a bit too civilized. Exposed continuously to the joys and ease of a good life, to the secretaryship of an Anglican church—an Anglican church, God up above, that had to do with Missis Queen and all that—to the security of owning a house, to good food and lots and lots of other civilized people, it had all been a bit too much. This high-handed, stupidly domineering attitude, she conjectured, seemed a kind of disease that only the civilized enjoyed.

Mrs. Mac came up to the cistern, looked over Dinah and her wash-tub disapprovingly and, in an awesome silence, walked cockily towards the front of the yard. Suddenly the silence was shattered. It was that voice. That loud, mocking laughter again.

7

THIS time she was positive. She had heard that voice before. Many times too. She stared at the door from which it came, half in surprise, half in a kind of shock which crept slowly upon her and seemed to mock her loudly. She hardly had time to collect herself before she heard the loud voices of a man and a woman coming from behind the door. As she listened more carefully to the woman's voice, her worst fears were realized.

The man was demanding that the woman get up and prepare him some breakfast. His voice was weak and strained, lacking all the force of the command his words sought to imply, and, if anything, seemed to have a tone of fear and timidity for the person to whom it was addressed. The woman barked back scurrilously and for the next few minutes there was a heated exchange of words, the woman having the better of it.

Eventually there was a pause in the conversation, after which the man mumbled something. Suddenly the woman exploded.

'You not gettin' me out of here one damn! Not till I ready to leave. I don't care a damn if I disgracing you or not. The people them outside is nothing but a dirty pack of hypocrites. Claiming that them is Christian yet every night them gone to obeah-man an' revivalist church. I laugh an' talk as I like an' yu not getting me out till ah ready to leave, so jus' go to hell an' leave me out!'

Not her, Dinah kept mumbling to herself. Anyone else but her. They could never get along down in the Dungle. They never would.

She tried to pull herself together. It may have been hoping

for too much, but perhaps the woman inside would not reveal her. She knew her whole attitude was a façade. She realized very well the last thing in the world the woman inside would do would be to keep her mouth shut. Yet she was composed and she hated herself when she sensed the real reason for her composure. She knew then that she would have to make that woman shut her mouth. And she knew full well, too, that it was no longer a matter of not wanting them to know about her but of convincing herself that it did matter that they should not know. Again she flushed at her self-hypocrisy. But she was too lost in the jumble of her soul to mind. It was easy now to follow the façade that guided her consciousness. She bent over her tub and continued to scrub.

A quarter of an hour went by. Mrs. Davis had gone inside and was trying to feed the boy his porridge. Carlton had started the engine of the motor-bike, making a loud, stuttering sound, and was too intent on what he was doing to notice anything else. Old Mac was still on the roof, piling up a larger and larger heap of dry ackee leaves while his son still busied himself in the little kitchen.

Then the door opened with a squeak and the woman stepped out with a chamber-pot in her hand. She was scantily dressed in a semi-transparent blue duster through which it was possible to see her red silk underwear. From the corner of her eye Dinah observed the woman peering around her guardedly. Then she turned to look in Dinah's direction. Immediately Dinah looked away. The woman didn't seem to have recognized her at once, but went about doing what she evidently came outside for. She pushed away the board from under the tap and slyly slipped the urine from the chamber-pot into the cistern. Then she opened the tap over the pot and washed it out, allowing the water to run on it for some time to get rid of the rank smell. When she was through she turned round and began to walk back to her room. She suddenly seemed to have recalled something and stopped. Then she turned to look at Dinah. The chamber-pot almost fell out of her hand.

'Dinah! Is wha' de backside you doing here?'

Dinah kept scrubbing, pretending she did not hear. The woman rushed to her door, placed the pot inside, then came back towards her.

'Wait, wait, wait, but no Dinah dis, no?' she said, as if she had begun to doubt herself. She walked straight up to the tub, placed herself between it and the fence and looked with an inquisitive frown upon Dinah.

Dinah decided it was no use pretending any longer that she had not heard the other woman. She looked up as if in surprise. 'Mabel! My gosh, you frighten me.'

'Yu want to tell me dat you never did hear me a while ago when me did call you?'

'No,' Dinah replied drily. Mabel was quick to detect the unfriendliness in her voice and for this very reason was bent on pursuing the conversation.

'Or is going on yu going on like yu never did see me?'

'I never notice yu. Ah was washin', mindin' me own business.'

'Mindin' me own business eh?' she repeated half mockingly, 'same ol' Dinah, always mindin' her own business.'

Her voice had an air of superiority about it which irritated Dinah. It hurt her pride to think that this careless, dumb-witted virago could have the nerve to talk to her as if she had anything over her.

'Lawd, ah see yu still fightin' it, gal; how it go? De police boy take yu on fo' a few days? At leas' yu can live like a human being fo' a few days now; ah understan' dat whorin' gettin' tough these days.' She shook her head sympathetically and, with great delicacy, flicked off a spot of soap-sud that had dropped on the side of her duster.

'Yu don' 'ave to talk so rass loud,' Dinah said irritably under her breath; 'as a matter of fac', yu don' 'ave to talk at all, for ah not interested in one damn' thing yu 'ave to say.'

'Eh, eh, is what dis, me God? Yu think me 'fraid fe mek anybody know dat me come from Dungle? Is wha' de 'ell you goin' on wid like yu so strikin' nice.' Her voice was uncertain. She knew that she was no match for Dinah if she got her into a fighting mood. But she was counting on the fact that she would not resort to force, having sensed something different about her. The woman she now saw somehow appeared milder, subdued. She must be up to something, but Mabel could not figure out what it could be. She certainly hadn't left Cyrus. He wasn't the kind of man a woman left. It was her awe and love for Cyrus that had sparked off many a fight with Dinah.

Dinah had not answered her, which made her even more determined to be a nuisance.

'Wait little bit, yu really mean to say yu goin' on like yu don' know me. Tell me if is so. Yu fo'get dat me an' yu use to——'

'Listen!' Dinah suddenly hissed at her, giving a quick glance to the back of the yard to see if anyone was listening. 'Listen! In case yu wan' to know, ah come here fo' good, see. Ah done wid what ah lef' behin' an' ah don't wan' to hear 'bout it. It look like yu still livin' in de Dungle, though yu out of it in flesh. I pullin' myself out, body an' soul. Ah don' wan' to 'ave any link wid it, ah don' wan' to 'ave anybody remindin' me 'bout it. So jus' tek dis as a warnin', don' play de ass an' fool 'round me wid any Dungle talk.'

'Yu mean to say dat yu don' wan' de people dem fe know whe' yu come from. Yu hidin' it?'

'Yes, ah hidin' it; ah wan' people to t'ink me is human an' not beast.'

'Well, me no 'ave not'in' fe hide,' Mabel said stubbornly.

Dinah dropped the shirt she was scrubbing into the tub. She lifted one long, soap-sudded finger and pointed it menacingly at Mabel. Her eyes narrowed in the sinister fashion the other woman had come to fear. Her mouth twitched scornfully to one side.

'Well, from now on, you big lump of shit, you goin' 'ave something to hide.'

Mabel shuddered inside. She hadn't forgotten one bit the fights they had had. But she still counted on the fact that Dinah would not break a fight. She saw that she desperately wanted to give the people in the yard a good impression, though this puzzled her. Fortifying herself with the thought that she could use the knowledge she had of her past over her, she loudly exclaimed: 'Oh, so is what yu tek me fo'? Me say any blasted t'ing me please.'

'Well, if yu t'ink yu name bad-woman tell dem where me come from!'

Mabel took up the challenge.

'Is Dungle yu come from, jus' like me, is——' She hardly had a chance to say anything more. Lifting up the shirt she had been washing, Dinah swung it behind her and with all her might whacked Mabel on her mouth with it. She howled with pain and held her mouth for a few seconds. Then she sprung on Dinah, pushing over the tub as she did so. The two women fell to the ground, drenched all over with soap-water. Dinah was the first to spring to her feet. She snatched Mabel by her short, straightened hair, dragged her a few feet to the side of the fence and hit her head on one of the posts to which the zinc was nailed. Immediately Mabel sprung back, clawing and ripping away all the buttons in front of Dinah's dress. Before Dinah could retaliate, Mabel had also rid her of her underwear, so that she stood completely exposed to the people in the yard who were attracted by the fighting. Mabel's tactic of stripping the offender always failed with Dinah. Instead of scowling away in shame, Dinah helped herself off with the fragments that were still on her. She was now only a surging passion. The desire to destroy, to kill, had possessed her with the fervent completeness of an orgasm. A pang of terror ran through Mabel. She knew she could only run now. But it was too late.

By this time the whole yard was looking on, in addition to some passers-by who stopped to peer in. Mrs. Mac was having a fit, declaring in all firmness that she was secretary of an Anglican church, that she was ruined; her mother, for the second time since the morning began, had not spat in her little can for almost a minute; Mrs. Davis was trying desperately to keep the baby from looking while looking herself; she locked the boy in, but just as soon she heard from the keyhole, 'Look at them rolly-polly bottom, Gran'ma!', upon which Mrs. Davis shrieked, 'Junior!'and locked herself in with the giggling boy. Old Mac had actually flung away his broom and was bending so far over the roof to peer at the fighting women that only the heaviness of his boots could explain the miracle of his not falling over. Carlton and Mr. Davis were having a grand time, laughing wildly and sneaking forward every now and then to fondle the bottoms of the women under the pretence of trying to part them.

By now Dinah had completely overawed Mabel. She had ripped the screaming woman's duster clean from her and all her underwear, then had proceeded to hold her breasts and squeeze them till they almost crushed in her fingers. Mabel began to howl for her man.

'Benjamin! Help me, Benjamin!'

Benjamin was heard jumping from his bed and running to the door. Benjamin was seen to take one startled peep outside. Benjamin was heard to close the door. And not a sound from him again.

Dinah was now sitting on top of Mabel, battering the life from her. The woman's face was swollen. She bled from bruises all over her body.

By this time Mrs. Mac was pretending to be hysterical as she saw the crowd grow larger and larger at the gate, some of them even venturing to open it and come inside. Suddenly she fell dramatically on the shoulder of her daughter, reviving just long enough to fix her displaced wig. As the daughter led her inside to apply the smelling salts, she kept repeating that such a disgraceful scene would never, never happen in America. This was the only thing that could distract Old Mac, who ordered her to stop the blasted boasting about America. The old man had an abnormal hatred for America and everything that had anything to do with it, including his stepdaughter.

'It's true, I ain't tellin' no lie!' the stepdaughter said defiantly. 'Harlem's a civilized place; you'd never find anything like this happening there.'

'God damn yu to hell,' the old man said, raging.

'You ain't civilized here,' the stepdaughter insisted. With remarkable vigour the old man dashed for his broom and as the stepdaughter dragged his fainting wife to the kitchen he showered them both with dry leaves. Mrs. Mac's eyes suddenly popped open and glared up at her husband. But by now the old man had been completely carried away and he dosed the astonished women again with another shower of leaves.

'Rebecca!' she screamed, dashing with her daughter to the safety of the dining-room as another shower of leaves came down on them, 'Rebecca, get the prayer book, Satan let loose, everybody gone mad!'

At length Mabel was so battered that when she saw no help forthcoming she deserted her pride and begged for mercy. This was the moment for which Dinah waited. Snatching the other woman by the neck and squeezing it she leaned her lips to Mabel's ear and whispered menacingly: 'Now yu goin' to do what ah tell yu. Don' open yu mouth 'bout one t'ing yu know 'bout me, or else, so 'elp me God, ah kill yu rass nex' time, yu hear! Yu hear!'

She gave Mabel's neck a final squeeze, satiating her passion with the wince and howling agony. Then she sprung from her, picked up the clothes from the ground and flung them in the tub, and, quite oblivious of the gaping onlookers, walked calmly to her room.

8

IT WAS coming on to dusk. The sea was as calm as a nanny, and just as grey. Cyrus and his fellow fishermen sat in a circle on the damp, black sand, mending their nets. They were discussing their favourite subject, Ethiopia, and a mildly heated argument had just sprung up between two of the men, the rest of them taking sides. It all began when Brother Emmanuel, a short, bull-necked locksman, stated that Ethiopia was just a part of Africa and not the whole of it as some of the Brethren were wont to think. Brother Brisco had immediately taken him up on this hotly debated point. He made it clear to Brother Emmanuel that what he had just uttered was a blatant piece of blasphemy, that Africa was just another name for Ethiopia, but the white man, in his wickedness and deceit, had split up the country into divisions, saying that only one of them was Ethiopia.

'Ahh, me god-brother, yu mek de oppressors dem still foolin' yu; I remember when I use to go to school teacher use to tell me de same lies dat yu repeatin' now. She use to show me one little flat book she call Atlas, where them cleverly write down dem propaganda. But when dem run I out of de dirty school de spirit of Rastafari come to I an' tell I dat I is god an' dat if I seek into I, I will find all t'ings an' all knowledge dat de oppressors try to hide from I. De white man 'ave to get 'im knowledge from book because 'im is a' inferior being, but as 'cordin' to I being a black angel an' a son of de holy Ras I only 'ave to seek widin I to find de true an' livin' truth. An' yu know what,

Brother, when I seek unto I is like I discover dat all dat dat stupid teacher use to tell me is lie, lie, everything, especially dat Africa an' Ethiopia is not de same place.'

'Of a truth, me Brother, of a truth,' Brother Emmanuel quickly retorted, 'but yu can't say dat de white man don' teach truth sometime; remember Brother Solomon say dat if dem never did 'ave sense dem wouldn't be as successful as dem is in certain t'ings. I did go to elementary school too, an' although mos' o' wha' de teacher did teach me is lie, yu can't say dat it was everything.'

'Ahh, Brother, but yu don' understan', yu don' understan'. De white man is full up of a certain kind of knowledge. What yu call thrash knowledge. 'Im know how to mek motor-car an' plane an' skyscraper. 'Im know 'ow fe mek big gun an' big bomb so dat 'im can blow up 'imself. But dat is jus' de knowledge of de t'ings of de earth. Plane an' skyscraper an' bomb, de 'oly Ras tell I dat them is there only 'cause them appear to be there, de 'oly Ras tell I dat dem is there only 'cause I will them to be there. Dem is jus' de extension of my flesh, see what I mean, Brother, an' when my flesh dead an' gone, same time them dead an' gone too. Nothing live longer than I. An' anything dat don't live longer than I is trash. Jus' like de flesh here, Brother. But wisdom, Brother—real wisdom, de wisdom of life—well, dat is de secret of de black god Rastafari. Only de black man know de secret of life, an' 'im find it through the divine inspiration of Rastafari.'

'Wisdom, yu speak wid wisdom, me god-brother,' piped in old Zacharry the chanter, a peppery old zealot, who, though he no longer went to sea, since he was not strong enough, still helped the fishermen to mend their nets and hoped for what they could give him.

'Furthermore,' continued Brother Brisco, as he licked his thick black lips, half hidden by the mass of brown, woolly hair, 'furthermore, yu know well dat all dem teachers and doctors and lawyers is nothin' more dan treacherous agents of de white oppressors. Yu can never trus' dem!'

Cyrus had remained quiet all this time and the men now all looked towards him to hear what he had to say. But he didn't seem even to have been listening. Instead, he was staring far out to the red, subdued horizon. His eyes were narrowed in a

67

thin, reflective slit as he seemed to brood on something not of this world.

'Me god-brother seem to be dreamin' of far-off lan',' said Brother Money-man; 'maybe 'im can tell we 'bout de milk an' 'oney and de palace dem we goin' fe live in, an' de white servants dem dat going serve we; tell we all yu dream, Brother, for yu surely seem to be inspired by de 'oly spirit of Rastafari.'

But before Brother Cyrus could say anything Brother Brisco quickly interjected, 'Wha' yu say, me Brother, a dream, far-far lan', yu soun' as if 'eaven is so distant, as if we not going to reach there in a matter of months.'

'Yes, I go wid yu, me Brother, I go wid yu, but——' Brother Money-man tried to defend himself, but he didn't have a chance with Brother Brisco. Placing his net to one side, Brother Brisco stretched forward his rather twisted neck, opened his eyes wide with an expression of mild surprise and sympathy and immediately set out to rid this poor Brethren of his ignorance.

'Me god-brother, it is clear dat yu 'ave not been followin' up de lates' development in de 'oly brother'ood of rasses. Yu mean to tell me dat yu did'n' know dat from more dan a month ago we sen' two delegate to Ethiopia to plead our case to de 'oly Emperor an' dat we expectin' a reply from dem anytime now?'

'Yes, of course——'

'Yu mean to tell me dat yu didn't know dat quite possibly dis reply even come already, for not long from now a meeting goin' to keep in Brother Solomon house? Ah could'n' manage to hear de details but ah willin' to put me head on a block dat they hear from de delegate them an dat they goin' to discuss de date we goin' to leave. Yu mean to tell me dat yu didn'——'

Brother Brisco stopped suddenly as they heard a start from Cyrus. They all stopped what they were doing and stared at him. They knew that he had been smoking the holy herb not long ago and was quite possibly revelling in the divine visions of Rastafari. Maybe, they thought with one accord, maybe he would even get a sign telling him when they would be leaving Babylon for the promised land. Many others had already received such premonitions. Cyrus was in a stooping position. He held his net in both hands, raised in a kind of supplication towards the greying sky. His eyes were now wide open in a remote, transfixed expression. A pleasing, half-smiling ecstasy shone from them. Despite his rather awkward position, he gave the impression of being completely relaxed.

'Me god-brother, jus' a while ago, me was walkin' in 'eaven: me see de pretty green lan', me see de flowin' white robe an' de horse an' de milk an' de alabaster. An', me Brother, far-far off in de distance me see a great white light shining an' when me look good me see dat is de 'Oly Emperor. An' 'im say to me, "Cyrus, I see dat yu 'ave suffered at de 'ands of Babylon long enough, yu pay well fo' de sins dat yu forefathers commit, an' now de time come fo' yu to return to de promise' lan'." An' ah say, "Yes, Father, 'oly Emperor." An', me god-brother, jus' as ah start to walk towards me heaven ah hear ah cry behind me, an' when ah look, guess who me see? Dinah! Yes, Brother, me see her wid her han' an' foot dem tie up wid some heavy chain an' she was beggin' me fe come an' let her loose an' carry her wid me. Ah never know wha' fe do, so ah look back towards de 'oly Emperor an' ah hear like 'im say to me, "She is de Black". Dat is all, Brother, jus' "She is de Black". But ah could see dat I was de only one could free her, an' ah could see dat 'im did want me fe free her, although all dat ah hear 'im say was "She is de Black". So, me Brother, ah jump up an' mek after her to free her, but, Brother, although she tie up in heavy chain, an' although ah see dat she want fe come wid me from de look on her face, she still run, she still run. An' then ah turn 'round fe look an' see if de 'oly Emperor still there, an' wha' 'im would say. But . . . but when ah look, me god-brother, 'im . . . 'im gone.'

'Gone!' they uttered, spellbound.

' "She is de Black". What it could mean?'

They were still lost in the mystery of the vision when suddenly from behind them they heard a familiar cackle. They all spun round to see Rachael, who had crept up quietly, laughing down on them. They glared angrily up at her, but their glances left the old woman unperturbed.

'Yu hear de vision? Yu hear wha' yu should'n' hear? Woman, yu know dat wha' we talkin' 'bout is sacred?' It was Brother Brisco who finally managed to shout threateningly at her.

'Me don' hear not'in' an' me don' see 'ow it would matter even if me did,' Rachael replied calmly, shifting her walking stick from one hand to the next, 'but lawd, oonoo Rasta seem to 'ave somet'ing up oonoo sleeve like hell. Going on fidgety an' holdin' secret council like mad dem las' few days. Is wha' goin' 'appen. Oonoo plannin' fe attack de government, or oonoo get news dat de time fe go back to Africa comin'.' Her voice had its usual flat sarcasm. It annoyed the Brethren to the core to hear this decrepit old bitch making fun of their religion. Their eyes blazed madly at her until suddenly old Zacharry, who felt himself best called upon to handle this situation, sprung to his feet, and pointing his fingers reprimandingly at her face, belched his indignation at her.

'Hence, thou lingering piece of vapour! Out of my sight, thou daughter of Jezebel! Obliterate, you blasted washed-up old agent of Babylon! Move, before I offer you up as a sacrifice to the devil!'

Old Zacharry's gestures and his show of wrath were so ridiculous that the rest of the Brethren could not help laughing. Rachael, who had become quite used to his bursts of indignation and his habit of calling anyone who annoyed him a washed-up agent of Babylon, returned his stare calmly and when he was through laughed softly and mockingly at him. Old Zacharry, finding himself laughed at from both sides, resorted to a venomous outburst of curse words, interspersed here and there with his favourite 'washed-up agent of Babylon'.

Singing her favourite tune, Rachael walked on in the direction of the foreshore road. She had just passed a clump of cacti on which some worn, ragged clothes, mainly women's under-wear, had been hung to dry when a figure darted from behind one of the huts. She stopped, wondering who it was. Suddenly the figure appeared in full view and she relaxed when she recognized him. 'Big White Chief!' she exclaimed. 'Is what de rass-clate yu doin' frightenin' people fo'? Is wha' 'appen to yu now? Yu married de white woman yet?'

'Not yet, not yet,' the man said in a hushed, hurried manner. He was short and black, jet black, with a flat face, a broad heavy nose and thick lips which he kept pulling inside his mouth and licking so that they always appeared moist, and with a sprinkling of spittle on them. He seemed constantly to be in a hurry about something, but at the same time seemed quite uncertain what it was he was in a hurry about.

'I must give the sweet girl time,' he said affectionately, looking about, then at the back of his hand which had no watch on it. 'Just out from England, you know, not yet acclimatized, the poor darling.'

'Ah see,' Rachael commented teasingly, 'yu waitin' till she get used to the hot sun an' these stupid Jamaican people, no?'

He nodded, then commenced to complain about the bad treatment he was getting from Whitehall as his home leave had been long overdue; it was only a strong sense of duty to the mother country that kept him in the wretched island. Suddenly he looked down upon his black hands and complained bitterly about the fact that, despite the hot weather, he had been so office-bound that he was beginning to lose his tan. He ordered Rachael to get his bathing trunks and to see to it that the car and chauffeur were ready, for he intended to go to the beach. And damn the office. Suddenly he seemed to have remembered something. He looked at his hand where the watch should have been and hustled off in the direction of the road. A few yards away he stopped, turned round and hurried instead towards the sea. As he passed the laughing Rachael he glanced down at her with pitiful disdain and shook his head in resignation. 'These natives,' he was saying.

Eventually Rachael managed to pull herself from the spasm of laughter she had fallen into and got up. She walked on past the little patches of black swamps, stinking with decaying debris; past the little containers—old pans, the husks of coconuts, rusty old enamel basins—in which the children insisted on easing themselves. She always tried to look away, but they never failed to attract her eyes. A sickening, cloying stink. She could smell the filth of adults any time without it troubling her. But the filth of children she could never get used to. There was ingrained in it a certain rawness, rotting, rotting which made her stomach sick.

She hurried on to Mary's hut. On her way she passed Brother Glory, a huge, broad, frightening cultist who tied his head with a red cloth and wore a patch over one eye with a flour-bag skirt around his loins and a wide, sweaty green scarf thrown over his shoulders. He was grunting under the strain of a large black pig which apparently had died on the road and had not yet been taken up by the garbage-truck. It was just beginning to smell. ' 'Ow much of it ah mus' leave fo' yu?' he asked Rachael as she passed him. She sniffed the pig to see how far it had gone. 'Leave a pound fo' me, but yu not gettin' more dan sixpence. De damn' t'ing start smell a'ready like carrion.'

'All right, Sister,' Brother Glory said, and walked on.

When she entered the hut Mary was sitting on a box darning her daughter's dress while the girl sat on the bed doing her homework. Mary looked up at Rachael and beckoned to her to be careful not to disturb her daughter in her studies.

'Ah 'ave great news, but is only yu one me tellin' now,' Mary whispered. Rachael sat down and yawned, knowing that the only thing Mary could speak so excitedly about was her daughter. And of her she felt she had heard enough.

'Wait till yu 'ear wha' goin' 'appen,' Mary said, her eyes beaming.

'Well, is wha'? A white man propose to her or something?'

'Not yet. But now ah 'ave better news, wait till yu hear is wha'.'

'Well, rass-clate, if yu tellin' me tell me no.'

'Yu hear 'bout de free scholarship dem dat government start give now to de pickney dem in elementary school?'

'Free scholarship? Me no' know not'in' 'bout no free scholarship. Wha' yu mean by scholarship?'

'Lawd, Rachael, but yu illiterate fe true. A scholarship is when government pay fo' yu pickney fe go a' secondary school so dat dem can higher dem studies.'

'Higher dem studies? Den is wha' yu an' yu pickney business wid dat for? That is backra business. Wha' de rass yu goin' sen' yu pickney fe higher her studies fo'? Is bust yu wan fe bus' de pickney brain? Education no mek fo' neager people, yu know.'

'Jus' move off! Yu see me pickney look like dem other little dry-head, black pickney dem 'bout de place. Yu no' see she 'ave backra blood in a her. Is her father she get de brains from. Me black an' stupid, but her sailor father give her all de brains she need.'

She stopped speaking and glanced lovingly at the girl on the bed. One hand held the book she was reading and with the other she played with the brown, curly locks that came down to her shoulder. 'Lawd, me angel, me angel,' Mary sighed.

'Why yu don' bow down an' worship her?' Rachael asked, her sarcasm lost on Mary.

72

'Yes, but is wha' dis scholarship business yu tellin' me 'bout? Ah still don' believe in too much a dis studyin' fe black people. Look 'pon Mr. Solomon him, yu see 'ow funny-funny 'im gwan. Them say dat 'im was big-big Anglican parson, 'im try fe study more dan wha' 'im teacher dem could teach 'im. Send 'im stark mad. Dat is why 'im 'ad fe leave de Church an' join up wid de Rastafarian them. An' look 'pon Big White Chief, yu did know dat 'im is a very educated man. I knew fe certain dat 'im was big-big in de Civil Service an' was due fe some big promotion an' it get to 'im 'ead. 'Im fall in love an' wanted fe married English gal. T'ief government money fe impress her. When them sen' 'im to prison an' 'im lose both de gal an' 'im job 'im go off 'im 'ead same time. Education! Is education an' too much ambition cause it. Black people mus' learn fe know dem place. Is right here we belong. Right down a' dutty-ground ya.'

'Yes, but ah keep tellin' yu dat yu mus'n' rank me daughter wid black people. Yesterday me daughter do her scholarship exam. She say she do well an' ah know dat she always come at de top of her class. She goin' get dat scholarship. She goin' get educated more dan any woman in dis here country. An' after dat she goin' go to university. Den she goin' back to Englan', yu hear me? She goin' Englan' an' she goin' married a rich Englishman, an' she goin' come back here fo' me an' tek me fe go an' live wid her in her palace, yu hear me?'

'An' wha' yu goin' do in de meantime,' Rachael enquired sarcastically.

'Don' worry 'bout me. Me still 'ave little flesh 'pon me body. Me can still whore it. An' when de whorin' slack off me can go an' clean people house fo' dem. Me will do anything till me daughter ready fe take me to her palace.'

Just then someone knocked softly on the zinc which made up one of the walls of the hut.

'Who dat could be?' Mary frowned.

'Why de backside dem don' come round? Yu no 'ave not'in' fe 'ide.'

'Is who dat?' Mary went to the zinc and asked. A woman's voice replied from outside.

'My God, is Mabel,' Mary said.

'Mabel! Is wha' she doin' down ya? Is her death she lookin' fo'?'

'She say we mus' look fe see if Crocus anywhere 'round dis side.'

Rachael went to the door and peeped out. She could make out no one in the darkness. Mary therefore whispered back to the woman outside that she may come in.

'Wha' de hell yu doin' ya?' Rachael asked her as soon as she entered.

'Ah come fe fix somebody—tu'n down de lamp little bit, ah don' want nobody fe see me.' Mary neglected the request, since Rossetta was still reading.

'But if yu wan' fe fix somebody,' Mary said, 'why de hell yu 'ave to come down ya. Yu know dat if Crocus see yu 'im beat yu to death.'

'Is Dinah ah come fe fix.'

'Dinah!' both women exclaimed at once.

'Is wha' de two a' yu could 'ave now? Oonoo don' live near one another any more,' Rachael said.

Mabel explained the fight she had had with Dinah. When she was through Rachael asked: 'Den' wha' yu 'ave to come to de Dungle fe fix her fo'. Is dat me can't understan'.'

'Is a piece o' obeah me goin' wo'k 'pon her. Is de only way ah can get me revenge. Ah goin' to make a obeah-man set de Dungle 'pon her so dat no matter wha' she do she will 'ave to come back here, she goin' to dead right here in de Dungle. Ah went to a obeah-man, him charge me plenty, but them say that 'im as good as gold. 'Im say dat ah have to come back to de Dungle an' dig up some o' de earth an' carry it back to him mix up wid grave dirt. Is it 'im goin' use an' work de obeah 'pon her.'

She lifted the paper bag she had in her hand and showed it to the women.

'Is dis 'im goin' tek an' kill her; an' 'im goin' bring her right back here before she dead too, 'cause ah know dat is de worse thing she would want fe 'appen to her. Oonoo jus' watch an' see.'

'Ah don' like this,' Rachael said. 'Dinah was me frien'. Is a wicked t'ing to do to her, even though ah know she mus' come back some day!'

'Me neither,' Mary added. 'Suppose somebody was to do dat to me daughter?' The meaning of what she said seemed to have

74

come home to her only after she had stated it. The thought chilled her, for she hunched her shoulders, held one hand to the roof and said in a loud, menacing voice: 'Lawd Jesus, ah would kill dem, ah surely murder dem. Me daughter, me sweet-sweet brainy, brown daughter, me little, pretty puss-puss.' She ran to the bed and held the somewhat startled girl to her breasts protectively.

'Yu better go now before Crocus see yu; ah don' wan' no murder in de place tonight,' Rachael adviced Mabel.

'All right,' Mabel said, 'but me no care a rass-hole wha' any o' yu wan' fe say. Me goin' get me revenge. Ah goin' bring her right back here an' kill her dead wid obeah.'

'Min' it don' fall back 'pon yu, gal,' Rachael said in her most ominous tone, and walked out of the hut behind Mabel singing her song.

As Mabel walked away a shadow moved from somewhere in the vicinity of Mary's hut. It came closer and closer to Mabel. Then it stopped and afterwards continued to shift in and out of the tracks between the shanty hovels as it trailed, unseen, behind her.

9

Less than a week after she began living with Alphanso, Dinah found herself becoming restless. She was afraid to admit to herself that she was bored. The novelty of the place had held her interest for the first three or four days, but after that she began to wonder what it was in it that had overawed her so much when she first came. From the few conversations she had with Mrs. Davis and Carlton she soon came to realize that they weren't much better off than she had been. In fact she soon found that quite a few of them were much worse off.

These people, these men and women whom she had so stupidly felt that first morning were so civilized, so different from her, turned out to behave and think in a manner not very different from the way she was used to. They got up and drank their bush-tea in the morning as she was accustomed to. They went to bed after stuffing themselves with cod-fish and flour, and sometimes with nothing at all, same way as down in the Dungle. The children might not have appeared as starved, but they still ran about the place naked and uncared for. There was just as much swearing and fighting and cursing, despite Mrs. Mac's frantic protests that they were living in a decent neighbourhood and that she was secretary of an Anglican church.

At times, indeed, there seemed to her to be even more violence and fighting than in the Dungle. Perhaps it was because there were so many more people. This was one of the things that really amazed her after a time. Though the rooms were better than those of the Dungle, there were about twice as many to each of them. The women and their children, their many, many children, their old, sick, unwanted mothers, and their men, two-night-standers and weekenders, temporary daddies and uncles whom the tough little children smiled upon with mocking cynicism, they all piled into the little rooms, in their tens and their fifteens and their twenties. Always, always there was the laughter and the babbling of the women, the cry of babies, at frequent intervals the screams of a fighting or a killing, and every now and then the chimes of 'O Faithful Love' going up for the marriage of some old dying couple seeking in the end their peace with the god who had been too respectable for them to live with. They had their concrete walls, sure, they eased themselves in privacy and sometimes had the part of an egg for breakfast, but she didn't see where it made them much the better.

She soon discovered that the area was considered by outsiders just as much a part of the slums of Kingston. And in one sense it was decidedly the worse part to live in. For the people were all trying so desperately hard to deny that it was. Blast them! The stupid, pushing, hypocritical fools. Striving, striving, striving. But getting nowhere, going down if anything, a horse in quicksand. Sensitive like mad too, she realized. Always ready to curse you and tell you of the gutter you were coming from. And they were so good at describing the gutter.

She was sure they weren't any different from her and yet she worried. She was not quite sure why each moment she should catch herself thinking, longing. But the knowledge of what she thought so abhorred her consciousness that she always drove it to oblivion. She determined to hide herself from herself. For this longing in her could not be real. It was a freak, a conspiracy her mind was working on her. What longing, though? She would tell herself that there was none. She was out of the wretched Dungle. She wasn't as happy here as she thought she might have been, but it was only because she was seeking to go yet farther. She was ambitious. Nothing could hold her back. The only longing within her was the longing to move forward. It was so.

And it was that longing which drove her to go to the government unemployment office that next Monday morning. She had told Alphanso of her intention and he seemed pleased, though by then it did not really matter, one way or the other, just what he thought. Of all the people she was bored with none was more depressing than Alphanso. If she could even have detested him it would have been better. But he was just there, big-jawed and clumsy and negative and loving.

The office was to be found way over towards the centre of the city. It was a part of the Ministry of Labour, a series of wooden, two-storey structures, the converted mansions of the old plantocracy. The office she sought was on the corner, separate from the other buildings. When she arrived she was immediately alarmed at the size of the crowd. At first she thought that it might have been a fight and hurried to the scene, for there was nothing that terrified and fascinated her more than the sight of a man outstretched on the asphalt, all crimson in his own blood.

After the initial shock and disappointment of discovering that nothing in particular had happened, she soon sensed that although the size of the crowd might have been normal, there was, none the less, something wrong that morning. She had lived too long in the Dungle not to know when a crowd was becoming a mob. She could feel the tension creeping up about her, growing surreptitiously. Quick-slow like.

She sensed the tautness, the rising passion, in the shouts and barks of the men and youths. She sensed it in the women at the back of the crowd with their hands on their hips tipping on their bare toes to peer over the shoulders of the men into the office. She sensed it in their eyes, the anger and the longing, the hope and the despair, the brown eyes with the yellow tinge gaping into the office, believing against all hope that by looking in they would at least be one step nearer to their goal. And she sensed it, too, in the laughter of the women. She knew that laugh well. It was the laugh of pain. The laugh of hostility that came from the biting, dry wit of the wretched.

She pushed herself into the crowd. For an instant she lost herself in the collectivity. The din and the merriment and the anger ploughed up something in her. She barked and bellowed and laughed with them. But as a large black woman with a basket on her head stepped on her toes she cursed aloud and the act of feeling her pain brought her back to herself.

Suddenly from one side of the door a little brown-skinned man with a gleaming bald head, which he had a way of clasping with his palm every now and then as he became exasperated, began shouting at the crowd. The reckless shifting of the crowd brought him in and out of view so that now she saw his gleaming brown eyes, now his white teeth, now only the top of his shining head.

A few people bothered to notice him.

'Is wha' 'im fo'?' a meagre woman with hideously bony features enquired loudly. Another woman nearby, flamboyantly dressed in a green and purple outfit with the skirt hugging her beneath the breasts and the blouse choking her—she was obviously a religious, the penitent type, the type who could curse most if you crossed their temper—beamed her eyes on him suspiciously and hissed her teeth.

' 'Im look like John-crow parson perch 'pon 'im pulpit.'

' 'Im is a P.W.M. man,' someone near Dinah shouted.

'People's Workers' Movement,' another repeated with disbelief. 'But 'ow that? Him party no jus' win election? Me no expec' fe see another one 'o them fe de next five years again.'

'Maybe is de money an' rotten salt-fish dem buy we vote wid during de election dem come back fo',' a little man suggested from the rear.

There was a burst of laughter. A P.W.M. supporter nearby, angry at this unfavourable reference to his party, shouted back: 'You never know 'bout de half-rotten bully-beef an' secon'-han' underwear dat de J.N.P. candidate dem carry down an' bribe de voter them with. Me would 'a' prefer a man fe give me five shilling fe vote fe 'im dan fe wear brown people old drawers. But de Jamaica National Party is a middle-class party an' dat is why dem t'ink dat all we deserve is secon'-han' middle-class under-drawers.'

'Yes, is true, is true!' a female supporter of the P.W.M. chimed in, and immediately broke into the party song.

'Oh, shut up, shut up!' a man in the middle of the crowd barked in a loud, booming voice. He seemed in his late twenties, was neatly dressed and had the sprinklings of a beard. On the left bulge of his pigeon chest was a gleaming brass badge indicating him to be a member of some league of the unemployed.

'Shut up, all a you! You is all a damn' pack a fool. How long

you goin' to tek to find out that none of de party them 'ave any
interest in you all. Is only when election time come that them
fool 'round you. Before election time you backside out o' door,
an' after election you backside out o' door and you belly bottom
burn you wid starvation same way. "Put me in power an' I
shall give you paradise", that is all you hear from those son of a
bitches. "Paradise, my people, I will give you paradise." An'
the only paradise I know is when I had to go an' haul me little
sister from Paradise Street whore house.'

There was another scream of bitter laughter. The little
brown man near the door was still trying to get a hearing.
'T'ings is different now, my people,' he shouted. 'My wonderful
Jamaicans, I come to bring you tidings of great joy. It is my
party, the P.W.M., that's just been put in power. If it was only
your votes I was interested in why would I bother to speak to
you now?'

' 'Cause you like to butter you bread soon,' a large woman in
a bright red dress answered.

'Fellow Jamaicans,' he continued, as if he had not heard their
laughter, 'I've come to warn you of a conspiracy. The Civil
Service is full of nothing but J.N.P. supporters, the jobs are there
and they're keeping them from you so that they can give them
to their party followers. But our dearly beloved leader has
heard about this scandal and I tell you something. If they
continue this nonsense one more day they're going to regret
it. For our dearly beloved leader, that wonderful supporter of
the under-privileged, that remarkable prophet who was inspired
by the words of God to come and lead his people out of the
trepidations of poverty and starvation and who still has every
intention of doing so, fellow Jamaicans, this great leader of
yours, Seymore Nathaniel Montesaviour, has heard of this
injustice being done by the J.N.P. Civil Service and at any
moment is liable to come down here and bring justice to this
wicked place.'

Dinah pressed and squeezed between the hot sweaty mob
till she had wormed herself to a spot just a few yards from the
door. At this point it was impossible to go any farther. In any
event, the sight inside the office gave her little encouragement
to go on. From where she stood she could see the high iron
railing which divided the office in two. On one side the crowd

swarmed and bustled. One or two tried to sit down on the hard wooden benches, but they soon sprang up again screaming that people were breaking wind in their faces. Some stood on the benches and barked at the civil servants with their towels round their necks and their glasses of ice-water in their hands.

'Hey, you little jeesy-tail boy behind de desk. You t'ink you better dan any o' we here. That tie you 'ave 'round yu neck, an' that damn' towel yu sportin', is them we goin' use an' hang yu. Give we the wo'k yu keepin' from we. Wo'k or we go on real bad!'

Another woman nearby got up on the bench, drew her skirt up above her knees, narrowed her eyes, widened her nostrils and with her left hand placed on her behind, which was shot out in cursing fashion, she jerked her right forefinger menacingly at a young clerical officer who was in the act of lighting his cigarette.

'Look 'pon dat little load o' shit. 'Im don' even drop out o' egg-shell yet an' 'im goin' like 'im is any big white executive.'

'Like is not our taxes paying fo' them,' an expectant mother with an enormously large belly added. She was almost bottom heavy as she wobbled her way towards the bench. Her chest was braced backwards and her two wiry hands swayed loosely from her shoulders. She literally bounced the other women away as she made for the bench.

'But see here!' another woman who was telling her listener what a dirty stinker her former employer had been—a lousy poor-show-great, going off to England and the Continent to spend her vacation yet not having enough money to pay her maid—and who was interrupted by the push of the pregnant woman, protested: 'Is wha' 'appen to this woman? She mus' be t'ink dat dat belly she 'ave in front of her is a iron shield.'

'Walk off!' the pregnant woman replied angrily, 'leave me an' me belly alone. At least people know that is man me sleep with when me go to bed a' night-time.'

'Walk off again!' came the quick reply, and by now the people nearby, smelling a possible quarrel, had begun to cluster around them. 'Is wha' you goin' to do wid dat baby when you 'ave it? Is 'ow yu goin' mind it? Is 'ow yu goin' feed it? See here, if yu go on foolin' 'round me ah will tell you is 'ow yu goin' 'ave fe look after it, yu know.'

'Tell me! Tell me!' bellowed the pregnant woman, taking up the challenge.

'Yu know is 'ow yu goin' to mind it? You know is 'ow yu goin' to mind it?' the other woman repeated, warming up, and the crowd almost licked its lips as it waited expectantly for the final word lashing.

'I will tell you! Is you eye-water yu goin' give it fo' tea! Is yu nose-noght yu goin' give it fo' porridge! And is banana trash yu goin' give it fo' clothes, for you don' 'ave no silk to cut.'

The roar of laughter that greeted this last remark meant that the pregnant woman was finished. She tried to laugh with the rest of the crowd and retreated to the back of the office at the earliest opportunity.

Dinah had heard it all, but this time she did not laugh. Somehow he began to feel sorry for the crowd. It was strange that she should feel sorry for anyone but herself. But for the moment she had separated herself from the crowd. And she couldn't help being impressed by a certain quality in it. She had never seen poverty quite like this before. Where she came from there was complete poverty, and so there was no poverty. For in the Dungle poverty was a way of life which she neither hated nor loved but which seemed to have a frightening compulsion about it. Here, however, it was different. They might have come from the country; they might have had a good job once; when they were young they might well have got good pickings while they whored. But they had all fallen. They were all little pieces of garbage thrown aside by their worlds. In the Dungle you could be easy, you could be patient, you could even be happy in your complete loss of hope. Unless you were a Rastafarian there was nothing to look forward to except poverty, and of that there was plenty. Here they were striving. They were rolling on their bellies and their heads were buried in the dust. But they were conscious of where their bellies were and she knew they constantly felt the dust around them. She felt, too, the strange anger that came from them. Yet she could see that even in their anger they were failing. They could only curse themselves. But they knew it wasn't real. Always they laughed at themselves as they cursed themselves.

'Get back, I say!' she suddenly heard a voice from within the office. Two or three youths had begun to climb over the railing that separated the civil servants from the crowd. The youths were shouting back that they had been coming to the office for nine months and hadn't got any jobs. They wanted to know if it was true that there was politics mixed up in their decisions as to who should get jobs, as the man outside had said.

'Get back,' the office manager repeated as he lifted the phone and called the police. The youths climbed back over the railing when they heard him giving the alarm, but still shouted menacingly. There was going to be blood and murder there today. They wanted work! Work!

Dinah was beginning to get nervous. She had an instinctive hatred of policemen. But she was trapped by the crowd. Her temper rose as she heard the man with the bald head sparking off again about the party bias of the Civil Service. His words were beginning to catch on the crowd. The anger in them was coming out. At least in this they were succeeding. She burned in the realization that even in this little success they were being used. She hated the politicians about as much as she hated the police.

One of the three youths finally struggled his way outside. 'Mr. Brown! Mr. Brown! De civil-servant man inside, 'im call fo' de police an' fo' de minister!' he shouted to the man with the bald head. This seemed to have been the moment he was waiting for. 'Oh yes, good,' he said. 'The minister can't handle this one. Is de Master ah goin' to call. Is time we 'ad a showdown wid dem damn' civil servants in this place. Tek over till ah come back.' He pushed his way through the crowd until he reached the fencing that separated the unemployment office from the other buildings of the ministry. Then he climbed over and ran towards the telephone booth across the road.

10

A<small>N ANGRY</small> murmur waved through the crowd as two mesh-wired jeeps from the police riot squad, each with around twelve policemen, all helmeted and ready with their tear-gas bombs, arrived. Behind them a large black Vauxhall driven by a stiff police corporal pulled up. The corporal got out, majestic in his red, white and blue uniform. He opened the rear door and a white superintendent stepped out.

'Babylon!' an aloof Rastafarian standing a little way from the mob shouted. 'But one day thou shalt fall. Thou shalt soon fall, Babylon!' He folded his arms with the old flour-bag cape around his shoulders. He held his head aloft, proudly, and with deep abstraction forgot once more the seething mob as he stared towards the east.

The pigeon-chested youth with the badge of the league of the unemployed began to curse. He poured his wrath upon the politicians, those merciless, selfish, opportunistic pack of tricksters; he reviled the middle classes, ambivalent, hypocritical, puritanical sons of bitches who licked the asses of the white upper class while they pretend to live in peace and harmony with them; he raged against the upper classes, the thieving merchants and their four hundred per cent profits, their bribery of the politicians, their contempt for the masses whom they had fooled, through their control of the Press, into believing that they held power in their country under the treacherous farce of democracy. He had just started on the police when they finally reached him after beating their way through the crowd. He received a few heavy blows from their batons for his cheek, and, under the hiss of the boiling crowd, they dragged him off to their jeep.

From inside the office the sound of cheers and boos went up. The Minister of Labour, a tall, well-groomed coloured man with curly brown hair and dressed in a brown suit with a maroon waistcoat, had entered the office from the back entrance. He had begun to speak and the crowd outside pushed even harder to get to hear what he was saying. Beside him was the office manager, who was now glaring at the crowd in the manner of a junior master looking at a group of schoolboys he had just reported to the headmaster.

'Listen to me!' the honourable minister was saying. 'Since we kicked the last government out of power we been taking stock of the situation, and believe me, my people, it bleeds my heart to know what a mess that vicious government has made of the country.'

'We want work, not words. We tired o' words!' a woman screamed from the back of the room.

'Yes,' the honourable minister replied, 'but if we is to give you work we must clear up de mess that de country is in first.' He tried to speak in the dialect, but unfortunately he had been too well bred and it came off stiltedly.

'Finish wid words, finish wid words, an' give we wo'k an' food!' the same woman repeated, edged on by a few, less bold, around her.

'Oonoo must give us time,' the honourable minister continued. 'In a few years my party shall make you all happy and contented, you will all have job to go to in the morning, your women them won't even have to go to work if they don't want to, for my party don't believe that women should work——'

'Is true, is true!' a woman in front of him agreed, and the honourable minister breathed a quiet breath of relief when he observed that, at least, he had a part of the female support. The crowd outside weren't hearing much of what he had to say, however, and the supporters of the opposite party had begun to heckle him loudly.

But suddenly from the road another shout went up.

'De Masah! De Masah!' was the cry. It was the Premier. His car had pulled up in the middle of the road beside the crowd.

The little party man with the bald head who had called him now rushed to the car. His was the glory of opening the door. 'Master,' he said with fervour and bowed. The Master stepped out. He was an elderly man, almost seventy. Yet he was a tall, imposing figure. Elegant in the extreme. His great shock of brown hair, with the delicate streaks of white, stood up in unruly majesty on his large, long head. His features all came forward in a graceful, pointed sweep—his forehead, his nose, his chin, his armoured chest, his long feet. As he stepped out of the car he straightened himself and from his exalted height surveyed the scene. He almost seemed to sniff the atmosphere as, for a moment, with kind condescension he glanced down at the silent crowd. They squirmed under him, mute, un-moving, petrified. Each lost his being in the collectivity, and the collectivity killed its being in him. He was the totality, the very essence of the moment. Every move he made, each shift of the wry and gleaming eyes, each turn of the head, each subtle change of countenance—a smile, a reprimanding gleam, a touch of anger, a little bit of sympathy—was imbued with an almighty vigour and gave the moment life.

Then his face broke into a broad smile.

'Heh, heh, heh, heh, heh,' he cackled with a deliberate, delightful ruefulness. And almost at once, with subtle and incredible swiftness, his whole personality had changed. He had descended from the heights at which he had enraptured them. He was human once again and a sympathetic warmth began to emanate from him. Suddenly he had become a kind and loving father. He would not admonish his children. He loved them all with an eternal fondness.

'Heh, heh, heh, heh, heh.' Oh poor, helpless, darling little things, he seemed to say.

This was the moment for which they waited. The magnetism was over. They had been overwhelmed in his mystic splendour and now they had been permitted to come back to themselves. The more diehard of the opposition were silenced while the others, for the moment, deserted their party and joined in the jubilant uproar.

'Massah! Massah! Big Massah! Montesaviour!'

'Come an' give we wo'k!'

'Come an' save we like you did in 'thirty-eight!'

'Save we, Big Massah! Save we!'

The shouting went down a bit when they saw that the Master was helping another person from the car.

'Gloria!' they roared, as they recognized her. 'Gloria!' It was the Master's long and faithful secretary, a gracefully built, well-groomed negress with a quiet, confident smile.

A way was made through the crowd for the venerable figure, and with his arms around the faithful Gloria, he walked firmly forward until he reached the top of the steps by the door of the office. The crowd had begun to cheer again. Those nearest to him reached out to touch his garment. A few of the bolder women threw themselves on his shoulder and at his feet. He neglected the older ones. He kissed the younger and prettier. On the steps he turned towards them.

'Ma people,' he began softly, 'I been hearing a lot of nonsense about what's goin' on in this office. From I been in the opposition I been hearing about how they only give job to their party supporters; ain't that true, Gloria?'

'True, true,' Gloria replied severely.

'An' I hear too that during de election people from this office was campaigning against me; I hear that dis place is a den of opposition to ma government.' His voice became louder and louder, angrier and angrier as he spoke until by the time he said the last word it had become an unintelligible squeak.

They loved it. The hostile grimace on his face gave vent to their sense of destruction. The supporters of the opposition now completely deserted their party. The collective anger of the crowd was now infinitely more important to them than party loyalty. It was release. The great man felt the way they did. He had identified himself with their anger, with their rage, with their destructive hate. There was no longer any guilt in the way they felt. They poured out their souls with him.

'Break dem!'

'Fire dem out!'

'Kick dem out!'

'God-damn civil servant dem!'

'T'ink dem nice!'

'Fire fo' dem!'

The Master, with his chest forward, his thumbs stuck in his waistcoat, paused in his rage. He gave them all the time they needed to express the anger of their souls. Gloria crept up close to him and whispered something in his ear. He shook his head vigorously in recollection and squeezed her closer to him.

'An' listen to me, listen! I also hear that a certain man in this office been makin' rude remarks in public about my relationship with my secretary here. Well, this is the last straw; ain't that so, Gloria?'

'It is, it is,' she said with determination.

'This is the last straw. Make them trouble me; make them say nasty things 'bout me. But nobody say nothing 'bout this good woman here!'

'Fire dem out!' the crowd roared again. 'Fire dem out!'

Clenching his fist, the honourable Premier marched into the office. The crowd now had their complete freedom. Those already in the office began climbing over the iron railing. The civil servants folded up their books and fled, only one of them rushing back to rescue his towel from the back of his chair. They began crawling all over the office, opening books, sipping ice-water, the more ambitious sitting behind the desks, scribbling away at the blank pages.

Outside the police stood helpless. The crowd jeered them mercilessly. 'Why you don' arrest the Massah?' they screamed at them.

The superintendent sat in his car and fumed as a few pregnant women nearby began passing slighting remarks about him. Dinah was caught in the midst of it. She was still half scared. She still sensed that something would break out soon and moved towards the back of the mob. But at the same time she was unable to resist the temptation to bark and scream with the rest.

'Ah want to live like human!' she heard herself shouting, and to her surprise and delight a few people near her took up her words. 'Like human!' they screamed. 'We wan' fe live like human!'

By this time the Master had made his final pronouncements to the civil servants. He warned them against speaking out in opposition to the government and giving jobs only to supporters of the other party. He demanded that the man who had made slighting remarks about his secretary be fired at once. It was all said for the mob's benefit, for by this time there were no civil servants to be found within a hundred yards of the place. Neither for that matter could the honourable Minister of Labour be seen, since he had also spirited himself away with the civil servants, thinking it best to leave things to the Master.

Several of the party henchmen, led by the little man with the bald head, who was now beaming all over, made another path through the crowd for the Master. He waved and kissed and hugged all within his reach. Every now and then he turned and gave the good woman by his side an extra squeeze. That pleased them no end. Somebody started singing the party song and they all joined in.

> 'Montesaviour is me leader till ah dead,
> Montesaviour is me leader till ah dead,
> I will never starve or hunger
> I will never live to want,
> 'Cause Montesaviour is me leader till ah dead.'

The couple went inside the car and drove up beside the superintendent's. There was just enough space between the two cars for the superintendent to get out and salute. The Master pushed out his head and bellowed, 'Listen, Maxwell!', then he lowered his voice so that the crowd could not hear him and said angrily: 'What the hell you sitting there like a bloody fool for? You going to wait till that mob smash up the blasted place?'

'But, sir——'

'Don't "But, sir" me, sir, you have a duty to perform.' He now raised his voice for the benefit of the crowd. 'An' your duty is to keep the public peace, to protect the public! Ain't that what that nice Scotland Yard inspector told us at the cocktail party in England, Gloria?'

'Exactly what he said,' she confirmed.

'Yes, Massah!' they shouted, 'tell 'im, dem is to protec' we, not to brutalize we!'

The Master lowered his voice again. 'Now you just get that blasted mob out of here fast,' then louder: 'You hear me, do as you're paid for!'

'Yes,' they roared, 'mek 'im know 'im place! Mek 'im do wha''

89

we pay 'im fo'.' Then the Master's car drove off. They shouted with joy after him until he was out of sight.

It took a full minute before the superintendent collected himself. Then his jaws bolted forward, his shoulders hunched, he held down his head and stared up at the crowd like a bull about to attack. 'Chaaarge!' he ordered the constables.

For a moment the crowd remained baffled. They couldn't believe he could be that insolent. How could he dare disobey the Master so blatantly. But as they saw the constables moving forward hesitantly with their tear-gas bombs and batons their rage broke loose again and they charged on them. The constables were taking no chances. They saw plainly the anger of the mob and they knew they could not cope with it. They flung down their weapons and fled to their jeeps.

'Chaaarge!' the superintendent, now red with rage, screamed hysterically. The pregnant women around him advanced menacingly. One of them came forward and slapped him across his neck, another spat on his trousers. He took one long look at their eyes, swallowed, and retreated to his car. The crowd scattered before it as it drove off rapidly.

By this time Dinah had managed to struggle her way through the mob. She heard a tear-gas bomb go off and the scream of the people nearby. She looked towards the jeeps and saw that they were unable to move. The mob was battering down the sides of the vehicles in an effort to get at the frightened constables. Several of them had deserted the jeeps and had taken to their heels with a part of the mob behind them. From inside the office she could hear the smashing of furniture and the ripping of pages.

She began to run. First up the Queen Street, then on to a narrow lane off it, not answering the people she passed who kept asking her what had happened. But even when she was more than a quarter of a mile away she could still hear the ghastly sound of their voices. 'Wo'k!' Wo'k or is murder!' 'Wo'k!' 'Food!' 'Wo'k!'

II

'READ it,' she said breathlessly, thrusting the letter into her daughter's hand. 'Read it an' tell me wha' it say, quick.' Rossetta took the letter from her mother. Her heart, too, was pounding wildly. She tore open the envelope. Slowly she read the contents of the letter which said that the government was happy to inform her that her daughter had been awarded a free place to a secondary school.

Both of them stared with disbelief at each other in the little hut. Then Mary broke out with a loud scream of joy. She lifted her smiling daughter and carried her above her head outside for the world to look at her. 'Me daughter! Me daughter!' she repeated. 'Me daughter win scholarship. Me daughter goin' to go to high school an' sit down wid big people pickney. Lawd ooh! Me pickney, me pickney, me one sweet, brown pickney!'

Soon she had created such a commotion that everyone had rushed towards her to hear the news. Some shared her joy with her. They took hold of the girl and gave her a hero's piggy-ride. Mary, now completely unable to control herself, kept jumping about, rolling on the ground and howling with ecstasy. She kissed all the men she came across, much to their distaste. She got hold of the peppery old Zacharry and plucked his beard, kissed him while she did so.

'Woman!' he belched, 'the spirit of Beelzebub has taken hold of thee.'

She caught Rachael's cynical gaze and immediately promised her a job as nanny and a pension when her daughter had married her rich white man. Another man soon got a job as butler in her palace, a third was to be gardener and a fourth had been made a cook before she finally found herself in front of Brother Solomon's shop. Ordinarily she would not have dared to approach Brother Solomon uninvited. But now she felt she could approach the biggest and the best. For soon would she not be one of them? However, she thought better of the idea of offering Brother Solomon a job as tutor of her grandchildren. She walked inside and told him the news. He nodded calmly, revealing by his expression his gladness for her. He invited her to the back of the shop so he could give her some idea of what the scholarship would involve.

'Is a bright girl you have,' he said after she had sat down. 'You can praise yourself very much fo' bringing out what was in her.'

'T'ank you, Mr. Solomon. T'ank you.'

'But you mus' realize that this might have difficult consequences.'

'Like, like wha' so, Mr. Solomon?' She was beginning to feel nervous, but her faith remained strong. She listened carefully.

'Well, you going have to buy good clothes for her to go to school; you have to give her good food, people can't study on hungry belly, you know. But that is not all. When Rossetta go out an' see how Babylon live, when she meet new friends, what you think going to happen? Here will satisfy her no more.'

'No, ah don' wan' to cross you, Mr. Solomon, but no, not my Rossetta, she will always love me, she will always wan' to stay wid her mother till she ready fe tek me out o' de wretched place. I believe in her, Mr. Solomon, an' she believe in me.'

'I admire your faith,' he said sincerely; 'continue believing place, an' you'll continue being happy.'

'You jus' watch an' see, Mr. Solomon. We both goin' up. We both goin' reach the top of the hill.'

'With your faith you very well might,' he said softly.

She stared up at him and started at the wide vacancy of his expression. 'So you really believe in me Rossetta; you believe we will get to de top of me dreams, right to de top, don't it, Mr. Solomon?'

'You're sure you will, don't you?' he asked, looking at her admiringly.

'I sure-sure, Mr. Solomon, I sure-sure.'

'Then already you have,' he told her.

She was not sure she understood. But she could see that he was in some strange way happy for her. She held his hand and squeezed it joyfully, then left.

12

THAT same night the Rastafarians held a meeting in the Dungle. As usual the meeting place was in a small area enclosed by a bamboo fencing near the sea. There was a clear blue sky and it was one of those nights when the stars were numerous and daring, hanging close above like eyes of happy ghosts. The sea was calm and warm, with a raw luscious stinkness.

By ten o'clock they had all arrived. They sat in a neat semicircle, the five elders in the midst. They were all dressed in proper colours. Some were dressed in robes, like the elders— green and gold and red. They held their head aloft as they spoke their words of wisdom, calmly, soft-like with a gentle dignity, for they were all aware of the spiritual presence of the Holy Emperor. The older ones who were not elders stood up above the rest, not because they felt they were superior, for here there was complete equality, but because to stand in the divine presence was a special privilege which was given to the old and wise. They were little withered souls as they stood there seeking every now and then the support of the bamboo fencing for their weak frames. But they were proud as they folded their old flour-bag capes around their shoulders. The staffs in their hands were held firmly, with unwithering zest.

That night there was a special guest. Sitting beside Brother Solomon was a young man from the university who had come to address them. He was brown-skinned, short and wore spectacles. Despite the shabbiness of his clothes, it was not difficult to detect his difference. His face was too smooth. If he appeared

94

relaxed he gave the impression too much that he was making a deliberate attempt to appear relaxed. His expression was serious, perhaps too serious, for the Rastafarians with their piercing sensitivity could detect somehow that he was trying to impress upon them his awareness of the seriousness of the occasion. But this very fact defeated itself. For in detecting his effort not to appear condescending they sensed a certain kind of condescension. They eyed him suspiciously, and yet not without friendliness.

The meeting was called to order by Brother Solomon with a short prayer to the Emperor Selassie. Then they all stood up and sang the hymn *Here We Are in This Land*. Their voices were like trumpets in the distance. They sung with the dignity of zealots marching to the lion:

> *'Here we are in this land.*
> *No one think how we stand*
> *The hands that are on us all day.*
> *So we cry and we sigh*
> *For we know not our God.*
> *So we'll always be crying in vain.*
>
> *Our forefathers cried;*
> *Feel the pangs of the chain*
> *See the blood running out of his vein.*
> *And our slave masters did pierce*
> *Our forefathers' hearts*
> *So they die like a brute in the chain.'*

As soon as they were through, one of the elders with the flour-bag cape sprung forward. He almost fell to the ground, but at the last moment managed to support his undernourished frame with his staff. With his left hand held to heaven, his head aloft, his beard conical and stiff and his long woollen braids almost down to his shoulders, his spare frame, silhouetted against the bamboo fencing, seemed like a hungry wolf at bay.

'Brethren!' he screamed, 'why is I here? Why is we here?'

''Cause we forefathers sin, Brother!' came the loud chorus.

The old man cocked his head and waited for the chorus. He nodded meditatively as they shouted, then proceeded to enlighten them. 'Yes, Brother, it is written in the scriptures. *Lamentations 5 verse 7*, "our fathers have sinned and are not: and we have borne their iniquities".'

'Word of wisdom, Brother!' the chorus echoed at this knowledgeable quotation.

'And, Brethren, what was de price dat we did have to pay fo' we forefathers' sin?'

'Slavery! Slavery to the white man!' they answered back.

'Yes, Brethren, we is de children of Israel, we is de sons of Ethiopia, we is de princes of de earth, but because of our forefathers' wickedness we was shipped away to this land of bondage, to this land of Babylon which de white slave masters call Jamaica. Our inheritance is turn to strangers, our houses to aliens, my Brother!'

'Wisdom, Brother, wisdom!'

'We is orphans and fatherless, we eat de filth of de earth!'

'While de white man and de black traitors live off de fat of de land,' came the reply.

'We neck is under persecution, we labour an' have no res'.'

'Babylon! De police! De black traitors, Brother!'

'But you hear what de scriptures say! You hear wha' *Lamentations 10* say; it say, "Our skin was black like an oven because of the terrible famine"; the famine is slavery, Brother! Is slavery dat tu'n us black because we had to clean out de oven at de great house too often! An' now de white man rule over we, but will it las' for ever, Brethren?'

'No! Judgement shall come! Babylon shall fall!'

'Hear de sacred word of Rastafari, me Brothers. *Revelation 18* say, "An' he cry mightily wid a loud voice an' him say, Babylon de great is fallen, an' is become de habitation of devils and de bowl of every foul spirit an' a cage of every unclean an' hateful bird" . . . an' you know wha' happen me, Brothers, you know wha' goin' happen, 'im tell we in *Revelation 21*, a mighty angel tek up a big-big millstone an' 'im cast it down 'pon dem, you know who dem is?'

'De white masters, de black middle-class traitors, them lackeys de police! All shall burn! All shall burn!'

The gathering had now been worked up to a state where they could hardly remain seated. They clenched their fists and plucked their beards in anticipation of the final quotation with which they were sure the learned elder would end his speech. 'Thus, Brethren,' the old man barked, he paused, stared abstractedly at the sky, then suddenly, with a final plunge that saw him to the ground, he shouted with agony, 'thus with violence shall de great city Babylon be thrown and shall be found no more at all!'

'No more at all!' they retorted.

'Fire an' damnation shall befall dis stinking land of Babylon!'

'Fire dem out!—de Conquering Lion of de Tribe of Judah shall burn up all de white oppressors, an' all de brown middle-class traitors shall fall an' be devoured before de great day of repatriation!'

Suddenly from the rear a youth began to beat a drum. A bandy-legged locksman, holding a picture of the Emperor which exhibited him in his full regal colours, holding a sword in one hand and with his mighty right foot on an unexploded Italian bomb, began wobbling around the group screaming with froth-spattered mouth: 'Selassie! Old Alpha! Invincible and visible! Redeemer of Israel—not de fictitious Israel of de Jews, but de true children of Israel who is de black race! Burn dem out! Consume dem wid fire!'

At this point Brother Solomon sensed that the meeting ran the risk of getting out of order. He therefore called one of the Brethren and told him to start a hymn. The man was well chosen, for with a loud, ghastly roar that deafened even the most clangorous of the cultists, he began to sing *King Rasta is Now on the Wheel*, a favourite hymn:

> 'King Rasta is now on de wheel,
> The knowledge of truth is now flowing
> If Israel can't hear they must feel——'

By this time almost the whole group had been called to attention by his roar and as he completed the first verse they were ready with the chorus:

> 'Our redeemer is calling us home.
> We see there is no truth in Rome.
> Our heaven is in Ethiopia
> With King Rasta and Queen Ethiopia.'

Almost everyone was singing by now except for one devout old salt who, with his eyes closed, kept repeating his favourite verse: '*Jeremiah 8, verse 21*,' he said reverently, and then proceeded to quote: 'For de hurt of de daughter of me people is I hurt; I am black; astonishment has takeneth hold 'pon me.' He said it in a plaintive, wistful voice with a bewildered kind of resignation, hardly noticing the others as, in their swaying and singing, they pushed and tossed his frail, astonished little frame. Their equanimity by now completely regained, they all droned in with the final verse.

> *'For centuries we've been down-trodden,*
> *We could not believe we were born,*
> *But we trust in King Rastafari*
> *For he is our guide and our shield.'*

After the song, the excitement subdued, they sat down once again. Two men left the meeting and in a few minutes were back, one of them carrying something which he held carefully across his palms. It was a chillum pipe containing the holy herb. As the cultists whiffed the wild acrid aroma of the ganja they held their heads to the sky and sighed. The more devout reflected on the eleventh verse of *Genesis*: 'And the dove came into him in the evening; and lo, in her mouth was an olive leaf pluckt off.' And was not this leaf the holy herb they now smoked? Who dared fly in the face of the holy word of Rastafari? The white man knew the wisdom of the herb and in his vicious plot to keep the black man in ignorance he had made the holy herb illegal and branded it marijuana. Had got the police, those dark treacherous sons of Babylon, to raid them and batter them for the sake of the weed of wisdom. But Babylon shall fall and shall be consumed in the endless damnation of fire and melting brimstone.

The chillum pipe passed from hand to hand. Each cultist held the long stem gently, reverently, took a deep puff and, as it swelled his lungs, embraced himself with fervour. When the pipe reached the student from the university the young man took it nervously, then, after a pause, with a sudden burst of courage he sucked the pipe determinedly and passed it on. Those Brethren who saw him smiled, half in condescension.

Brother Solomon got up and introduced the student. He told them that, as always, the people from the university were on their side and tried to do what they could for them, but that it was largely futile since they had to depend on the middle and upper classes for support to survive and they all knew what those pack of oppressors give. The student would be talking about Jamaican society and the farce of independence. Not that they did not know all these things already, for the omniscience of the holy Ras communicated to them through the un-perverted scriptures of the Bible and the Holy Key, which they were able to interpret because of the divine influence of the holy weed, had given them insight into all things.

'You can sum up Jamaica, me Brothers, in three little lines,' he concluded. 'If you white, you all right; if you brown, stick around; if you black, stand back. Still, it is good to know that the young men at the university think the way we do, so let us give him a big hand and listen to him carefully as him say him piece.'

Brother Solomon sat down and the student rose slowly in the sound of a polite clapping.

'Friends, Brethren,' he began, pausing and appearing to choose his words carefully, 'not very long ago the island of England obtained its independence from Jamaica.' He paused, but it was clear that no one had seen the humour, or, if they did, it was obviously not considered witty. Somewhat flustered, he continued. With an assumed fervour he passionately denounced the colonial past, what he called the heritage of slavery and the present capitalist system. He condemned democracy as a farce and castigated the brown-skin middle class who were the only ones that had anything to gain from it, referring time and again to their pathetic self-hate and subservience to English culture, he wailed with agony at the tragedy of the black Jamaican who after three hundred years of brain-washing and oppression had come, he claimed, not only to despise himself and his blackness but had almost completely come to accept his inferior status in his own country. Then in a final declaration of unrestrained anger, he threw his hands in the air and uttered:

'This, Brethren, this is the true heritage of colonialism which the crafty myths of multi-racial harmony and democracy are used to smother! Brethren, far from being independent we are still slaves. The worst kind of slaves. Mental slaves. All Jamaica, except you the Rastafarians and an emancipated few, are the slaves of an alien culture. And, most tragic of all, it is the Jamaican himself who is now his own slave-master. This, Brethren, this is the true heritage of colonialism!'

'Another Solomon,' they screamed with one accord as he sat down, proud, and not a little surprised at the tumultuous response he was getting.

'Show me a bastard white youth of his age who could digress such wisdom so magnificently, an' with such overstanding,' an elder challenged.

'A sweet black angel,' another suggested, 'a descendant of the Negus!'

'Even if now he is trapped by the guiles of Babylon when we go to Ethiopia we shall see him by the bank of the beautiful river,' another elder prophesied with certainty.

'Yes! Yes! By de bank of de beautiful river at de foot of de great Emperor. Sing him a song, Brethren!'

They greeted this last suggestion with wild enthusiasm and proceeded to bestow on their guest the great honour of singing for him the first verse of *Man is an Angel and God is Our King*:

> *'Babel is raging*
> *Man is an angel and God is our King*
> *Kingdoms are falling,*
> *Read Revelation*
> *The Negus is leading*
> *The Agamegnon.'*

When the song was through there was another round of the chillum pipe, and after a respectful interval the student quietly took his leave. A hush of expectancy now gradually began to dawn on everyone. They had suspected vaguely that something else was to come. It had been whispered over the past few days that a revelation, some incredibly good news, was to be made that night. All of them would like to think they knew. But they forced such thoughts from their heads. It was too unbelievable to think, to dream even, that the news would be what they all knew they wanted it to be. They must be patient. That was the divine injunction. It was the sin of impatience on the part of their forefathers which had condemned them to Babylon. Rastafari in his omniscience knew what time was best for them to leave. So they would be patient. Yet their hearts beat stoutly within their breasts as they inhaled the holy fumes and stared at Brother Solomon. Yet they dared to hope.

When they had all been purified, and the chillum reverently put aside on the stand to the right side of the folded flag of Ethiopia, Brother Solomon got up once more to speak.

'Brethren,' he began solemnly, and with a severe fluttering of their hearts they noted that he held a letter in his hand. 'Brethren, you must contain yourself, you must bolster yourself for the great news I have to give you. For it is a truth that the human soul is even less capable of holding great joy than it is of holding great sorrow . . .'

It was true, then. Almighty God, Rastafari, it was true. The time was coming. Agony began to breed in their eyes. Joy began to swell their souls. The sweat dropped from their beards, one by one, and in the light of the little kerosine lamps they were like pellets of molten gold. . . .

'Brethren, as you all know, with the money we had saved from the sweat of our brow we sent two delegates to Ethiopia to see after our repatriation. There was some doubt in our hearts then as to whether we were guilty of transgression or not by anticipating the activities of the Holy Emperor, but now you can dispense with these fears, for, as we decided, it was the spirit of the Holy Emperor who had come within us and given us the courage and patience to suffer the indignation of working for Babylon and depriving ourselves in order to save the money to send off our two delegates. Well, today we received a letter from our two brothers now in heaven across the seas . . .'

Now they could hardly breathe. An excruciating ferment began to soar within them, a simmering thrill began to move and wake, and there was such restrained fury in it, such a blithing pain.

'They said, first of all, that they had gotten an audience with the Holy Emperor . . .'

No! Unbelievable! They had seen Him! Had heard His voice! Had spoken to Him. Had walked in the path of His own footsteps. The delegates, Brother Tom and Brother Jeremiah, men whom they had known all their lives, had spoken to Him! Him who has created all things. The power of the trinity: 'Behold the hour cometh, yea, is now come, that thou shall be scattered, every man to his own, and shall leave me alone, because the faith is with me.' And perhaps . . . perhaps, even, they had touched him! Brother Tom and Brother Jeremiah? . . .

'. . . The Emperor said it was true that he has land ready and waiting for us, that he was aware of our plight and suffering, and that the days of our suffering were near an end. He has agreed to send one of his many warships, one of the very types which he used to destroy the Italian fleet, to take us back home. The only thing left to decide fully now is time. For the moment, the date the 27th of October is set as the day on which the ship will arrive unless words come to the contrary. This, Brothers, is the great and wonderful tidings.'

They consumed his words with open mouths. For seconds, minutes after Brother Solomon had taken his seat, they remained petrified where they were. For a time some of them tried to shout, but their voices remained choked with disbelief. At last the full weight of Brother Solomon's words sunk into them. Released, all at once they leaped in the air with great jubilation.

'Repatriation!' they screamed. 'We goin' home, we goin' home! Israel is redeem! King Rasta a come fo' 'im pickney them!'

'Him come to break up oppression!' one of them screamed.

'To set the captives free!' retorted another.

'To take away transgression!' said a third.

And then they all joined in, 'And rule by equality!'

All was now in turmoil. The elders, rejuvenated with new energy—already the signs had begun—threw away their staves and skipped around the bamboo fencing, others threw off their capes and hats and scratched themselves with ecstasy, others soared up to the top of the high mounds of filth and grappled for the sky, and, when they could not reach it, screamed: 'Africa! Ethiopia, I come!' And still others, in sheer deliriousness, dashed for the black, murmuring sea and, fully clothed, plunged themselves in. One enthusiastic youth had to be held back by his more restrained elders as he started swimming in earnest to meet the ship that was coming for him. Perhaps they would never have spotted him had he not stopped to ask one more knowledgeable than himself the way to the Black Sea. He was advised that perhaps it would be wiser if they all departed together since then there would be no difficulty in recognizing him as a true child of Israel.

Their voices could be heard for miles away. The little kerosine lights began to light up one by one, as others in the Dungle woke up to enquire into the reason for the tumult. But they were too overjoyed to speak to anyone. Only gasps of excitement of the songs of joy could be heard from their lips.

> 'The Lion of Judah shall break every chain
> And give us a victory
> Again and Again.'

The chorus rang out again and again like thunder in the freakish darkness of the night. It took a full hour before the meeting was brought to order again. The date of the future meeting was announced, as well as the preparations that were to be undertaken for the celebration of the coronation of the Holy Emperor which was not long due. Then the meeting came to a close with the formal singing of the Ethiopian national anthem:

> 'Ethiopia, the land of our Fathers,
> The land where all Gods love to be
> As the swift bees to hive sudden gather,
> The children are gathered to Thee.
>
> With our Red, Gold and Green floating
> With the Emperor to shield us from wrong,
> With our God and our future before us,
> We hail thee with shout and with song.'

Then they all scattered and went and spread the good news. Joy never knew such violence, such complete possession. As they moved about the cardboard huts, the old zinc cabins, the muck and grime all covered now with the blanket of night, their bodies rocked to the rhythm of their favourite marching song.

> '*When I go to Zion I'll never leave again,*
> *When I go to Zion I'll never leave again,*
> *I'm goin' to de Mansion*
> *King Rasta come an' prepare.*
> *When I go to Zion I'll never leave again.*'

So now all was happiness. All was the release of pain and the anticipation of more release. All was joy. All except Brother Solomon. He was the last to leave the meeting. He sucked the last fumes from the chillum pipe, wrapped it in the flag and placed the bundle under his arms. Then he got up slowly and walked to his hut. His head was bowed under the low ceiling of the sky. His eyes never left the ground, they stared vacantly, in rheumy distraction. He locked himself inside his hut.

In the distance he could hear their voices like children in the clouds. And he could also hear the sea, no longer just murmuring. He could hear it coming forward—black sea, wide sea, endless, remote and haunting sea; he could hear it going backward; he could hear it coming forward, he could hear it going backward. Forward, backward; forward, backward; forward, forward, and back and back again. . . .

13

SEVERAL days after the incident at the labour office Dinah managed to get a job. She was told about it by Mrs. Davis one morning after she had loaned her a cup of sugar which she knew she would not be getting back. The woman who used to have the job had become pregnant again and had to leave. She had gone to the house of the employer up in the residential section of St. Andrews and was told to turn out to work the next Monday morning.

Over the past few weeks a guarded kind of friendship had developed between Dinah and Mrs. Davis. The Saturday morning before she went out to work Mrs. Davis beckoned to her to come to her room after she had emptied her chamber-pot. Dinah could tell from the gleam in her eyes and from the cautious glances she made about the yard before letting her in that some kind of mischief was in the air.

'Come in quick,' Mrs. Davis whispered hoarsely, dragging her inside and closing the door behind her.

'Is wha'? Is wha'?' Dinah enquired, beginning to get alarmed at the countenance of stupefaction and mystery which Mrs. 'D' affected.

'Lawd me gal,' she said, 'me sorry fe you.'

Mrs. 'D' put her right palm to her jaw and tilted her head as if in pain. She stared at Dinah without speaking, her expression a mixture of fear and pity.

'Fo' God sake, is wha'? Talk up, no!'

'Dinah,' she said, and the word came out with a heavy sigh, 'Dinah, you know is wha' 'appen?'

'No, is wha'?'

'Them a work 'pon you.'

'Say wha'? Say them doin' wha'?'

'Obeah, Dinah, dem a work obeah 'pon you.'

'Jesus Christ, is who? is who?'

'Dinah, you have to promise me you not goin' call me name at all; me no wan' get mix up in a no more crosses than me in already.'

'No, me won't mek anybody know is you tell me, but is who?'

'Dinah . . .'

'Yes . . . is who, who?'

'Dinah . . . is Mabel.'

'Mabel! Ah kill her! Right now, God slap me down dead if ah don' kill her!'

'Wait, Dinah, wait!' Mrs. Davis held on tight to Dinah as she moved towards the door. Heavy brown sweat began to drop from her round black face. She saw that Dinah meant what she said.

'Dinah, listen to me. Is no so you fe do it. You wi' only go prison and lock up. Is no so you mus' get back at her.'

'Then how else? Why the hell she don' lef' me out? Jesus, ah know ah could feel something following me 'bout them pas' few days. Ah could tell dat some duppy was 'pon me.'

'Si' down, gal,' Mrs. 'D' encouraged, and pulled her down on the bed.'

'But is how you get fe fin' out say she set obeah 'pon me, "D"?'

'The other morning me go to the latrine early, 'bout four o'clock, is de soup me did drink de night before gripe me, me 'cotch de door halfway an' was a stare outside when all of a sudden me see Mabel a creep up, den she tek out one little black bag an' sprinkle some dirt she tek out from it in front o' you doorway, then she dip into de paper bag an' tek out anoder little bag, dis time one brown one wid a white cord string 'round de edge. She tek out a whitish powder from it an' sprinkle it 'bout de place, but mos' o' it she t'row over de dirt in front o' you doorway.'

'Jesus Lord! Me remember de mawnin' me did get up an' see de white somethin' in front o' me door. But me did t'ink is flour. Me did t'ink it strange dat it should a tek so long to wipe 'way but me never pay it no mind. Jesus, "D", is mek you never tell me before now.'

'Me did 'fraid, Dinah. Me never wan' get mix up wid Mabel an' her obeah; suppose me go trouble wha' was'n' my business an' it tu'n 'pon me. But dis mawnin' me conscience wouldn' let me keep it back any longer. Me had to tell you 'bout it.'

'Is wha' you t'ink it is Mabel put there, "D"?'

'Me can't be sure but de dirt mus' be grave dirt mix up wid somethin' else, some kind o' oil-o-fall-back, me think!'

'Oil-o-fall-back! Wha' dat?'

'Jus' what it say. It set a spirit 'pon you dat no matter how much you try you mus' fail, you mus' fall back to whe' you did start, no matter how near you reach you goal you mus' tumble back down. As a matter of fac', ah hear dat de spirit help you on in any thing you trying so as to taunt you; you see whe' you goin' but as soon as you reach, wham! you fall right back.'

Not hearing her say anything, Mrs. 'D' looked fully at Dinah. She gaped in amazement at her expression. 'Dinah, Jesus Christ, is wha' happen to you? Why you sweating so? Look 'pon me! Stop starin' into not'in', Dinah!' A thought suddenly pierced Mrs. 'D'. Perhaps it was the spirit taking hold of her now. God Almighty, it was her fault! If she had kept her mouth shut maybe nothing would have happened. She thought she too was beginning to feel a bit strange. Yes, her head was getting to feel a bit light. Suddenly she sprang from the bed and headed for her closet. Frantically, she pulled open the big drawer at the bottom, took out a little key and with it opened another little drawer farther up. Out of this drawer she took out a little brown paper bag. The sweat dropped from her face even harder as she took out the contents. A stench suddenly hit the air. Holding her nose with her left hand, Mrs. 'D' proceeded to sprinkle the ingredients all over the floor, but particularly in the corners. Then she rushed for her Bible, opened it at *Psalm 23* and after crossing herself seven times began saying, 'Hail Mary full of grace'.

'Say it, Dinah! Say it wid me!' she said as she ended her chant for the fifth time. But by this time Dinah had regained her composure and simply mumbled along with her until she had completed the chant seven times.

'You see,' Mrs. 'D' said with a sigh of relief and a deep grunt of satisfaction as she kissed the Bible and closed it, 'is only dis can work when duppy come 'round you. You did see one awhile ago, don't it? Is wha' it was like, Dinah gal? Tell me, you don' have to be 'fraid any more, de Lawd is wid dee.'

'Me never see no ghost. Who say me did see any ghost?'

'You never see not'in'. You mus' be mad, you should a see you face how you was lookin'. De spirit did even start come 'pon me until ah t'row it off wid de spirit o' de Lawd.'

'Well, even if a spirit was in here it was'n' dat was worryin' me. Is wha' you say Mabel set de spirit 'pon me to do.'

'You mean fe mek you fall back?'

'Yes, you t'ink it goin' work, "D", how me mus' stop it?'

'It would work if it did have anythin' fe work 'pon.'

'Wha' you mean?'

'Well, you no have not'in' fe worry 'bout. Is Jones Town you live: you no have nowhere to fall back to, unless is down ah Dungle you come from.'

Dinah turned to face her in alarm. For a moment she thought that the last statement was meant specifically for her, but on looking at Mrs. 'D' she could tell that she had referred to the Dungle innocently.

'But is still not a good t'ing to have 'pon you. Suppose you was fe try an' move up out o' Jones Town, you could never do it.'

'You sure is oil-o-fall-back, "D"?'

'Yes, me could tell from de smell; de smell die out after a while, but in de early mawnin' as soon as she tek it out me could smell it.'

'So now me 'ave to go to a obeah-man to get off de spirit off o' me. Christ, ah feel fe jus' end everythin' an' kill de dirty bitch an' mek dem 'ang me!'

'No, no, hol' you temper an' tek me foolish advice. Don' go to no obeah-man. You can't trust dem these days 'cause dem 'ave a way o' working wid one anoder and once one o' dem know dat him fren' set obeah 'pon you 'im will only tek you money an' don' do a thing.'

'So den wha' me mus' do?'

'Go to Shepherd John.'

'Shepherd John? Is who 'im?'

'You never hear 'bout Shepherd John?'

'No, no.'

'Gal, you not livin'. Shepherd John is de greates' healer an' revivalis' leader you 'ave in dis Kingston. Nobody no better dan him. People come to 'im from all over de islan' wid all sort o' complain'—sore foot, bad stomach, leprosy, deafness, blindness, ghost—you no have nothin' dat 'im can't cure. An' is only de word of God 'im go by when 'im work. 'Im 'ave 'im own church, 'im own "mother" an' angel dem an' everything. But you don' 'ave to be a member o' de church fe get him fe heal you, though 'im will try an' encourage you fe join. Mek me give you de address.'

By this time Dinah was beginning to find the odour too much for her. She had not seen Mrs. 'D' sprinkling the powder around the room and so could only conclude that something must be terribly wrong with her belly. She was tempted to ask her if she still had the gripe which the soup had given her several mornings earlier but thought that it would be better if she just left. After listening carefully to the instructions as to how she should get to Shepherd John she thanked Mrs. 'D' and dashed for the fresh air outside.

The Monday morning was hot like hell. Alphanso had left early and for that she was glad. Of late just the sight of him was beginning to irritate her. There was something about that man which was too comfortable. It wasn't that he thought that he was God on earth when he put on that austere blue uniform in the mornings. It was just that he became so contented in it. That heavy navy-blue uniform with the broad, ridiculous cloth belt seemed to be a kind of shield to him. He held his hand over his head and hid behind it every day so that no one could touch him, for no one really ever saw him, not the white superintendent whom he feared so much and pretended to be so hostile towards, not the black irascible sergeant who would penalize every man below him if he was not properly addressed, especially if it was after the inspector had ordered him about, no one except perhaps her, and when he took off his uniform he was such a snail without his shell. She delighted in pouring salt on him, especially when he so hopelessly tried to take her. But even that was becoming tedious. Oh, he was such a stupid, contented, black, country fool.

She began to feel irritable and swore as her dress fastened halfway down and refused to budge further. She took it off and put it on again. It was with mixed feelings that she was going to this job. She knew well what those St. Andrew middle-class types gave. But that wasn't what really worried her. For if anybody in that damn' household dared to be fast with her she would know how to fix them. She wasn't brought up in the Dungle for nothing. But it was her pride that was trembling with pain. She was going to be a domestic. Wait on brown people. Carry out their chimmy. Clean them floor. Yes, ma'am; no, ma'am, them. She would have to make herself humble. She, Dinah, would have to humble herself. She wondered if she could do it. She wondered.

But on the other hand there was a strange desire on her part to be on the job. Regardless of what it entailed, it was something new for her. She had never worked for anyone since she had become an adult. Work . . . get money . . . spend it . . . and work again for more money. Something nice about that. Sound good. Sound secure. Sound like what nice, decent people do. . . .

But blast it, though. It was just this that revolted her. Work and get your pay and come back again for more and that's a good girl. There was something about this which made her sick and want to vomit in as much as it attracted her. Why should she work for anybody at all? Why should anybody work for anybody else at all? It was such a nasty, bitchy world, but she would lick it yet. Ah, that's the spirit, she consoled herself against her own revulsion as she closed the door behind her. But Christ, the sun was hot, yes!

She got off the bus at the Hope Road in front of the Royal Botanical Gardens and walked across the newly built housing estate. Her eyes roamed over the bright new concrete walls—blue, light green, black, pink and white; oh, the white one was so pretty—completely white outside except for the two black clay pots with the long, slender green ferns in them. And the housewives with their brown and olive-skinned legs pouring out of their Bermuda shorts and their gardener boys with their black torsos gleaming in the sun. Such domestic bliss. Her with her little spade, he with his shear, both intent on manicuring the pretty green lawns.

For a long time Dinah forgot herself as she walked across the broad, clean roads of the estate, peering into each of the little units of peace and joy. Wonderful, wonderful. Round, closely clipped willows. Fat little dogs always sleeping; strange, she always thought dogs ran around and sniffed at other dead dogs . . . now it was wonderfully different; when they weren't sleeping they were chasing the canaries and the grass squits, it was so strange to see a dog not chasing crows. And look at the fat, smiling little brown babies being pushed in the prams. Nice baby, powdered baby, happy, little, pretty, brown baby. And look at the women in their stiffly starched drills pushing the prams. Look——

She stopped dead in her tracks. She had almost crossed the estate and for the first time she could come to her senses. She looked. She was a young girl. From the lumpiness of her features and her unstraightened hair you could tell that she was recently from the country. She had eyes only for her young missis' baby. She made sure always to push the pram in the shade of the trees on the roadside. Sun mustn't touch baby. Sun not good for baby skin. Her face betrayed neither strain nor contentment. She wasn't happy, sure, but neither was she angry. All she seemed concerned with was baby. She must keep nice baby out of the sun. Sun bad. Sun not good for pretty baby skin.

Dinah's eyes remained glued on the girl for a full two minutes. She passed her unmindfully, turned up a road with the name of some lovely flower still with her eyes on baby. And Dinah remained where she was. Staring, now at herself. Her feelings were too intense for rage. Somehow in those past few minutes she seemed to have seethed herself out of anger. Only a numbness trapped her. She pulled herself together, and walked to the southern end of the estate. She crossed over to the other side of the road, turned right and then left as she had been told until she reached the road that ran alongside the mountain. The numbness had sunk to somewhere in the depths of her and there it lingered. She could forget it. Somehow it didn't seem to matter. For a moment nothing seemed to matter any more.

14

THE house was a large, 'L'-shaped green and white structure with a flat roof. It was situated a little way in from the road on one of the little gradients at the foot of the hill. Most of the front of the yard was taken up with a pear-shaped swimming pool. In the hot morning sun the water gleamed a fresh, blue-green radiance, with every now and then little ripples trickling over it as a cool mountain breeze fluttered by. The lawns around the swimming pool were velvet-green, the leaves of the grass being broad and growing thick together gave the appearance almost of being a carpet. On the strip of lawn around the pool were the low, evenly placed almond trees, all like green umbrellas with spots of gold where the leaves had changed colour, casting their shade on the western side of the pool, a little of it falling on the path that led from the road to the house.

To Dinah, as she walked in the shade of the almonds, this was complete peace. There could be no worrying here, she was sure. Not with the tall, carefully clipped, spikey edges that enclosed and protected the green yard, not with the little mountain of acacias shielding you from behind, and all these canaries and ground doves and grass squits—that they wouldn't even hop an inch away from where they clustered as you passed them was sure sign that even they felt the safety, the complete security and peace, that pervaded the atmosphere.

The house was one of those new kinds which had no veran-dah, and the path led into a large open garage in which was parked a blue Volkswagen. Beside it was space for a much larger car. She walked along the concrete path in front of the house, looking at the glass windows, their beautiful forged iron framework and the long, pink curtains behind them. A little way down she stopped in front of the mahogany door and after a pause, in which she was not quite certain what to do, she knocked. There was a brisk walking inside, the door opened and Mrs. Watkins, a tall, very pale woman with her wavy hair combed in a bun that rested conspicuously on the top of her head, stared blankly at her.

'Yes, what do you want?' she began, then, recognizing Dinah: 'Oh, you are the new girl.'

'Yes,' Dinah said, hesitantly.

'A bit late, aren't you, it's after eight-thirty. I said you should be here by at least eight.'

'Yes, ma'm, but the bus——'

'Oh, don't you start on me with that already. I know very well that the buses are always late, but that's no business of mine. Anyway, be that as it is, you'd better come to the kitchen and let me tell you what you are to do.'

She walked away from the door, half closing it. Dinah pushed it open and went inside after her. Mrs. Watkins was just about to enter the kitchen when she heard Dinah's footsteps behind her. She spun round and gaped at Dinah with astonishment. Dinah, suspecting that already she had made some great blunder, stopped where she was.

'I beg your pardon!' Mrs. Watkins exclaimed, a questioning frown of amazement on her brows. Dinah was at a loss what to say or do. The only thing she could think of was to retreat to the door, hoping that whatever it was she had done wrong would be undone in the process. But she couldn't help herself from asking falteringly.

'What it is, ma'm?'

'What it is? You dare to ask me what it is? I can see that the chances of your staying here for any length of time are very slim. Will you kindly walk around to the back entrance. And if you don't mind I'd be happy if you used that entrance in the future.'

'Yes, yes, ma'm,' Dinah stuttered, almost falling as she backed out of the door.

'Well!' she heard Mrs. Watkins exclaim beneath her breath as she closed the door and walked towards the back entrance.

She was completely confused. She knew she despised Mrs. Watkins, but what was worse she felt now a desperate need for the job. She not only hated Mrs. Watkins, she was afraid of her. And because she was afraid of her she had to obey her. It was incredible, this paradox that perplexed her soul. Why did she not run from the place now? Why did she walk to the kitchen, despite the fact that she knew that nothing but humiliation was waiting for her there. She had lived all her life without suffering such assaults on her pride as she had just experienced. She was in no desperate need, for there was always Alphanso. And yet she walked to the kitchen. A strange, humiliating awareness came upon her. She tried to throw it off. It could not be true. But her very anxiety to deny its truth revealed how true it was. She was going to the kitchen because she wanted to go, because she had to go, because in her fear of Mrs. Watkins she felt a compelling urge to be near to her and at her command.

The door of the kitchen was open and Mrs. Watkins was inside waiting for her.

'Come in, come in,' she hurried her up, then she pointed to a woman in the corner peeling potatoes.

'That is Ruby. She does the cooking and the washing and you help her serve in addition to cleaning and taking care of the house and furniture, do you understand?'

'Yes . . . yes, Mrs. Watkins,' she said, unable to look away from the two small brown eyes that stared down contemptuously at her.

'Now follow me and let me show you the place.'

She walked out of the kitchen behind her mistress into the dining-room. The walls were spotless and of a light cream shade and the glazed tiles of the floor of an intricate black and white design.

'You shine the dining-table after every meal,' she said, pointing to the gleaming, oblong-shaped mahogany table with the firm, straight chairs around it.

'And the bouffet,' she said, pointing to a tall, square bit of furniture a shade darker than the rest the use of which Dinah was not quite sure about, 'be careful you do not scratch it. The wood is extremely rare and expensive.'

The dining-room extended into the living-room, the two joined at right angles. She was shown the large, grey, three-piece suite; the stained-glass centre table on a large Persian carpet which she was particularly warned about; the long, gleaming stereophonic set with its three separate speakers—if she wanted to spend the rest of her days in the work-house she could afford to be careless—and on the wall opposite the pink silk curtains that hung from the ceiling were the pictures of four men all grand and proud with their moustaches and walking sticks, waistcoat and golden watch-chain running in a loop somewhere across their breasts. Three of them were white and one a mulatto. As Dinah glanced over the pictures she wondered how the last one managed to find itself there. He tried to appear proud, but it was nothing compared with the stature of the rest. She pitied him as for a moment he seemed about as out of place with those three great figures as she now felt herself.

'Now is not the time to stare at pictures, girl; come on,' she heard Mrs. Watkins calling.

Then she was shown the main bedroom; young Mr. Watkins', who was at the university, bedroom; young Miss Watkins', who was at public school in England, bedroom; the guest room; Mrs. Watkins' sewing and rest room and Mr. Watkins', whom she later learned was a lawyer, study room.

'Now, if there is anything you don't understand ask me,' Mrs. Watkins said as they came out of the third bathroom. 'Never touch or do anything you're not sure about. Do you understand?'

'Yes, ma'm; yes, Mrs. Watkins; me understand, ma'm.'

'Very well, then, take the vacuum-cleaner and start with the dining-room, it badly needs cleaning.' Dinah was astonished, as no matter how hard she tried it was impossible for her to detect one speck of dirt anywhere in the place. Nevertheless, assuming that this was another of the mysteries of high living, she went towards the store-room behind the kitchen where the vacuum was kept.

As she walked through the kitchen she heard a strange whining sound coming from the opposite corner. At first she thought it was somebody crying, but on looking saw that it was Ruby the cook. She was still peeling her potatoes, her eyes intent on what she was doing. She was a well-built woman, around fifty and with black and well-carved features. Looking at her, Dinah realized that she was not crying but laughing. It was a low, piercing, whining giggle which began slowly, quietly, then gradually rose to the point where her whole body vibrated with its motion. Then it stopped suddenly, the woman would then wipe her eyes with the back of her palm, sniff deeply and sigh, 'Lord Jesus save me from the cross,' a silence would follow and then the whole process would be repeated.

Dinah began to rage, thinking that Ruby was laughing at her. She went to the store room, took out the cleaner and as she walked back through the kitchen she heard the woman whining again.

'What de hell sweet you so, gal?' Dinah asked her angrily.

Ruby stopped laughing and after a pause, as if suddenly becoming aware of the fact that somebody was staring at her, she looked up at Dinah with a blank expression. 'Ma'm?' she enquired mildly.

Dinah was puzzled by the woman's expression. She knew that lower-class Jamaicans often used the word 'ma'm' when talking to each other as an address of disdain, but somehow she got the impression that Ruby was saying 'ma'm' to her, as if she was her mistress.

'Ah say is what you laughin' at?' Dinah repeated in a milder tone.

'Laughin'? Me laughin', ma'm?' the woman asked, obviously puzzled.

'You want to tell me say that you wasn' laughin' jus' now.'

'No, ma'm——'

'Wha' de hell you calling me "ma'm" for?'

' "Ma'm"? What I calling you "ma'm" for,' she repeated, 'is thirty-seven years, ma'm.'

'Thirty-seven years,' Dinah repeated, puzzled and irritated. 'What 'bout thirty-seven years?'

'Thirty-seven years since me gran'mother sen' me out fe work. Have manners, she say. Always say "ma'm" to people, no matter who. Is thirty-seven years me working fo' de Watkins. Three generation o' dem.' She gave one of her whining little laughs again.

'Well, you goin' to say you never laugh jus' now?' Dinah asked, by this time realizing that she had not been the cause of Ruby's laughter.

'Laughin', ma'm?'

'Yes, laughin', giggling, is wha' de rass-hole wrong wid you?'

'Well, if you say me was laughin' ah guess ah was laughin', ma'm. Is thirty-seven years.' Dinah lifted up the vacuum and continued to the dining-room as Ruby began once more to mount her strange whimpering titter which always broke off just before its climax.

She left work at six that evening and arrived a little before eight the next morning. For the second time she hardly touched her lunch, for the food that was prepared was completely strange to her. What a way to do the fish? She had never seen potatoes made up in that manner before, and served cold too. And that thing that Ruby called pie. She vaguely recalled the name from the time she used to work as a girl just up from the country, but she had never tasted it before, and when she ate a slice which Ruby gave her she felt immediately like vomiting. As a matter of fact, she felt like throwing up everything she ate. She could not complain, however, as she did not want anyone to start wondering what part of the jungle she came from. So each lunchtime she suffered silently.

Around three days after she started working Mrs. Watkins told her that she would be expecting some visitors for tea that afternoon and that she should put on her uniform and get herself ready to serve.

'Uniform, ma'm?' she quizzed her mistress.

'Don't stand there gaping at me like such a wretched fool, girl, what do you mean "Uniform, ma'am"? Don't you know what a uniform is?'

She was going too far now, Dinah felt. She was taking a liberty with her and that she would not put up with. No, she wouldn't.

'Go to Ruby and she'll tell you what to do,' Mrs. Watkins said, and began to walk off.

'Yes, ma'm,' Dinah replied. She stared at the woman walking off. Her tall, upright frame, her light skin and the austere bun of her wavy hair. Suddenly an impulse seized her. She had no reason. She could not explain her anguish, but she had to do it.

'Mrs. Watkins,' she called, her heart beating heavily. It was the first time she had called to her by her name. It was perhaps the first time she had addressed her at all without being first addressed. In calling her mistress's name she received an inexplicable thrill. The woman was just about halfway down the passage to her rest room; she turned briskly and looked at Dinah. For a long moment the two women stared at each other. In that one moment, Dinah was sure, a unifying intimacy enveloped the both of them. It had its essence in a complete animal nakedness. There was for one moment a complete consciousness of each other's role as mistress, as servant, which completely negated itself, so that they remained, both of them, woman.

Mrs. Watkins was the first to break away. She flustered a bit, patted the bun on her head for no reason that she knew and enquired angrily, 'What is it?'

Dinah, despite the elation she felt, was also confused. She blushed, then stammered, 'You could tell me where ah could find the uniform, ma'm?'

'Girl, are you trying to provoke me? Are you sure you're in complete control of your senses? I said ask Ruby and I don't want to hear or see you until this afternoon again.' She hurried to her room and slammed the door behind her.

The perplexity of her feelings were now almost unbearable. She was convinced that she hated Mrs. Watkins, she hated the place, the food, the orders she got, all of which so completely humiliated her. She could smash everything, she could almost kill in her rage. Yet she stayed on. She wanted to be facing Mrs. Watkins always, she wanted to hear her bark at her, she wanted to be commanded, to be pushed, to be kicked, because it was her, Dinah's, command, her pushing, her kicking, even if they came from another person. Her soul raged with humiliation and bitterness, but in the humiliation and bitterness there was the sheer pleasure of pain. She became convinced now, more than ever, that she needed Shepherd John, whoever he was.

Ruby, between her whimpering, told her where in the store-room the uniforms were kept and later helped her to dress into one of them. It was a stiffly starched white uniform like the one she had seen the girl pushing the pram with.

By four o'clock all five ladies had arrived. To Dinah the remarkable thing about them was that they all looked so much like each other. Their dresses were all of silk in some drab floral colour and they were draped up in the same odd places. They all walked alike, they all held their tea-cups alike, they all talked alike. They were all very light-skinned, except for the one called

Mrs. Brooks, and one of them, Lady something or other, she thought she heard them say, was obviously of pure white stock. She was the eldest of the lot and the veins stuck out from all parts of her neck and face in a manner that revolted Dinah, as much as it fascinated her. The odd thing was that Mrs. Brooks, despite her disadvantage in shade, didn't, after a time, seem in any way conspicuous. In fact, in the delicate way in which she held her cup, in the way she crossed her legs and expressed approval at everything else that was said, or disapproval when it was required, in the exotic and obviously cultured way in which she squeaked and chattered and neglected her hand during the game of bridge, she seemed the very embodiment of the whole group, more like it and more of it than anyone else among them.

For the next hour and a half they drank their little hot cups of tea—and it never ceased to amaze Dinah how it was that they could drink so many hot cups of tea on such a hot afternoon— they ate fantastic little sandwiches that Ruby had so skilfully prepared, and they nibbled delicately at the cakes and biscuits.

They left most of the sandwiches and cakes behind then. Dinah, who was not hungry, could consume only a little of what remained. Ruby never seemed to eat anything. So, like most of the other meals, the greater portion went to the garbage-box.

15

I T HAD to be tonight. Things were bad over the past few weeks. There was hardly a sailor to be seen in Kingston and the few that were available were quickly grabbed by the younger and better-looking women.

Age catching up with me fast, Mary thought, remembering the days of her own youth when she could afford to pick and choose her customers. Still, she had no remorse in the knowledge of her age. For she had Rossetta: her daughter was beautiful and brainy and had colour. She would get a rich white man soon and take her away from her poverty. It was just a matter of a few years now and she still had enough flesh on her body to whore it until the time came.

But her daughter couldn't go to high school without clothes or with an empty stomach. She had done her part by getting the scholarship. Now she had to get the money to buy her clothes and food. And she had to do it the only way she knew.

Tonight the sailor-men were swarming the city. Two ships had come in harbour unexpectedly on Friday night and a third yesterday morning. There had been literal panic among the whores down at Hanover Street and the rest of the red-light district. The pimps were almost running over each other and the vice squad of the police was almost driven out of its wits trying to keep up with them.

She was sorry now that she didn't operate with one special brothel. Nowadays the pimps had themselves so well organized that it was difficult business finding a stray sailor on the streets. They were even driving cars these days or, if not, the cab-drivers would pick up the sailor-men as soon as they came off the ship and take them to their own contacts.

Furthermore, even when she did manage to pick up a sailor-man it was another problem finding a brothel to take him. On a night like this most of the beds were in full use and the permanent girls got first choice. And in addition to all this there was the risk of being arrested for soliciting. There was no law against whoring in a brothel, but once you get out on the streets they lash you with soliciting. It wasn't fair, she thought, not fair at all.

Yet she knew that she could never have been a brothel prostitute. It wasn't just that she would never want her Rossetta to grow up in such a place, though that would have been enough to prevent her, but that she couldn't tolerate the 'mother' of any brothel. Those keepers really thought they owned the whores that lived in their place. A cunning, scheming pack of bitches, that's what they were. They lend you money when things were out of season, you get in debt to them and then your goose was cooked, you soon find yourself grinding out all your flesh only for those bitches. Even with her, the mother of the brothel which she used tried to be domineering, though the men she carried there always paid for the use of her room without any trouble. No, she would have nothing to do with those women.

The night was dark and it threatened to rain. She hurried by the railway station, passed the warehouses, taking in the familiar smell of stored food, coffee and peanuts, sugar, rum and cod-fish, pimento and rice, all mixed up with the musty board dungeons, the raw, sordid smell of the murky sea and the stink disinfectant powder that the Chinamen used to clean out their wholesale groceries. Another ten minutes and she had passed the little Chinatown with the narrow alleys behind the shops, the mess of expensive-looking garbage in front of them and every now and then the contrasting smell of pop-cheow. Cautiously now, she turned off the Harbour Street so as to avoid the water-police station, made a semicircle among the nasty little back lanes where the only signs of life were the mangy mongrels with their heads buried in the garbage-boxes and every now and then the eerie, bellowing sound of an old condensed-milk can falling and rolling to the gutter which had the effect only of emphasizing the dark, musty, mean silence, and finally was back again on the Harbour Street.

She finally settled down between an alley which separated two large banks, from which point she had a good view of the waterfront and at the same time avoided the lights of King Street. She was tired and so she sat down on a clump of discarded money-bags near to the gutter. She jumped to her feet on hearing a familiar Yankee curse-word in the distance and hurried down to the corner, but her face fell as she saw that they were all already swarmed by pimps. She was too disappointed to move from where she stood at the corner, and lingered hopefully as they approached her. But the pimps were in full control. With amazing skill they were carrying on an endless chatter with the sailors, their American slang was even more perfect than the sailors themselves and whatever it was that they were saying seemed to be amusing the sailors, as every now and then the silence was shattered by their loud guffaws. As they passed her she could just hear one of the pimps, who was wearing a pair of sun-glasses, saying:

'Lemme tell you, Mac, this here land is one of multi-racial harmony; man, I tell you, there's all kinds of gals here, Chinese gals, Indian gals, black gals and lots of white gals too—but take a tip from me, Mac—try the blacks first. I ain't kidding you, man, when I say, try the blacks . . .'

Several more sailors passed escorted by pimps. A little later she saw two of them walking alone. Quickly, she straightened her dress and lit a cigarette. As they came to within a few yards of her she crawled out of her corner and stood in their path.

'Hi, sailor-boy,' she said.

'Hi,' one of them said half-heartedly, dropping a bit behind his friend, but as she came more into the light, and he had a better look at her, he turned away and hastened to catch his friend.

'Hey, I talkin' to you, pretty-boy,' she said, running after him and desperately holding on to his sleeve.

'Hey, lay off, will ya,' he snarled, pushing her hand away.

'Listen, you won' get a better bargain dan me, come on——'

'Don't ya hear what the guy says?' the other sailor, a tall slimy fellow with mean eyes suddenly said. 'He says beat it, Granny, go mind the kids; now scram, huh?'

She swallowed her saliva and slunk back to her corner. Rossetta, she must get clothes and food for Rossetta, even if she had to steal, even if she had to kill. But they kept passing her, either neglecting her completely or throwing her off as she came under the light, and there was one she held on to so frantically that it was not until he had spat in her face that she could bring herself to let him go. And now it was beginning to drizzle. But Rossetta, she must get good clothes and food for Rossetta.

Another hour and a half of waiting, then suddenly her eyes brightened. If not him, then no one else would take her. She stared hungrily at his huge frame in the distance. He struggled from one side of the piazza to the other, clutching the bottle tightly in his hand and taking a gulp every few minutes.

Despite her desperation, she couldn't help but shudder as he came closer to her. She could smell the rum in him from several yards away. The front of his shirt was wide open and revealed a red, hairy, powerful chest; his uniform was moist and dirty and the front of his pants stained with vomit.

She walked in front of him as he crossed the corner, and he stopped. He gaped at her stupidly, wobbling and hardly managing to keep his balance. He widened his bloodshot, bulging eyes at her; they closed involuntarily and he widened them again. Suddenly he growled something at her as he stuck out his tongue and licked off the little spots of stale vomit which had dried on to his face.

'Hi,' she said, 'looking for fun, eh, Mac?'

He continued gaping at her stupidly, grunted something then walked closer to her.

'Gesh me a bed,' he growled, still squinting at her.

'Sure, Mac, come wid me.' She walked up to him and held on to him tightly. Hurriedly, she led him along the Harbour Street, across King Street, in the direction of the red-light district, straining under his massive weight. But as she walked past one of the back lanes she became aware of heavy footsteps trailing her. She looked back and her heart sank. It was a Special Constable. It was no use trying to run, so she stood where she was, the sailor stopping with her and asking, 'Whazzup?'

As the Special Constable came closer, she recognized him to

be 'Street-hawk' and she sighed a little with relief, knowing full well what was going to happen.

'Whe' you teking him?' he enquired, taking out his notebook.

'Christ Almighty, Street-hawk, you can't give a gal a chance.'

'Listen, woman, ah 'ave no time to higgle an' haggle tonight, tell me whe' you teking 'im so dat ah can collect afterwards, or else on behalf of Her Majesty I is arrestin' you for illegal soli——'

'All right, all right, is Golden Orange, an' no more dan a third.'

'Ah never tek any more, ah never tek any less,' he said, writing down the name of the brothel in his notebook, 'an, remember, no funny business wid me.' He stuck the notebook in his breast pocket and walked off briskly.

The American by this time was leaning on the wall of the shop, gulping down the last of his rum.

'Gemme a bed,' he kept saying. 'I wanna bed.'

'Come, sailor-boy,' she said, pulling him along, 'you soon lie down.'

The Golden Orange was an old two-storey building on the right side of the road in the direction of the East Queen Street. It was flanked on either side by two more brothels which didn't cater for street-walkers. She sighed with relief as she came to the narrow enclosed stairway on the left corner of the building. It was a difficult task getting him upstairs, but when one of the girls came down to help, Mary promptly ran her off with curses. She knew those women and what they gave.

Immediately at the top of the stairs was a little bar well stocked with rum, juices and peanuts. In one corner was a juke-box and in the other a fat, mulatto woman with pouting mouth and sneaky, half-closed eyes glared up from an armchair.

'Wanna dance first,' the sailor suddenly said. 'Don't ya think I'm drunk, baby, you just get me a bottle of rum and music, 'cause I wanna dance before I get ma bed.'

He took out his wallet, turned his back to her, and, after considerable fumbling, handed her two dollar bills. 'Doncha think I'm drunk, baby,' he said, putting his wallet in his pocket. She led him to the room in front. There was a large speaker in one corner carrying the sound from the juke-box inside the bar and several tables and chairs near to the walls so that a large enough space was left in the centre for dancing. On the walls were the familiar decorations—semi-nude women in all kinds of poses, large men with shot-guns saying 'Buy something!' the flags of most of the more widely known countries, with, of course, one whole wall devoted to the stars and stripes of America. The girls were all dressed in shorts or panties and bikini tops, all dirty and smelling. Several of them were dancing in the corners. The others were waiting impatiently on the pimps.

Mary went to the bar and ordered a flask of Appleton. She discovered to her delight that one of the bills was a five-dollar note. She punched several tunes, took up the bottle and glasses and returned to the dance-hall.

'Hey,' he said, as soon as she sat down, 'how come all them gals so naked?'

'That's how they dress here, Mac.'

'Then how come you ain't naked too?'

'Don't worry, you soon get all you want,' she said, coming up close to him and inhaling the vapour of his stinking breath, the rum and his vomit all mixed together.

'I wanna see you naked now, so take them off, take them off.'

His large palm suddenly swiped her across her neck. She fell upon the table. He ripped away the front of her dress and tore off her bra. 'That's better,' he said. His hand tightened upon her breast. She screamed with pain. He laughed, dug his fingernails even deeper into her flesh, then with another sudden swipe he slashed her down on the table again. Then with sudden gentleness he undressed her, smiling and humming *The Star-spangled Banner* to himself as he did so. He took off her shoes, kissed each gently and rested them on the table.

'Now let's dance,' he said, dragging her to him.

It was sheer torture. Every step he took his heavy boots came hammering down on her toes. He saw she was in pain and he laughed his filthy-smelling, rich laugh and, coughingly, as the music finished he pulled her to the ground and fell upon her.

'Not here,' she said, hardly able to bear the pain of his fondling. 'Come with me.'

He became gentle again and began to run his palms over her shoulders soothingly.

'I don't hurt you, baby?' he asked, as if with deep concern.

'No, come,' she said, and led him to the room.

The fat mulatto woman got up from her chair, walked past

them and stood in front of one of the doorways. Mary stopped with the sailor in front of her.

'Whazzup now?' he asked. 'She want to dance too?'

'No, she want the money for the room first.'

'Oh, she want the money for the room,' he repeated with mock agreeableness. 'How much?'

'Depend on how you taking it, long time or short time.'

'I ain't know, jus' tell me how much.'

'Three dollars.'

'No, five dollars tonight,' the mother corrected.

The sailor handed over the five dollars and she left. They went inside the room and she closed the door without locking it. He took another gulp of the rum, dropped down on the bed, then began to stare at her. He laughed.

'Come here,' he said.

She walked up to him, beginning to be a bit nervous. There was something about him she didn't like. She had been out with drunken sailors before. As a matter of fact, she liked being with them when they were drunk, as it made her job much easier, and you could always pinch them of everything they had. But there was something about this one she didn't like. It was in the way he grinned his teeth, in the way his eyes narrowed on her when they were open, in the way he kept laughing. But she knew she had to get that money for her Rossetta. She had to get good clothes and good food if she was going to mix with brown people pickney. So she walked up to him.

'C'm'ere, c'mon, don't be afraid,' he encouraged her. He dug into his pocket, then held out his hand. 'Look,' he said, almost jubilantly, 'dollars, Yankee dollars; hee, hee, hee.' As soon as she was within reach he grabbed her by her forearm, wrenched it, and dragged her on the bed. She howled with pain and he slapped her across her face. Each time she made to scream his hand came crashing down on her mouth until she tasted the blood gurgling down her throat. With his left hand he held her down on the bed by her neck while his other hand began to roam over her body. Every part of it he touched he pinched severely. His fingers were like the jaws of a crab. She could feel the blood spouting from her flesh each time his fingernails eased out of it.

And each time she tried to scream the left hand left her neck and battered her across her mouth. He was laughing hysterically now, as his right hand with the thumb outstretched moved nearer and nearer to the pit of her stomach. Suddenly she winced with agony and with a mighty effort tore herself away from him, screaming at the top of her voice. But his laughter drowned her screaming. His red eyes bulged wildly. He took the dollars from his pocket again. 'Pretty,' he said, 'pretty, pretty Yankee dollar, hee, hee, hee.' He approached her slowly, craftily, then made a dash for her. She slipped away from his grasp just in time and he crashed into the wall behind her. Her eyes suddenly caught sight of the rum bottle at the foot of the bed and she dashed for it, snatching it up by the narrow end. By this time he was up again and coming after her. She raised the bottle, timed his approach, and as he was upon her she crashed it upon his head. He screamed and fell to the ground in a splash of blood and rum and dollars.

She ran for the door and was about to go outside when she suddenly dashed back in and ripped his wallet from his back pocket. Already he was beginning to stir from the effects of the blow as she hurtled through the door and made for the stairway.

'See here,' she heard the keeper shouting behind her, 'is wha' the rass-clate you carrying on inside me place, eh? If you cause any policeman to come in a me place dis night, God blind me if ah don't dig out your bombo-hole.'

Suddenly she heard the crash of glass as someone swiped away a table. She turned and saw the sailor struggling frantically towards her. His face was completely covered with blood as well as the major part of his clothes. She threw her hands in the air and dashed for the bar. 'Lawd God, she kill 'im!' she screamed; 'she kill 'im in a me place!'

The sailor grappled down to the foot of the stairs shouting for the police on the top of his voice. Two constables patrolling the area had heard the screaming and were already heading for the brothel. As they saw him they ran forward and held him up.

'Who done it? Who done it?'

'God damn ya, didn't you see the gal that just ran through here?'

'I know there was something fishy about that woman that just ran past us,' one of the constables said. 'I told you we shoulda hold her. Look after him, I'll go after the bitch.'

He ran off in the direction that he had seen Mary go, whistling for aid at the same time. Soon he was joined by two patrol cars and around six other constables.

'She couldn't be far, circle her and close in,' he told them.

Mary, as soon as she came out of the brothel, had dashed for the lane which ran parallel with Harbour Street, then she turned up another, then down again, hoping that she would lose anyone who might try to follow her. But then she heard the whistle of the police and the sound of their sirens. If only she could reach the western side of the waterfront before they caught up with her she was sure she could lose them then. She ran with all her might, forgetting all the pain she had just suffered.

But the sounds around her became louder and more frequent. She couldn't see them, but they were all around her. Suddenly she heard a shrill loud whistle to her right. She ran in the opposite direction down a narrow lane with zinc fencing on either side. But suddenly from in front of her she heard the same stark shrill. They were taunting her. If she could only see them. They were nowhere. They were everywhere. They were closing in on her. The whistles were coming nearer and nearer, louder and louder. Why didn't they just take her? They knew where she was but they were tormenting her. As long as she had a chance they knew she would run. And the agony was prolonged. The whistles became more shrill, the sirens louder and louder. She ran through an opening in the zinc fencing and found herself in a completely exposed area where a building had just been pulled down. She could see their flashlights darting in the night and she could hear their footsteps. The whistles were now unbearable, piercing. They were everywhere, mocking her, taunting her. In front of her, behind her, beside her. Footsteps, whistles, sirens, flashlights. She darted back through the opening in the fence.

Suddenly she saw one! Then she felt it. The baton slashed her across her breasts. From behind another swiped her across her back. Then a third came crashing down upon her ear. She fell heavily to the gutter, her teeth biting into the slimy filth.

16

THERE had obviously been a devil of a commotion either in or near Mrs. Mac's house. Dinah could sense it as soon as she came off the bus that took her from work. She hurried down the narrow road and soon discovered that it was in fact her own home that was the centre of attraction. Whatever had happened seemed to have passed its climax, for the women who stood nearby were laughing and talking among themselves, digesting to the full the excitement that had just taken place. More than the usual number of children were running about the street in the vicinity of her gate, taking advantage of the fact that at last their parents had found something else of interest other than barking at them. And the dogs were numerous and active, seeming themselves to have caught the atmosphere of laughter and free-for-all excitement.

Dinah hurried through the little crowd, opened the gate and went inside, realizing that she had at once become the object of attention. She went straight to Mrs. 'D's' room and knocked. Everywhere was locked up and not a sound came from the main building. She had the odd impression that there was something abandoned about the yard, as if a hurricane had just passed through it. There was no answer, but Dinah knew that Mrs. 'D' was in, since the white and red string which she hung at the top of her door when she was out to prevent evil spirits from entering was not there. She knocked again and after a long pause she heard a soft almost frightened voice, which she just managed to detect as Mrs. 'D's', ask, 'Is who dat?'

'Is me, Dinah, quick an' open up.'

There was an eternal ruffling and shifting inside as Mrs. 'D' broke off whatever it was she was doing. Then the door opened slowly, Dinah slipped in, and quickly it was closed again.

'Is wha' de hell goin' on?' Dinah enquired as soon as she stepped inside, holding her nose immediately as the stink odour of the room hit her.

'Me gal, hell pop loose ya this afternoon.'

'Say wha'? How it go?'

'Mabel man come fo' her from down ah de Dungle. My God, Dinah, you know dat wid all the style dat dat gal pull 'pon we is down ah Dungle she come from! Her man is a terrible bearded man, look like a Rasta. 'Im come wid 'im gang an' haul Mabel out ah de room an' gi' her one piece ah beatin'. Lawd, although she was such a bitch me couldn'n' help feel sorry fe har! 'Im rip all o' her clothes from off o' her an' bus' her ass wid a cow cod. Den 'im go inside her room an mash up everything there. Den 'im dump her in ah' 'im donkey-cart wid de coconut and drive her 'ome. Gal, one crowd gather up outside ah de gate for you can imagine de screamin' Mabel put up.'

'Serve de bitch right. But, tell me, wha' dat other bitch Mrs. Mac do all dis time.'

Mrs. 'D' held her stomach and laughed beneath her breath. 'See here, God, me have fe tek bad something mek laugh; she come outside when she hear de commotion start an' when she see de Rasta man dem she drop down an' faint same time. We 'ave fe lif' her up an' tek her inside. When she get up an' hear de screamin' she faint same time again. An' when she get up again she start put up one piece a praying an' she don' stop yet.' The two women tried to restrain their laughter. Suddenly Mrs. 'D' became serious.

'But, Dinah,' she said, 'is you me sarry for now. Mabel not goin' stop at anything now fe mash you up now dat she gone back to de dogs. You mus' go to Shepherd John right now, you mus'.'

'Yes, me did 'ave every intention ah goin' tonight. Tell me de address again.'

Dinah left for the church around seven o'clock that evening. It was not very far away, only a mile or so in the middle of the Trench Town district. To reach the church she had to walk off the paved road on to one of the innumerable little dirt tracks that led into the large clusters of tiny hovels and huts which were partly hidden from the road by a maze of thick, hoary, green cacti.

She walked for about a hundred yards down the dirt path, asked her way to the church, was told to turn right, then left, then right again and it would be on the second corner on the left. It was another world inside there hedged in by the cacti. It had a character different, too, from the type she now experienced in Jones Town. The people all seemed the same. They all had the same hemmed-in look on their faces, as if they had never gone outside on the road before. They all seemed prisoners of the hoary cacti. They seemed to linger and crawl and slave for the cacti. The thick, flat, heavy green cacti, with the grey streaks and the tall spikes, were like living bludgeons: greedy, green and greedy for their lives. There was a strange silence in the place. Even the noises that the hungry babies made, the whimpering of the old women, the knock of the dominoes on the raw wooden tables in the little arid openings that the men made as they gambled, even the sounds that the children made as they played without laughter, they all added to the silence rather than detracted from it. There was always a hush, always a pressing, eerie, squalid hush forced down by the bludgeoning cacti, by the little arid, dusty patches, by the complexity of the narrow, crooked pathways which lost themselves in an unending maze. They all looked at her as she passed, but they did not see her, for they could see nothing but the forbidding green bludgeons and the arid patches; they answered her, but they did not hear her, for they could hear nothing but the whimpering of the old people and the choking of the dying babies. And every now and then a dog crossed by in a rickety sidelong crawl, its tongue half out of its head; and now a cat, half of its fur gone, the few remaining sticking up out of the scab and sores, the tail long and wiry; and then a pig, six ribs, seven ribs, squeaking silently, seven little piggies trotting persistently behind it, one bleeding, half chewed up, but still alive, still squeaking in its mouth.

She finally found the church in an opening larger than usual between the cacti. The yard was wide, dry and had an appearance of complete barrenness with the brown earth upon it loose and dead. The back and one side was fenced in by the cacti, now more tall and imposing than ever; the other side was made up of old, rotten zinc sheets and the raw, hooped staves of cod-fish barrels. On one side of the yard were three small huts made of old soap-boxes and the round bottoms of zinc barrels patched together. On the other side of the yard, after a space of about ten yards, was the church, a relatively long building taking up almost the whole of the zinc-and-barrel side. It was made of rough, irregularly shaped lumber shavings—the light brown cedar, mixed with dark mahogany, the smooth greenish streaks of the straight mahoe and the tough *lignum vitae* still distorted with its crude, greenish-grey bark spotted with little lumps of sap—they were all cobbled together, each strip held insecurely to the other by pieces of strings and wires and old rusty nails, and the top was covered over with the sides of discarded tar drums.

In the space between the cluster of little huts and the church was a tall white pole with painted black rings at intervals of about a yard from each other. Tied to the top of the pole was a red flag at one end of which was a black cross patched on upside-down with some other material and at the top end was painted in white 'REVIVAL ZION BAPTIST OF GOD', which was the name of the church. Immediately below the flag was a wooden sign on which was scrawled in an irregular mixture of common and capital letters, commas and full stops, 'THE WAGES OF SIN IS DEATH'. Between the 'S' and the 'I' of the word 'SIN', however, another hand had scrawled in black paint the letter 'K' and, as Dinah was to learn later, this was the source of profound mystery among the church members. Everyone, of course, knew that the letter was not written by human hand, there was none in the area who could be that blasphemous, and even if there was, it was certain that they would have been struck dead the moment they had attempted to interfere with such a sacred object. The mystery, however, was in deciding whether the letter was made by the hand of God or by Satan. Some held that it was a sign from God showing that he had not forgotten his poor black pickneys; others held just as firmly that it was the work of Rutibel, the fallen angel and Satan's closest assistant, who was trying to cast an evil spell upon them because of their faithfulness to God, and their persistent righteousness in the midst of misery and temptation. Dinah could hear the voices of people inside the church and in the background the soft rattling of drums. She walked cautiously across the yard, looking curiously for a moment at the sacred stones on the ground surrounding the pole: white stones, red stones, stones resembling the heads of sheep, stones like the bones of dead men. In front of the door were two clay jars in which were planted ferns; a few were green, most of them were brown and withered like the earth.

She went inside. The scent of their bodies and clothes swept upon her. Perfumes, cananga water, perspiration, leaves and flowers and herbs all combined to give a strange, exotic, ambivalent stench. It was sickening, it was sweet, it was nauseating. But in its very nausea, in the effect of total revulsion it had on her, there was a syrupy, molasses-like nostalgia. The soft beating of the drums, the hum of their voices, the herbs, the stench, swirled in the depths of her. Senses overwhelmed, palate cloyed, in an instant she was purged. And she woke up in a wistful atmosphere of white and purple dresses, starched drill pants and white shirts, blue, purple and red turbans, backless wood benches under a solitary, odd electric bulb. Dreamy, dreamy. The hard dirt floor; bumpy. Altar on raised platform. Unleavened bread and crackers and fast cups. Glasses and pitcher of consecrated water. Red candles at each corner of table. Two black candles below on either side of the basin of water. Flags and placards, and Christ with long, sad face and nice black beard. HOPE. FAITH. CHARITY. BY THE SWEAT OF THY BROW SHALL those pretty flowers fading. Moses with long wise beard white as lilies, and crotons and ferns and nice-nice flowers and herbs in the earthen vase on the altar. It was wonderful. It was sweet. It was strange and different and nice. She sat down.

Several of the women began looking in her direction. They whispered something among themselves and then one of them left the group and went through the door at the front side of the church. A little later the same woman returned with another, older, woman. The latter was dressed in a black silk dress, longer than the rest, and around her waist was a purple cord towards the end of which was tied a pair of scissors and a long steel whistle. Her turban was tall and imposing and made of red, blue and purple cloth.

' 'Evening, I is de Elder Mother. You come to join de service,

Sister?' she asked Dinah in a quiet but firm voice, the other woman falling a few feet behind her.

'Ah come to see de Shepherd,' Dinah replied. Instinctively, she took a dislike to the woman she faced. The tails of her eyes went too far round to the side of her face, her lips were clamped together too firmly. She seemed a woman who was used to giving orders and getting them obeyed.

'You can't see 'im now. Service jus' goin' start. If you wan' you can stay an' wait in de service an' you see 'im afterwards.' She began to turn away, as if it didn't matter what Dinah answered, only pausing another moment to add, 'It would do you good.'

Dinah remained seated and watched the woman as she walked up the dirt aisle, stepped up on the wooden platform, and, standing on the left side of the altar, raised slowly the whistle to her lips. She blew it hard and loud. There was a stir as everyone rushed to their proper places. A late couple hurried in from behind and Dinah noted with surprise that the man accompanying the woman was Sammy, the garbage-man.

The drum stopped beating. A moment of silence. Then suddenly it started again, this time louder and the rhythm now set to a quick, fixed pattern. Suddenly, through the front door, a figure appeared. He was tall and almost jet black, with clearly defined features, eyes wide apart, gleaming and condescending, a carefully shaven moustache, neatly pressed, dark navy-blue suit, a stiff white shirt and a long black tie with a silver tie-pin. In his right hand he carried a long wooden staff with a brass handle and in his left hand was a large black Bible. His majestic purple and white turban stood at least fourteen inches above his head.

The Elder Mother walked down from the altar as he entered and joined the Water Mother, the two armour-bearers and the Daughters of the First Order in the front row. With a loud confident voice the Shepherd broke into the first line of the hymn *Just As I am Without One Plea*, as he walked on to the platform keeping time with his staff, urging on his followers with a 'one more time, Sisters', and an 'Ahmen, Praise de Lord'.

In a few minutes the service was in full swing. Everyone was singing heartily and adding their 'Alleluias' and 'Yes, Lords'. Already one or two of the more devout were beginning to feel the spirit coming down on them, though restraint was necessary at such an early period of the service. Several more hymns were sung—*Where Shall I Go?*; *At the Cross, at the Cross*; *Glory Be To God, He'll Set Me Free Some Day*—mournfully, sweetly, wailingly. It was such a far land their voices took them to, such a far-far land. Away, away. Sun, Moon and Stars—They Shine So Bright. It was not just the milk and honey, not just the voice of God they heard, nor even the happiness of Jesus by their sides. It was the awayness. Oh Wandering Sheep, lost and forlorn. Barren, desolate desert. Endless, arid nothingness. Day After Yesterday. Poor me, poor me. Lost and far away. Remote poor me. Dissolving me. Sweet, sweet release.

'Sisters, Brothers!' Shepherd John broke in as they neared the end of a hymn, 'de spirit of de Lawd is sweet. Las' night de spirit o' de Lawd come inside of me as ah lay down on me bed an' meditate. An' de spirit say, John, ah know dat you an' all you followers suffer, ah know dat it is a wicked an' a tough worl'——'

'A tough worl',' his followers repeated. 'A tough worl'.'

'A worl' o' sin an' shame an' corruption, a worl' o' sodomy.'

'Ahmen!' they all agreed.

'A worl' o' temptation an' wickedness. But I is de Lawd Jesus——'

'Alleluia!'

'I see an' I know all t'ings. I see dat my children suffer but their sufferin' will not be long cause blessed are de poor——'

' 'Cause theirs is de kingdom o' 'eaven,' they chorused heartily.

'An' de spirit say, John, you is me appointed shepherd, you will lead me people till de day o' righteousness——'

'Praise be to God, Alleluia!' they rejoiced with fervour.

'Hol' on to you brush, John, de spirit say, hol' on to you brush an' don' fall to temptation. Like de good shepherd lead dy sheep out o' de wilderness o' wickedness. Let dem not lust after de t'ings o' de worl'; let dem not envy de white man an' 'im riches, or de brown man an' 'im education——'

'Yes, dear Lawd!' they echoed. 'We hear you, Lawd!'

'Let dem know de path of acceptance an' goodness——'

'Praise be! Praise be!' It was growing in them, the spirit. Short. Quick at first. Little tickling sweetnesses.

'Jesus! Alleluia!' They shivered.

'Let dem be patient an' follow my ways till de day of

judgement shall come. Den ah hear a great soun' like a t'under-clap an' all was silent!'

'Ahmen! Ahmen!'

The Shepherd then moved back to the table and drank a glass of consecrated water, sprinkling some of what was left in the glass around the platform, then he went about rearranging the contents of the table in the mystical pattern that only he knew.

In the meantime, the first armour-bearer rushed up to the platform and read the *One Hundred and Nineteenth Psalm*. 'I will keep thy statutes,' he ended, his eyes closed tightly and the tears spouted from them. 'Oh forsake me not utterly!'

No, God. No. They kneeled. They begged. Forgive them. Forsake them not.

And the labouring began. The tickle trickled to the brown stream. The river came down. Came gushing down. Down the veins of their flesh that swelled with heat. It was such an agony. Such a sweet, gurgling, rushing agony. It twisted the flesh that wrapped their necks. It wrenched their shoulders. Every muscle writhed. Torment. The river knows no bank. Everything goes down before it. Trees, houses, cows and rich man's castles, donkeys and American motor-cars. It was Gabriel, mighty, rhapsodic Gabriel. She held on to her sister. For joy, for pain. But Gabriel would not let go and she fell to the ground in ecstasy. And now Shadrach. Meshach. Abednego. They flung them to the ground. They burned them in the mighty furnace of their power. They ravished them and twisted them in the dust. Burn and burn and burn again. Eat up the dirt with out-stretched limbs. Dying, fluttering birds. Crawl under Michael. Calm, sweet, tormenting Michael. Run from Rutibel. Oh merciful, almighty God. Run. Black cloak spreading like wings of bat. Run, Shepherd John! Do, Shepherd John. Use your staff! Can't speak. Use your staff. Useless. Dust.

They screamed in the voice of the unknown tongues. Those that were too possessed were calmed down by the Mothers and armour-bearers and Shepherd John. Those that were slow were held and whirled and lashed with the staff. They leaped with anguish. They rolled and moaned in a blissful, divine paroxysm. Oh, what a writhing joy. What pain relieving pain. Oh, sweet, sweet, excruciating release.

Dinah remained motionless. At first she was tempted to

laugh. She had never taken these mad pack of zealots seriously. She was even beginning to get uneasy as she caught Sammy's eyes gaping at her every few minutes. But as the service progressed something in the atmosphere began to overwhelm her. She came to realize that the men and women before her had something she longed for. It was simple and plain. They were untormented. By their singing and dancing and spiriting they had scraped their misery from themselves. They had ravished and exhausted their living hell. So now there was only the dead nothingness of joy.

17

THEY left in little groups at the end of the service, wondering at Shepherd John's great gift of prophesy and the almighty spark of his tongue, singing and humming softly their songs of praise. Dinah soon found herself alone in the church except for the Shepherd and one of the Daughters of the Second Order. A little later the Elder Mother had returned. She stopped at the door, shrouding it with her stout frame like a glum ghost. She stared at them severely but said nothing.

Every now and then the Shepherd took a look at Dinah out of the corner of his eye. Each time they beamed on her with a quick, furtive interest. He seemed anxious to get rid of the woman he was talking to. She, however, seemed to be relishing his presence and it was not till another half-hour before she managed to pull herself away.

Quickly, he walked over to Dinah. The Elder Mother took two slow steps forward so that she was in full view of them. She folded her arms and eyed them silently. The eyes were black and wide, the lips more tight and severe than the bolted door of a store-room.

He stopped about a yard from her. A balmy fragrance came from him. She was struck by the complete ease and confidence of his manner. There was no pride, no vigour, no fear in him. Only a perfect self-assurance. It was mysterious and powerful in its radiance. In an instant she had the uncanny desire to fall down at his feet and pour out her soul to him.

'Sister, you want to see me?' he asked, his voice was soft, reassuring.

'Yes . . .' she faltered, '. . . yes.'

'Call me Shepherd,' he said with a firm kindness.

'Yes . . . Shepherd,' she said with the embarrassment of an illegitimate child meeting its father for the first time and being told to say 'Daddy'.

'Woman, you have a troubled soul. People harming you.' He broke off and stared through her for a long moment, then he added, 'No, is not just people, something bigger plagueing you.'

'Is de Dungle, Shepherd, is de Dungle.'

He did not appear the least surprised at her statement. It was as if almost every day people came to him with the same complaint.

'It haunt you, no? It like Rutibel on you all de time?'

'Yes, Shepherd. Ah running from it. Ah try hard as ah can. But it not outside o' me. It inside. It drawin' me back. Ah don' wan' to go back but it pulling me hard-hard. An' on top o' all dat a woman set a spirit 'pon me dat ah go back. You can help me, Shepherd? You will help me?'

Another long moment. He studied every detail of her soul with his piercing black eyes. Yes, she was sure he could help her. But what was he thinking? The intensity of his look was beginning to frighten her. She was bare. She was ashamed. She wanted to fall at his feet and burst out her soul. Never before had she felt the way she did towards any man.

'Ah been waitin' a long time fo' you,' he said at last, but slowly, mysteriously, still staring through her.

'What, Shepherd?'

'You is no ordinary woman an' dat is why you 'ave no ordinary problem. Only Melshezdek can protec' you.'

'What . . . what you mean, Shepherd?' She was puzzled, but the mystery of his words throbbed her.

'You mus' renounce all de t'ings o' de worl' an' join de church. You soul is clogged up wid filth an' all de sins o' de flesh. But beneath it ah can see dat it is no ordinary soul. You mus' renounce all an' come an' join de church.'

'Yu mean dat ah mus' give up me job?'

'An' leave your man who yu livin' in sin wid an' devote yu'self to de t'ings o' de spirit.'

'But . . . but how ah will . . .?'

'You will live here at de church. Yu is chosen to be de head o' de Daughters o' de Firs' Order. But firs' yu mus' be purged an' cleansed an' taught. Yu will go 'ome now an' say goodbye to all t'ings an' come tomorrow. De lawd 'as great t'ings prepared fo' you. Now go.'

He turned and walked away. He whispered something to the Elder Mother as he passed her. She did not move or say a word, but neither did he wait for an answer. As he left the church the two women stood silently facing each other like two dead trees in a barren field. Their eyes remained glued to each other. Long and hard. A raw, animal hate vibrated between them.

Then Dinah turned and left. She was surprised at her own composure. Despite the terror of the other woman, she knew she was not really afraid of her. The calm mystery of the Shepherd quivered in her. She had a strange sense of triumph. But over what she did not know.

There was no excitement. No doubt. She only did what she knew she had to do. She went home and packed. She did not make Alphanso touch her that night. And the next morning, without saying anything to anyone, she left.

It was a peace she was heading for. She did not know exactly what it was. But she could sense its power. She realized, too, that it would be no easy task awaiting her. The turmoil would be great as she broke the shackles of her soul. But Shepherd John was great in his peace and confidence. She would have the blissful release she witnessed last night.

One of the Daughters met her at the gate. 'De Shepherd waiting,' she said simply, and led her to the small hut to the left of the yard. The Shepherd was sitting on a stool when she entered, staring at the earth. She walked in and stood in front of him. The other woman lingered at the door.

The room was small and dark. There was a little table with a Bible, a copy of the *Sixth and Seventh Books of Moses* and innumerable small packages and bottles. In each corner was a large stone, two bones laying upon each other in the form of a cross resting on the ground in front of each one. A tall pole was stuck in the earth behind him at the top of which a black candle burned. On either side of the door were two white basins. A flat wooden cross rested on each one and on top of each cross a red candle burned. To the left corner of the room was a large aluminium bath-tub half filled with water.

He seemed unaware of their presence for about a minute. Then he stirred from his meditation and looked up at her. She sunk into his stare with shame. He shook his head, but not in despair.

'Oh, you are stink with sin,' he said softly. 'What that?' he asked her, looking at the bag she held in her hand.

'Me clothes, Shepherd.'

'Take dem an' burn dem,' he said to the other woman, 'bring de robe an' de cananga water an' call de Water Mother.'

The woman obeyed. Dinah made no protest as she took the bag from her hands.

'Before yu can receive de mysteries an' instructions o' de pure life yu mus' go through a period o' purification an' cleansin'.' He washed her with his eyes again, then he added kindly: 'But it will not be very difficult. Yu will persevere.'

'Ah do anything yu say, Shepherd.' Her voice was humble.

The period of cleansing began with a purity bath. She took off her clothes and knelt on the ground in front of the tub of water. Shepherd John read a chapter from the *Sixth* and *Seventh Books of Moses*. He took a cup of water from each of the white basins by the door and poured it in the tub. He sprinkled some of the cananga water over the room, then poured the rest in the tub. Then the Water Mother came forward, helped her in the tub and bathed her from her neck downwards, being careful not to make any of the water touch her hair. The other woman kept her eyes constantly fixed on the black candle, while Shepherd John went from corner to corner, making the sign of the cross and in a deep pleading voice read the *Twenty-ninth Psalm*.

She was dried. Shepherd John walked forward, put away his Bible and asked for the oil of gladness. The Water Mother handed him a bottle of olive oil from the table. He poured some in his hand, put down the bottle and rubbed his palms together. He touched her on her forehead, on the tip of her chin, on the crown of her head and on both cheeks with his forefinger, then from her neck he made a slow downward movement, beginning first with her hands, then coming up from her ankles, then horizontally across her belly, making sure that none of the oil touched her pubic hair. As he balmed her he repeated the twenty-sixth verse of the *Eighteenth Psalm*: 'With the pure thou wilt shew thyself pure; and with the froward thou wilt show thyself froward.'

Dinah remained calm throughout. She was overwhelmed with the mystery of it all. The balmy fragrance, its esoteric acerbity, sweet, lemony stink, seeped into her nostrils, into her every pore, salving her soul. And the touch of Shepherd John's hand was like magic, every squeeze, every slide, every stroke, soothed her flesh to a lilting, calm vibrance.

He covered her over with a red robe, then led her to a small room adjoining the balming hut. Inside there was only a white candle, a mat and one small hole looking into the yard. There she was locked in and told to meditate on her sins.

Alone in the dark little room, she was at a loss what to do or think. She sat down on the straw mat, her elbows on her legs, her cheeks in her palms. She should think of her sins, but what were they? Was it the men she sold her body to? Was it the hate that used to rage within her? Was it her complete ignorance of God? Perhaps. But somehow she felt it could not be just that. Sin could not just be whoring and hating and ignorance. Sin could not be that small and petty. Sin could not have come that easily and could not be thought away that easily. There must be something more powerful in its evil. There must be some tormenting pain in its extinction. Sin was the enemy of God. So in its way it must at least be as powerful as Him. And what power was there in whoring, what power was there in poverty and filth and hate?

But what was it? Where was it? How could she find it so as to fight and kill it? She pondered hard and long, but in the end succeeded only in pondering on her attempt at meditation.

Suddenly the full consciousness of herself crashed in on her. The musty board walls, the darkness emphasized by the solitary candle with its shifting mysterious light. A terror crippled her. She felt like screaming, but her throat was clogged up. She wanted to run through the door, but she was even more afraid of what would face her outside.

Her eyes caught the little hole in the wall. She dashed desperately towards it. She gaped outside with one eye. Earth. Little patch of bare, dry earth was all the hole permitted her vision. But there was something in the parched, plain patch that snatched her. Her being became trapped in its sear, dry nakedness.

What was beyond the nothingness of the dusty patch? she wondered. Nothing but more barren nothingness. The thought fascinated her. The arid patch was a moment in a vast eternity. The patch itself was nothing, but the moment was real. She had discovered something. It was immense, too big for her to understand, but she knew her soul comprehended it. The more she realized the unreality of the barren patch, the more it receded into the vast eternal nothingness, unseen but implied by itself, so much more was she impressed with the certainty of the moment, with the conviction that only it was real.

Calmly she looked away. She glanced at the happy flickering of the little flame.

'God!' she whispered softly, and her hands moved gently to her breasts.

The next morning she was woken up and given a cup of mint tea. At around nine o'clock she received her second bath, this time the bush bath. The Water Mother and one of the Daughters prepared it for her by boiling in a large kerosine tin a mixture of tamarind leaves, aralia bush, rosemary and Jack-in-the-bush. After the boiling they buried the leaves with a silver threepence and wrapped the kerosine tin with calico. When it was cool she took off her robe and stood in the tub. The black candle was taken away and a white one put in its place.

Then Shepherd John took up his Bible and read the *Nineteenth Psalm*. When he reached the ninth verse the Water Mother lifted the calico-bound kerosine tin and slowly poured its contents on Dinah's head as the Shepherd repeated the ninth verse three times. One of the Daughters went outside and in a few minutes returned with a live white pigeon. Shepherd John took it from her and, holding the bird by its neck, he battered Dinah's body with it from her neck down. As he flogged her he repeated solemnly the forty-second verse of the *Eighteenth Psalm*: 'Then did I beat them small as de dust before de wind: I did cast them out as de dirt in de street.'

The bird began to flutter in his hand. It struggled for air; it swallowed deeply, painfully. It hummed a stifled death-whine as the life gushed wonderfully from it. The feathers shivered, the legs stiffened slowly. Then it was still.

Then she was balmed down again with the oil of gladness, this time by the Water Mother. She was robed and given a large breakfast of salt-fish, ackee and fried dumplings. Afterwards she went back to her confinement to prepare for the third and final bath.

At around the same time the next morning Dinah undressed herself for the blood bath. This time two candles, one black, the other white, were burning. Shepherd John wore his special red gown. He seemed more solemn this morning than on the other two occasions. The Water Mother, dressed in her full white robe and turban, and one of the Daughters of the First Order, also dressed in proper church clothes, officiated. There was also an armour-bearer, a tall, slim woman with deep, vacant eyes.

Consecrated water was sprinkled around the room while the armour-bearer recited the *Twenty-third Psalm*. The Daughter placed a black bag on the ground in front of Shepherd John.

He knelt down before it, held his right hand to heaven and blessed it. The bag was opened and a white rooster taken out. The Daughter handed Shepherd John a sharp cutlass and, resting the neck of the cock on one of the holy stones, he chopped its head off in one quick stroke.

Immediately he came towards Dinah and allowed the blood to drain over her body. The hot blood trickled all over her. She closed her eyes and took a deep breath. The blood was like a razor gliding through her flesh. For one long, excruciating moment she was sure that it was her own blood that flowed. She was pained out of consciousness and lost herself in the dense, sour-sweet enigma that closed in on her.

In the meantime the Water Mother began to prepare the bath-water. She took several of the herbs and oils from the little table—purity powder, oil of Rutibel-go, crystal musk, the essence of alabaster and Compellance powder—stirring them all together in the tub of water. Dinah was lifted off her feet by the armour-bearer and the Daughter, placed in the tub, and bathed down while Shepherd John read aloud the *Twenty-fourth Psalm*.

Without drying her she was balmed once more with the oil of gladness. Her robe was folded over her. Then each one, except Shepherd John, embraced and kissed her twice on her cheeks. As she walked back to her cell for the last period of confinement, her eyes caught sight of a figure at the door. It was the Elder Mother. It was the first time she had seen her since she had arrived. She stood her ground straight and erect and with her arms folded, she stared piercingly at Dinah, stout, silent, austere. Dinah at first thought it best just to walk by as if she did not see her. But as she neared the other woman she was impelled to stop and return her stare. With a pure, soft voice she said, 'Mother, ah feelin' good.' She smiled gently, without malice, and went on to her cell.

18

A ND the next morning she saw the sun. It was bright and
glorious. Its radiance sparkled everything. The cacti,
even the very earth, seemed imbued with its life. She
walked about the yard half in a trance. Her body was totally
relaxed, her mind was empty with joy.

Fortunately, a baptism had been arranged for the following
Sunday and Shepherd John planned to include her in it. So for
the rest of the week she was instructed in all the wisdom and
mysteries of the Church. She was told of Christ and all his
wonderful teachings, of all the good and bad angels, of Michael
the Angel of Peace and Minister of the Lord's Day, of Gabriel,
fierce and powerful, Minister of the Midnight Wind, of Raphael,
the Chief Archangel and Minister of the General Wind, of the
wicked Rutibel and of the wretched people who sold their souls
to him and his master Satan so as to be able to work evil on their
fellow men, of the gods of fire, Seraph and Nathaniel.

Shepherd John was patient and kind with her throughout,
explaining over and over again anything she did not understand. He told her how when people died their souls went up to
heaven to be judged, but that their duppy still remained on
earth and could be used for both good and evil.

At other times she simply sat at his feet and watched him
doing his spiritual work, healing the sick, the deaf, the insane;
giving baths and preparing tables for those on whom others had
cast an evil spell, helping out those who were going to court so
that they won their cases, and, more often than any other,
taking off the ghost of no-work.

Although the Elder Mother lived in the same yard she did not see her often. When they did meet, however, it was the same cold, silent stare that Dinah received. Although she was not afraid of her, Dinah could not help wondering why the other woman took such a dislike for her. She found it hard to believe that anyone could hate another in such a holy place.

On Saturday morning the Shepherd went out to make arrangements for transporting his members from the baptismal river the next day. Shortly after he left she went to the little room which had been given her and began to meditate on all that she had been taught. Soon she heard the door being opened and the Daughter stepped in hesitantly.

'Come in, Sister, come,' Dinah encouraged her. She was not sure how much the Shepherd would like it, but she felt like talking. The Daughter walked in slowly and sat down on the bed beside Dinah. She was no more than twenty-two, of a dark brown complexion and, as usual, her hair plaited in narrow rows. She smiled and gazed at Dinah with unabashed admiration.

'You is a Daughter o' de Firs' Order, no?'

'Yes,' she said, grinning broadly. There were no front teeth.

'Oh, me still confuse wid all these orders an' t'ings. Explain to me again, no?'

The Daughter, obviously pleased with Dinah's friendliness, moved closer to her on the bed.

'At de top yu 'ave Shepherd; den below 'im de Elder Moder; den below 'er de Water Moder an' de two armour-bearer them. Den yu 'ave de three Daughters o' de Firs' Order. Me is one. An' den you 'ave de three more Daughters o' de Secon' Order.'

'Ah see, an' wha' dem suppose fe do, again?'

'Well, yu know wha' Shepherd do already; de Water Moder she mainly in charge o' baptism an' bathin'; de armour-bearer dem read Bible in de service, set de altar table an' control de sister an' broder dem when dem get de spirit too strong.'

She paused. Dinah looked at her, still waiting for her to finish. The Daughter flushed. Then she said: 'Only de Elder Moder an' one o' de Daughter o' de Firs' Order live wid de Shepherd. De Daughter livin' wid 'im do anythin' 'im want.' She paused again, now even more embarrassed.

Dinah still looked at her expectantly. She opened her mouth as if to speak but at the last moment stopped herself.

'Well,' Dinah said at length, 'wha' 'bout de Elder Moder. Yu say nothing 'bout her.'

The Daughter took a nervous look towards the closed door, edged her way a few inches nearer to Dinah and whispered:

'De Moder, everybody fear her.'

'But wha' mek?'

'Her spirit strong. Dem say dat she know de Lawrence book by heart. Is she who did start de church, den she tek in Shepherd John an' train 'im an' mek 'im Shepherd. Now everybody love Shepherd John an' is 'im an' 'im spirit dat keep de church together. But she still hold de purse-string.'

'Ah see,' Dinah said, nodding her head.

'Shepherd John don' pay her no mind cause 'im know she useless without 'im. As a matter o' fac' if 'im wan' 'im can move away an' start 'im own church an' mash her up. Is only out o' de goodness o' 'im heart dat 'im still atolerate her.'

'Ah see, ah see. But tell me, why yu t'ink she hate me so?'

'Is so she hate any woman dat Shepherd pay too much attention. People say dat secretly she love 'im, but Shepherd won' 'ave anything fe do wid her. She don' get on wid any o' de Daughter dem but she can't do nothin' 'bout it.'

'Yes, but she seem fe 'ave a special hatred fo' me, yu don' t'ink?'

'Yes. I t'ink she 'fraid o' yu. Shepherd always say dat one day de choosen one will come along who God selec' as 'im mate. She fear dat yu might be de one.'

Dinah glanced at her, half in surprise.

'Me?'

'Yes, yu didn't know?' the Daughter asked. Her hand came to her lips as for a moment she thought that she might have revealed something which Dinah should not have heard.

'Yes, ah know, ah understan',' Dinah reassured her, not daring to believe her own thoughts.

The Daughter jumped up suddenly.

'Ah 'ave to go an' get clothes an' other t'ings fo' yu baptism tomorrow,' she said. 'Shepherd would vex if when 'im come ah don' gone yet.'

'All right den,' Dinah replied, 'walk good.'

The Daughter hurried to the door and as she was about to open it she turned to look again at Dinah. Her brown eyes were wide and childish with admiration.

'I t'ink yu is de right an' chosen one,' she said quickly, and left.

It was on that same Saturday night that the vowing service took place. By eight o'clock the little church was filled with their white-clad bodies and black eager faces. Many had to stand outside. The candidates stood around the sacred pole in the yard, silently, their heads bowed, holding their long white candles firmly, reflecting on their sins.

A feeling of grandness was dawning on Dinah. The moment was drawing nearer and nearer. And as it came closer it became more real. But its essence was still a mystery to her. She only sensed it. As yet she did not feel it.

Then came the piercing shrill of the Elder Mother's whistle. The service had begun and she could hear them rising within. Dinah took the privileged position of the lead which had been assigned to her. They were all looking. It was her joy and they were sharing it with her. Oh they were so wonderful. Those curious black faces indistinguishable in the dark. And those inside, how solemn and serene they all were. How totally unselfish. She could feel they were one with her. She knew they shared the joy of her nearing moment.

They walked slowly, with the humility of chastised dogs, down to the altar. They knelt on the mat in front of it. Nine of them. Nine wretched, lost souls with their heads bowed.

As soon as their knees touched the mat the congregation began to sing the hymn *There Was Ninety and Nine*. Their voices were mournful with penitence. They wailed with joyful anguish for their lost sisters at last come home.

Shepherd John's face was serene, confident and proud as he walked to and fro before his regained sheep. His robe was as white and pure as the skin of masters, his bearing upright and strong. When the hymn was through he held both hands to heaven. With a loud, clear voice he uttered:

'Sisters an' brothers, tonight is a great night.'

'Yes, Lawd!' they all agreed.

'A wonderful night, me Brethren, a solemn night.'

'Amen, praise de Lawd!'

149

'Let we sing fo' de souls of our new sisters, me children, now found at last.'

Again their voices filled the air.

> *'Take off his clothes of shame and sin,*
> *The Father give command . . .'*

Dinah clasped her palms together tightly. The moment grew larger. It was stretching for eternity, yet she could sense it so close to her. It was there in the altar and the herbs. It was there in the bare wooden walls and the ground. She sensed it in the painful, distant languor of their voices. She would feel it, yes. Eventually she would have her moment in her soul. . . .

> *'. . . My Son was dead and live again,*
> *Was lost and now is found.'*

The song finished, they sat down.

Holding the Bible in his left hand, to his heart, his eyes closed, his right hand forward, the Shepherd asked gently:

'Tell me, oh my lost Sheep, yu understan' de meanin' of all dis?'

'Yes, Shepherd, we do,' Dinah and the other eight replied.

'Yu know what is de wages o' sin, me children?'

'Death, Shepherd, death.'

'And yu know de path to salvation?'

'Christ, Shepherd, only Christ,' they all answered.

'Well, den, me los' sheep, repeat dis vow after me.'

'*I did eat de bread o' iniquity,*' he began slowly, giving them time to repeat his words.

> *'I did drink o' de wine o' hatred.*
> *I is de dawg dat eat de vomit o' me soul,*
> *I is de wanderin' sheep at las' come 'ome.*
> *Lawd teach me no' fe hate,*
> *Teach me no' fe envy de rich,*
> *Teach me fe know me place before me betters,*
> *Guide me in de right path o' 'umility.*
> *I make a promise from dis day on*
> *To follow de path o' righteousness.*
> *Dis is me solemn vow,*
> *Dis me can never break.'*

After the vowing service there was a period of waiting in which the congregation talked among themselves and the candidates remained in the front row praying. At twelve the holy march began. The Elder Mother blew her whistle and the chief armour-bearer lifted the long black pole on which was hoist the banner of the church, a white flag with a moon and several stars stitched on to it in a blue material and the name of the church written along one side in red silk. Immediately behind him walked the other armour-bearer, then the Water Mother, who took precedence on this occasion over the Elder Mother. Behind the latter came the Three Daughters of the First Order, followed by the Daughters of the Second Order. There was a space of about ten yards then came Shepherd John, pious, calm, radiant, leading his sheep. The congregation followed the candidates.

It was morning in their souls as they left their cactus jungle. Their voices had to contend with the innumerable blasts of the sound-system dances, of the swearing of the drunkards in the rum-bars, of the jeers of the idle prostitutes and urchins, the cars and hand-carts and the whistles of the peanut-vendors. But they held their peace. Only they knew the end of their journey. Only they felt the joy of the distance. The far-far land drew nearer with the end of each hymn, with the repetition of each step.

Place pass by. Out of the tortuous streets with the gutters on each side. Out of the hovels, the shanties, the bars, the sparkling coney islands, the whorehouses upstairs, the police-men, the scufflers, the shifting, aimless, ragged, drifting crowd.

Time pass by. One o'clock by the high walls of the Roman Catholic cemetery. Two o'clock and the Cross Roads behind. Half past two, up the Old Hope Road. The mansions were beautiful on either side of them, the lawns were damp with dew and the huge bulldogs sitting in stately grandeur on the palatial verandahs glared at them curiously out of the corners of their eyes, not bothering to bark. Three o'clock and the valley of the Hope River.

Down the side of the hill. The pace increased. How could they hold back. Already they could see the river, a gleaming unmolesting serpent piercing through the shrouded thighs of the mountains. Move on, Armour-Bearer. The pulse quickens. The blood gushes up. The moment calls.

At last they settled by the bank of the cooling river where it was smooth and dark. They were fireflies in the night with their candles in their hands. Black fairies in white floating with the dawn. Singing alleluia in the vague, ethereal mist. The mountains drank up their voices and poured new ones and back and forth and back again. Soft-soft. Dwindling through the shy, emerging gorge. Away to the far-far land. To the land that was nothing but all around them. Refreshing mist, mild dew, soft, juicy crushing shrubs. But only the mist saw their souls, the vague, indefinable, far and dissolving mist.

The Shepherd John stepped forward. He had changed into white drill trousers but still kept on his robe. Slowly, solemnly, his foot pierced the surface of the river. He took a bottle of oil of holiness from his pocket and emptied its contents all around him in the stream. Then, holding both hands to heaven, he invoked the blessing of God on the river. His voice resounded clear and pleading in the valley of the morning, like the unseen conch-shell bugling through the silent palms of a melancholy meadow.

The Water Mother took her place by the side of the river with her towel. The Elder Mother clipped her scissors in the air several times, cutting away whatever evil spirits that might have been present, put her whistle to her lips and blew hard and sharply. Immediately the chief armour-bearer came forward, held Dinah by the hand and led her to the river. The congregation began to hum once more the hymn *There was Ninety and Nine*.

Forward slowly. Where was the earth she stepped on? Where were the hills now, the fragrance of damp morning shrubs? Had they all dissolved into the water? Were they subdued under the glory of Shepherd John's angelic, waiting arms. The water. It burned into her ankles, knees, thighs and belly. She heard him utter, 'Dat which is bawn of flesh is flesh, an' dat which is bawn of spirit is spirit.'

She felt his hands resting gently on her shoulders. Pressing down. All receded. All fled to the land of the nothing. Water! She came up gasping with life. She did not hear his words. She could hear nothing but the splashing of the water as it fell back to its source, and made a thunder in her soul. The moment was grand. There was the sense of the overwhelming nothingness of eternity. But, still, she did not feel what she intuited should be its negative essence.

The Water Mother led her to the little thatched hut not far away, took off her clothes, dried her and gave her new ones. Neither said anything to each other while she was being dressed. But as the Water Mother was about to leave she said to her kindly:

'Ah know you feel it deep, even if yu didn't show it; not all a we can.'

Dinah held down her head and stared at the ground after she had left. She did not quite know whether she should be happy or ashamed. Perhaps she had disappointed Shepherd by not getting into the spirit. Just listen to them outside. Hear their ecstatic screams. Feel the ground trembling with their trauma. See them coming, pure-bleeding, frenzied infants of joy, the Water Mother trying her best to calm them down. They sat around her, lost in their shivering bliss. She sensed their joy and was happy with them.

But had she really disappointed herself? Was she expecting more than a sensing of the moment? She had conceived of the eternity of the moment. She knew its possibility. She realized its awe. She was aware of the reality of its complete negation. If not her mind, her soul. She could not have desired more. Not yet. She was content. Now at least she knew what happiness would be like.

They left as the hills began to pale with the first birth-pains of the dawning sun. The old truck was waiting for them and in another half-hour they were back to their church in the cacti. For the rest of the day they fasted, prayed and sang. Dinah locked herself in the little dark room with the candle and the hole. For most of the day she stared at the sterile, brown patch. Wondering where it began, where it ended and where in eternity it was. As night approached, a deep, haunting expectancy seeped into her.

The first communion service began at nine. Already the drums were sounding. One rattled lightly like a flock of white clouds playing with the wind against the background of the other, a deep blue, austere sky. They met around the sacred pole as they had done the night before and, with the blowing of the Elder Mother's whistle, walked slowly in and down the aisle, this time with their heads up with pride.

The congregation sung their songs of joy and clapped their hands. The armour-bearer read the Bible loud and passionately. Shepherd John preached his vision of salvation. The wind blew more swiftly, beating the little white clouds before it, intimating every now and then shades of the vast, eternal blue gaps.

Then the table was blessed. They, nine of them, came to the table. They broke the bread and ate. They drank of the sweet red blood. And the voice of the Shepherd poured into them:

'The wind bloweth where it listeth, and thou hearest the sound thereof, but canst not tell whence it cometh, and whither it goeth: so is every one that is born of the spirit.'

One of them screamed and fell to the ground in a quivering spasm which revealed without a doubt the presence of Gabriel. Another became possessed by Miriam and fell into a dreamy, swooning transfixion. The Elder Mother tried to calm down Gabriel with her scissors, while an armour-bearer went up to Miriam, kissed her on the cheek and led her gently to a seat near the front.

For the other seven the Shepherd decided that the spirit had to be brought down by labouring. He ordered the candidates to kneel down around the altar. Then he called all the officers and senior members of the church to him. The drums grew. And the trumping began. Around and around the altar they danced. Stamping their right feet. Bodies moving forward as the clouds in the wind.

Dinah felt them coming into her. The bodies hovering over her. The raw vapour of their breath as it gushed from them. Then up the bodies. The stamping of the left feet, the filling of the lungs with their deep groans. The blood in her grew warmer and warmer. Her pulse quickened and her heart crashed on her breast heavily like a sea on the cliffs in a hurricane. She soared with the wind that blew the clouds. But they were falling apart. Everything beneath was moving away. And the sweat of their bodies drenched her. An acid numbness seeped into her veins and melted away her flesh. The wind blew the clouds farther and farther apart. The pungent odour of the herbs filled her nostrils.

She tasted the sour-sweet vapour of their clammy flesh. Thumping, stamping and clapping. Forward and backward. Jesus! Alleluia!

Suddenly the clouds burst. The deep blue void crashed in. A power twitched her neck. Her shoulders contorted. A knifing quiver ripped from beneath her heart and lashed itself around her womb. The painful grunts, the piercing hisses, the raw sweat, the reeling vapour, the petrifying heat, and the bodies pressing in, round and round, eyes glazed and sparkling in black faces, mouths white and foamy with froth—all churning with the clouds before the wind. All gave way in awe to the deep, almighty abyss.

The moment was upon her. 'Jesus!' she groaned, and leaped up. Her soul strove out to feel it. But before it could she fell out of consciousness in a trembling spasm of expectancy.

She awoke in a fragrance of burning incense. The bed she found herself lying on was large and soft. The room was washed with a mild, glowing yellow from the light of a large, single candle. She sat on the side of the bed and held her forehead, which was still slightly dizzy, in her palm. A shadow loomed above her. She looked up with a start.

It was Shepherd John. But she could hardly believe it. He was transfigured. His figure stood before her, tall and erect, unmoving, like an angel of terror. He was utterly naked except for a long silk cloak which flowed behind him. His black skin churned with the twisting candlelight like a serpent across the river-bank under a stiffled quarter-moon. In his right hand he held a tamarind switch. She stared up at his eyes, petrified.

'So it came,' he said deeply, breaking the silence.

'Yes, Shepherd.'

'It was Melshezdek,' he told her with a tinge of pride in his voice.

'Y . . . yes, Shepherd . . . but——'

'I know,' he broke in. 'Only I could see. It was not complete. That is as it should be.'

Suddenly she threw herself at his feet.

'Ah mus' feel it, Shepherd. Ah mus'. Yu know de way.'

He allowed her to weep at his feet until the spasm ceased. There was a god-like silence. Then slowly she raised her head. She was helpless under him, totally devoid of will.

'Get up,' he said, his voice subdued but firm, pointing to the side of the bed. She obeyed.

'Take off your clothes.' She did as she was told and stood naked before him, still too overwhelmed to either think or feel. 'Lean over.' She rested the trunk of her body across the bed with her face sunk in it.

He took up the saucer of burning incense, went to all four corners of the room with it, speaking in a strange mystic tongue. Then he turned in an anti-clockwise direction three times, made the sign of the cross and said, 'Thy nakedness shall be uncovered, yea, thy shame shall be seen: I will take vengeance and I will not meet thee as a man.'

His hand went up. Then quickly the whip pierced through the air and sunk into her flesh. She bit the sheet and gripped it with all her strength. Yet as the pain rooted into her she felt a ticklish tinge in its quivering. No sooner had she felt it than it destroyed itself and filled her instead with a terrifying joy. Again and again the whip lashed into her. And each time the painful self-destruction became more intense, more thrilling, till she no longer felt the pain, only a divine, shocking heat that consumed every ounce of her flesh, every tissue, every drop of blood.

Long after he had stopped beating the last remnants of evil spirits from her she was still relishing the warm, vibrating ecstasy of the flagellation. It was not until she gradually awoke to the soothing touch of his hand as he balmed her over with the oil of gladness that she realized it was over.

He was now completely naked. He lifted her up in his arms. Their skin glowed in the flowing candlelight like enmeshed silkworms. He sucked her nipples, he kissed her gently on her cheeks, then he laid her down on the bed and whispered solemnly:

'Arise, shine; for thy light is come, and the glory of the Lord is risen upon thee.'

He came upon her with all his mighty gentleness.

Her soul swelled up to meet him. His flesh stole into her like a spirit. All was body, all was flesh, yet by the very totality of their presence, by the very power released by their contact, there was nothing of body or of flesh. Only an almighty, all-embracing surge. The moment grew, slowly, then faster and

156

faster, larger and larger. Now she could almost feel it. She enclosed him more tightly with her arms. Now it was upon her. Her body, forgotten, wrapped itself involuntarily around him.

'Jesus!' she uttered fervently.

Now she was the moment. It was all consciousness. It dissolved her into an infinite awareness of a passing self-destruction. 'Jesus!' she cried again. 'Oh, sweet father Jesus. . . .'

19

S HE sat in one corner of the cold, concrete cell, her head
buried between her hands and knees. Her daughter. How
did she eat? Who was there to protect her? They would
eat her up. The beasts around her would ravish away every
ounce of effort she had put in her.

'Help her, Massah God,' she prayed. 'Ah know dat ah
don' come to yu often, but yu know dat de heart is willin'
but de flesh is weak; protec' her, Massah God, please, do, ah
beg . . .'

She stretched out on the ground and wept once more. Her
throat was harsh and grating, her eyes were drained with tears
and burned. The muscles of her belly twisted together and
wearied out with pain. She was lost in the agony of her daughter.
Her mouth rested half open on the concrete. She did not taste
the little stream of urine that drained down into it from the
puddle of faeces she had deposited earlier when they would not
let her out. She did not smell the stench, nor was she bothered
by the swarm of flies that covered her flesh.

The large door opened and someone walked in. But it was
not until his heavy black boot sunk into her rib that she became
aware of his presence.

'You bring her? Yu bring me pickney?' she cried up at him. He
moved away scornfully, his heavy blue trousers with the broad
red seam newly pressed, his blue and white striped shirt stiffly
starched. He held his nose with his left hand, glanced quickly
out of the corner of his eye at the faeces, and held up his baton
menacingly.

'Yu nasty black bitch,' he shouted, 'ah could break yu stinking head wid me baton. Move!'

'Whe' she is? Yu bring her to me?' she pleaded, moving for the door. Suddenly his boot crashed into her back immediately below the spine. She spun half round with the impact, lost her balance and with the muffled whine of a dog splodged to the street beneath a wheel, she fell outside upon the gravel in front of the cell.

He locked the door behind him, cursing, and she struggled to her feet before he came too close to her again. Down the gravel path. He ordered her to the left, then up a small flight of stairs and into a little unfurnished room except for one long bench. He locked her in and she remained standing where she was, lost in a semi-stupor of pain and anxiety.

A few minutes later the policeman returned with a chair and placed it several yards opposite the bench. Then he said something and another person entered.

'Tu'n round!' he ordered.

She turned round to face another woman sitting in the chair opposite her. She was short, light-skinned and dressed in floral silk. She carried a small black handbag and a copy of the *Welfare Worker*.

'Sit down, dear,' she said kindly.

Mary was even more frightened of the woman than she was of the policeman. What could backra want with her? She hadn't done anything as bad as all that. She stared, bewildered, at the lady as she carefully took her spectacles from her bag and put them on. The movement of her pure, light-skinned hands, the delicate twirling of her fingers and the commanding eyes behind the spectacles filled her with terror.

'I said sit down,' the lady repeated.

'Y . . . yes, ma'm.' She fumbled on to the bench, sitting more on the edge, realizing that it was not proper to be too comfortable.

'Now, Mary,' the lady began, glancing at a pretty little black notebook with a gold crown printed on the cover, 'we won't waste each other's time, shall we?'

"What . . . what yu say, ma'm?' She had not heard properly.

'I said we'll come to the point at once. No time to waste.'

'Yes . . . yes, ma'm.'

'Now, you have a daughter called Rossetta, don't you?'

'You bring her? She all right. Me Rossetta, ma'm?'

'Were you the person who mothered this girl?'

'Ma'm?'

'Good heavens, don't you understand the Queen's English, girl? I said if you are the mother?'

'The moder, ma'm?'

'Yes. Mother, mumah, moder. Are you the mother of the child registered at the Denham Town School as Rossetta Reid?'

'Yes, ma'm. She is me own. She is all ah 'ave in de worl'. Is only she can save me, ma'm. Is only me Rossetta can——'

'I know. I know. She is in our charge at the moment. The school authorities reported her to us when she fainted from hunger in——'

'Lawd! me Rossetta, me poor Rossetta!' She wrung the skin of her belly in anguish.

'Please control yourself,' the lady said. 'It's important that you listen to what I have to say.' She paused for a moment, then continued. 'Rossetta is a very bright girl and has some future, as you might know.'

'If ah know, ma'm? Lawd, she is de brightest pickney in de worl'.'

'Yes, but no child can study or grow up properly in the Dungle. She has to have better conditions and that is what I've come to talk to you about. Now as long as you are in jail we are in full charge of her. But there might be some problem after you get out. Of course, if you have the girl's interest at heart there will be no problem, as you'll certainly agree with what we decide.'

'What . . . what yu mean, ma'm?'

'What I mean is that Rossetta has to leave the Dungle. It's a miracle that she has achieved anything under the conditions she was brought up and with you leading the life which you have. She has to make a clean break. She needs a good home and a good Christian upbringing from now on if she is to achieve anything. The board has arranged for her adoption——'

'Beg pa'don, ma'm? Wha' yu say, ma'm?'

'I said that the Welfare Board has arranged for her to be adopted into a good family. I take it you have her interest at heart and——'

'You mean say, ma'm, that you want to tek 'way me Rossetta from me? No! No!' she screamed, 'Ah wan' me Rossetta! Rossetta!'

The policeman rushed inside with his baton raised. The lady beckoned to him and he checked himself. They waited until she had regained control of herself.

'Now listen, girl,' the lady said more firmly, 'you're on a serious charge. You realize you could get years for this. In any case we would be in charge of the girl and even if, in the unlikely event, you were set free we could press the issue for keeping her. Now if you are sensible and sign for this adoption perhaps we could arrange something for you.'

'Arrange something, ma'm?'

'Yes, perhaps if the judge knew of your co-operation the sentence could be much reduced. Perhaps we may even be able to arrange for a probation.'

'But . . . but how ah can live without me Rossetta? How?'

'Whether you want to or not you wouldn't be seeing her for quite some time if you don't co-operate. The family who has been kind enough to adopt her at this late age is willing to have you visit her every now and then. You couldn't want better terms than that.' She paused, squeezed her thin red lips together firmly, and waited.

The anxiety grew in Mary. She was totally incapable of thinking about all that had just been said. Rossetta was the only thing that occupied her mind. An impulse suddenly seized her. She looked up at the lady and said:

'Ah can see me Rossetta now, ma'm?'

'If you signed the papers I see no reason why we couldn't arrange bail for you.'

'Anything yu say, ma'm. As long as ah see me Rossetta today. Now.'

The lady opened her copy of the *Welfare Worker* and took out a set of forms, already half filled out, from between the pages.

'Can you sign your name?'

'Yes, ma'm, ah can sign.'

'Officer, you'd better come and witness this signature,' the lady said. The policeman promptly came forward and watched Mary as she scrawled over the blank spaces pointed out to her.

'Now, me can see me Rossetta, ma'm? Me can go now?' she

161

said, getting up from the bench and handing the paper to the lady.

'Just be a bit patient. I'll see to that,' the lady assured her, folding the papers carefully and placing them back between the leaves of the magazine. Then she took off her spectacles, placed them in her handbag and closed it briskly. She glanced at Mary with satisfaction and approval.

'You could not have done a better thing for the girl,' the lady said. 'You may not realize it, but you've just given her the chance she needs to become a civilized human being. Good morning.'

About three in the afternoon they released her. And she ran. Every instinct in her pulled her on. She arrived at the Denham Town Primary School about five minutes before the students were due to be dismissed. She leaned against the gate, panting heavily, her eyes fixed on the classrooms.

Then the bell went. The sudden uproar. Screaming, running, ragged short pants, bare feet, the clapping of hands, hop-scotch at once, old pieces of board and knitted balls for cricket. Soon she was a buoy in their splashing, biting, rugged sea. She smelt their black, bony little unwashed bodies mixed up with dirty, dog-eared exercise books, tongue-licked slates, noses still slimy from the recent lashings; they bounced her, they pushed her, too careless with their raw spontaneous joys to notice her. But where was she? Where roamed her little soul? Ah yes, there was her little brown skin across the yard. No, she was not that tall. Her eyes shifted and darted. Then the heart leapt again. No, her hair wasn't that bad. Where was she, then? They were thinning out. Their voices were falling in the pit of her breaking soul.

She walked inside. She was not round the other side of the buildings. Frantically, she hurried from one classroom to another. She was down to the last room by the fence opposite the road. She was inside. The wind gushed in her lungs with joy. She was there. Her angel was sitting in the middle of the room, her olive cheek on her palm, reading.

'Rossetta!' she almost screamed, and ran for her.

'Mama! What happen to you?'

She flung her arms around her daughter. She crushed her to

her breast. She lifted her up to heaven and spun round and wept.

'They want to tek you 'way from me!' she cried. 'They t'ink me not good enough fo' yu no mo', an dem wan' to tek yu 'way from me. Lawd, me pickney, me puss-puss, me angel, dem never goin' tek yu. Never, never, never!'

She placed her at arm's length from her so as to devour every inch of her body. Then she squeezed her to her breasts again. Rossetta tried to say something, but she was too overwhelmed to hear her.

'Tek yu book dem an' come wid me, me pickney. We never goin' to part again. Only Massah God goin' break me from yu.'

Rossetta disentangled herself from her, but stood up without moving. She stared at her mother, then outside at the gate.

'Come, me pickney, hurry! Yu wan' dem to come an' tek yu from me again. Hurry, whe' yu book?'

'Mama,' the girl said uncertainly, 'they've said that I mustn't leave.'

'They! Who is they?'

'The people that been looking after me since yu left. They come for me in their van every evening and I have to wait for them. They would be vex if I leave.'

Mary's face grew serious with rage and fear. Till then she had never really believed that they seriously intended to take her daughter from her. But now everything seemed to prove that it was true. The lady really meant what she said this morning. It was not just a scare which they had concocted as an extra punishment for her. They really meant what they said. They were going to take her daughter from her. They were going to take her daughter from her. She repeated the thought over and over again in her mind, but still it was hard to believe. It was so impossible, so utterly unthinkable. It wasn't just that they were cruel, or spiteful. That was normal, and trite, and to be expected. It was just that it could not happen. They couldn't do it. They couldn't do it. They couldn't do it.

She walked slowly up to the girl, and held on to her tightly, possessively. She stared warily around at the gate. Every instinct in her was drawn up. Tense.

'Come,' she said, whisperingly. The girl hesitated at first, but she knew the countenance her mother now wore. So she took up her books and allowed herself to be led.

They crept to the back of the building, then over the fence, across somebody's backyard, down the narrow little lanes. Faster, faster, then into a trot. The girl was beginning to be tired. She complained, but the mother paid her no mind. She was the hen that crushed her chick. Soon they were across the Spanish Town Road and down the Industrial Terrace, then, at last, the familiar sight of the Dungle. Home. Her hut was there as she had left it. Home. She never felt such protection as the four crumpled cardboard-and-barrel walls now gave her. She never knew the stale stench of the trampled filth could be so sweet. Home. With her Rossetta close beside her.

'They try to poison yu mind against me, don't it, me love?' she asked, kissing her and for the first time beginning to notice the reticence in the girl. 'Ah know dat's wha' dem would try an' do. But dem can't tek yu from me. Never. Dem never goin' tek yu 'way.' Then she clasped her angel more firmly to her and gave vent to all her fear and joy in a long, shaking spasm of tears.

The news got round fast-fast that she'd returned. The moment made of her a heroine. Rachael and Sarah and Brother Zacharry, even Big White Chief, pickney and old people, they all came to her hut. Lawd, them was so glad to see her. What did happen? Oh, they did know it was the policeman then. Bitches. Stinking, dirty bitches. And now they want to take away her pickney. But Lawd God Almighty, what a liberty. What a dirty piece of liberty. But she trick them, though. They would never touch her and her one sweet pickney again.

Then they settled down to tell her all the news. About Mabel. How her man go up to Jones Town and bust her behind and carry her back down to Dungle. She as quiet as chicken 'pon him roost now. Not a word. Not a whisper. You would never think it was the same Mabel. She get what coming to her, but, still, you couldn't help feel sorry for her. Old Rachael shook her head.

'Ah tell oonoo all de while. Is no use. No use. Massah God know why 'Im put we down ya. 'Im mean say is ya we mus' stay. Wha' de use yu try an' run?' She paused and stared vacantly at them, then she shook her head again and added: 'Ah wonder how long Dinah she goin' tek fe come back. Ah don' know why, but ah miss dat gal so much.'

And of course they told her of the Rastafarians. This time it really look serious. All sort of letter-writing and publication. *Evening* newspaper take it up. Them coming from all 'bout Jamaica. Them full up the Dungle.

'Yu mean fe say dat them really goin' Ethiopia?'

'Yu damn' right is true. Them serious this time.'

'Date an' everything set.'

'Twenty-seventh o' October.'

'That is why ah never did use to laugh after them. I always did know dat one day them was really goin' pack up an' leave.'

'Ah wish ah was a Rasta woman now,' Mary said. 'Ah could leave wid me pickney fe Ethiopia now. De bitches dem would never set eye 'pon me again.'

'I not too sure; I not too sure.' Rachael was shaking her head again.

'Lawd, Rachael, don' set yu goat mouth 'pon de people them; yu always preachin' crosses.'

'Yes; 'cause dat is de only t'ing fe preach. I not too sure 'bout all dis preparation and ship coming fe tek dem back to heaven.'

'But it was in de evening newspaper. Mass Ramus from up de road read it loud-loud out a de newspaper dat de Rastas dem plannin' fe leave an' de date when de ship coming; yu gwine go 'gainst what yu see in black an' white?'

'Yes; dat is 'ow all de country Rasts dem get fe hear 'bout de repatriation. Yu t'ink dem country man is fool? Yu t'ink dat dem would sell out all dem 'ouse an' lan' an' all dem belongings if dem wasn' sure dat dem was leavin'; yu gwan t'ink dat dem country people is fool. Yu mek a sad mistake.'

But Rachel remained unconvinced. She did not bother to contradict their arguments. At times she had begun to wonder whether this time she might not really be wrong. It was one hell of a preparation they were making and they all seemed cock-sure about everything. But deep down she still held firm to her belief that it could not be true. It just wasn't natural. Nobody can leave the Dungle for good. Once yu born in it the world was the Dungle. The Dungle was the world. You were condemned to roam and wander freely there. But you couldn't leave. That for certain.

'Say anything you want,' she said stubbornly; 'bring all de newspaper you want; show me all de lan' dat de country Rasta dem sell out; I still say it can't happen. Nobody can leave de Dungle fo' good.'

And so they went on talking till Mary suddenly noted with alarm that the poor sweet thing was sleepy.

'Babylon! Babylon!' the cry went up.

The children on the street threw down their bats and balls and dashed madly for their parents. Some rushed for the inlets behind the sargossa. Doors and windows closed. And others ran and ran as far as their breath could carry them.

All moved except the Rastafarians. They were prepared. They knew that sooner or later the agents of Babylon would try to intervene. But they remained calm and confident. If this was a raid, then let them raid. Let them smash their huts. Let them tear their clothes to shreds. Let them burn up everything. They would simply be cleaning up the mess they had intended to leave behind. Brother Solomon had told them that if they remained calm nothing would happen, for they were guarded by the spirit of the Holy Emperor.

Two jeeps from the riot squad packed with policemen drew up in front of Brother Solomon's hut. Then came a Vauxhall and behind it another jeep. The driver of the Vauxhall jumped out briskly, his large red seam brilliant in the afternoon sun. He walked round to the other side of the car and opened the door. The inspector stepped out. He was a tall man with many wrinkles in his face, the inspector. His knees were large and brown beneath his stiff, austere khaki shorts. And he twirled a gleaming little cane between his fingers.

He walked a few paces, then snapped his fingers at one of the men in the jeep. A sergeant jumped out.

'You'd better come along with me, Sergeant Thomas.'

He glanced round and seeing Brother Solomon behind his counter walked up to him. Brother Solomon stood calmly, his arms folded.

'Listen, fellow,' the inspector began with a forced civility, 'there's no cause for any trouble this afternoon if you'll help us with what we've come about.'

'You can cause no trouble even if you try,' Brother Solomon answered.

The inspector continued as if he had not heard.

'It's not you we've come about. There's a woman who lives here called Mary. She has a daughter. We'd like to get in touch with her. Where is she?'

Brother Solomon remained silent.

'Come, fellow. You seem to have some sense. We can settle this whole business without violence. Simply tell me where the woman lives and you'll save us a lot of trouble. Or do you prefer if we searched ourselves.'

He waited a moment longer. Then, not hearing anything from Brother Solomon, he turned to the sergeant and said: 'Very well; I guess we'll have to find her our way. Order the men out, Sergeant.'

The sergeant barked a command and the men hopped out of the jeep, all helmeted and armed with tear-gas guns and batons and bayonets. They walked off the street, up the mound of dry filth. Sergeant Thomas pointed to a hut. Four men came forward; they walked a few paces in its direction, then stopped. Then two of them rushed forward and crashed the door open with their heels. They went inside, the other two fast behind them, while several more came up from the rear, their bayonets poised. A woman screamed inside. There was a crash and the whole hut seemed on the point of tumbling down. The voices of babies began to wail from inside. The woman screamed again then suddenly she came crashing outside. She tried to regain her balance and hold the baby she had in her hand at the same time. But the impact with which she had been shoved out was too great. She fell on her face. The baby slipped from her grip and rolled over in the muck, screaming.

'Ah don' do not'in'!' she screamed, holding her arm protectively over her forehead and wincing away from them. 'Ah don' do not'in', an' yu jus' come an' start beat me up.'

'Whe' she live? Whe' she is?' one of them barked at her, raising his baton menacingly.

'Who? Who? Ah don' know who yu talkin' 'bout?'

'Mary! De woman wid de brown pickney! She is yu frien'; whe' she is? Talk up, or ah bus' yu backside fo' yu!'

'Mary . . . Mary?' she repeated, her eyes wide with terror, not daring to look at the screaming baby.

'Yes, Mary! De whore dat cut up de sailor-man de other day!'

Slowly, nervously, her meagre hands went up, her fingers moved out painfully, as she pointed to Mary's hut. They left her at once and moved over to Mary's.

'Careful with the girl,' the sergeant warned.

They smashed the door open and went inside.

'No!' Mary's voice broke out. Then again the heavy, muffled thuds, the screams, the shaking of the huts. Suddenly the girl ran out. Mary dashed out after her.

'Rossetta! Stay by me; don' let dem get yu!' She ran after the girl and tried to hold on to her. Rossetta evaded her grasp and ran hesitantly towards the road.

'Rossetta!' Mary screamed frantically. But by now they were upon her. Two of them grabbed her by each arm. She struggled. She bit. She screamed. 'Rossetta! Don' mek dem hold yu. Run! Run, ah say!'

Halfway between the struggling woman and the inspector the girl paused, then turned haltingly to face her mother. Her stare gave first an appearance of confusion. But then she moved her eyes and glanced in a kind of bland perplexity at the dry, bare, scaly feet of her mother. When she looked up again all traces of confusion seemed gone. Her lips were slightly parted, twitching in a hard line on one side. For a moment she seemed almost to despise the toiling, frantic slut in front of her. But gradually the line at the side of her lips withdrew. The lips still remained parted, but a curious vacancy now over-shadowed her. She continued to stare at the mother, as if seeing her for the first time, as if hearing her from afar and somehow fascinated by the distant wailing of her ghastly, grappling voice.

'They come fo' me, Mama,' she explained in a strange, unaffected innocence. 'You always said that one day a tall brown man in a uniform would come for me and take me away in his car. I must go. I want to go.'

'Rossetta, they takin' yu 'way from me! Run! Run, ah say!'

She struggled with all her might. She bit and she kicked. They cursed and slapped her, while a third came to help keep her in control.

The girl paused a moment longer. The men with red seams were down there on the road with their arms. The big black car was there. The tall brown man in the uniform was there. He was waiting. He smiled at her as she glanced around at him. They were all waiting. She glanced back at the weeping, struggling woman, now half down on her knees, hanging from their grasp.

'Goodbye, Mama,' she said.

She walked down to the tall brown man in the uniform with the cane. He opened the door of his car for her. He closed it. And then they drove away.

20

WHEN he returned from the city he smiled at her and kissed her gently. Then he said, 'It is all settled now.'

'What is all settled?'

'We goin' to England.'

'England!' She put away the Bible she was reading and stood up before him.

'Yes. We leave in two weeks' time. Got all the paper them an' everything ready. Look!'

He opened the little leather bag that he always took around with him. She had come to love and fear that little dark-brown leather bag. Those papers and formulas and herbs and little secret mysteries inside. She loved to see him busying himself with them. It made him such a mystery. Such a man with power. A strange, gentle power it was.

Now she stared at him anxiously as he took the thick, bluish sheets from the bag and handed them to her.

'What them is?'

'This,' he said proudly, 'is your birth certificate, an' this your passport, an' this your ship ticket.'

'Me birth certificate! But 'ow yu manage get that. Me never 'ave one.'

'Yes. But, lucky fo' you, yu mother never forget to christen yu. It did give a little trouble getting it, though. Had to wet one or two hand before it came through.'

'Oh, so that was why yu was askin' me the other day whe' ah did bawn. Ah, yu never see smoke without fire.'

'Yes, everything settle. We leave fo' Englan' in two weeks.'

As if hearing him say it for the first time she started at his words. England, he said. Backra land. Where Missis Queen live. Unbelievable. She was going to live there too. She was elated and overwhelmed. Yet in that very moment she experienced a slight tinge of depression. She wondered why she was not more elated. She should have been. To a large extent she was. But the news she just heard was great. It was all her dreams. It should have been the realization of the moment she had desired most of all. Now she would be leaving completely. The Dungle and everything. For a land of life and dreams no longer dreams. It was complete fulfilment. She should be joyful. Yet the sinking tinge lingered. Increased. Gradually it eroded the moment. She sought to grasp it while it lasted.

'God, I's so 'appy, Shepherd. Yu mek me so 'appy. I can't believe it.'

'Yu will soon. Only two weeks to go. Next Sunday I tek me las' service.'

Suddenly she remembered the church. 'Shepherd. Wha' dem goin' to do when yu gone? They whole life depen' on yu.'

'I been t'inkin' a lot 'bout dem. I care a lot 'bout me sheep, as yu know, me choosen one. As a matter of fac', they is de main reason why I didn' leave a'ready. I been consulting de Holy Spirit often 'bout de matter an' 'im finally give me a answer.'

'An' wha' 'im say?' she asked, still not failing to wonder at his power of communion.

' 'Im answer was straight an' simple. In de en' a man 'ave de greates' responsibility to 'imself. Of course 'im mus' consider others. 'Im 'ave to consider others if 'im is to be completely responsible to 'imself. 'Im might even appear to consider others more. But dat is jus' appearance. In de en' is only you'self one yu goin' be responsible fo' on de judgement day. Hypocrisy is de greates' sin. An' de greates' hypocrite is not de man who deceive others, but who deceive 'imself. So de 'Oly Spirit tell me, me choosen one. So I mus' obey.'

'Yes, yu mus',' she said. Suddenly she reached out for his hand and squeezed it. She was ever more conscious of the happiness she should feel. But her very consciousness was the wind that blew away the soil on which the moment had planted. It was pain. She wanted to grasp the joy that gave itself to her. Her desire to grasp it was so strong that it almost cheated

171

the moment with its unreality. But she soon became conscious of her desire. She saw its grasping. She felt out tenuously for it. She knew she could not experience it. She knew the very act of trying destroyed itself. And so all she was left with was the increasing emptiness of what only existed. She held on to him tighter. Only in him could she forget. She had enough faith in him to believe that he was real. He expected her to be happy. She knew he expected her to be happy. So she was happy. See. She was smiling. She had encircled him completely with her arms. Her face was buried in the firmness of his chest.

'Wha' 'bout de Elder Moder?' she suddenly asked him.

'I tell her all about it already.'

'Yu tell her!' Despite herself she was growing frightened.

'Yes. I tell her to tek back over de church. De money ah use fo' we ticket is all mine, though she don' seem to t'ink so. But I 'ad no argument wid her.'

'But wha' she said when yu tell her we leavin'?' Dinah asked.

'Not'in'. Yu know 'ow she go on already. She only stare long an' hard at me wid her two big black eye. She wasn'n' ragin' or anything o' de sort. But she sure was'n' please. She jus' stare. As if she in another worl' starin' out 'pon me. Ah did'n' like dat look on her face at all. It was'n' nice.'

Dinah held on tighter to him. That was the last thing she had wanted him to say. So far he had always neglected the Elder Mother. He had been confident that she could do neither of them any harm. Though she spoke to him often with concern about the Elder Mother, she never failed to find assurance in his complete confidence in her inability to harm them. But now he had said that he did not like the look on her face. Of course, that was not saying that he was any more afraid of her or that he was any less confident in his ability to protect them. But his remark was still in some sense a concession to her. It was not so much her fear of the Elder Mother that now troubled her. It was just that what the Shepherd said meant a kind of victory for the Elder Mother; there had been a retreat, no matter how slight. The Shepherd was her sole protector. She wanted him so. She was infinitely proud of him. His retreat wounded her.

'Shepherd,' she whispered anxiously, 'I don' trus' dat woman. I never know wha' she goin' come wid nex'.'

'Don' worry,' he said. 'Sunday I give me las' service. The nex' Saturday we leave.'

And the blacks of their skin were like flute-notes in the night. Deep-deep and mellow: wailing in gleaming, fluent splendour. Across the dark-brown, silty shore. Upon the undulating, stale, delicious filth. When they did not move they were so many silhouetted majesties swallowed over with all the harvest of their expectancy.

Their movements were slow, determined, god-like. Even in the quick motion of their feet as they strode between the hovels; as they ran to the top of the mounds to stare and stare across the blue, the orange-flamed, the dark, steel-grey horizon, there was the restrained gentleness of certainty.

The ship would come. They talked. They laughed. The ship of the great Emperor would show itself in the morning with the glory of the sun. No, it would come in the evening-time, bursting through the molten fire of the eastern hemisphere, a conquering vessel of joy. Oh, but what did it matter? It would come. Sure as the holy land of Zion that waited now for them, it would come.

In the meantime they talked and laughed at what was past and dreamt of what was soon to be. Those of the city made friendly humour of their country brothers. The rustic Brethren laughed at themselves, but pointed out their own advantages, not that it really mattered. They had remained with the soil—the soil so small and cruel here but so fertile with everything that's joy back home in Zion. They had suffered more, had paid more for the sins of their forefathers, but at the same time had remained less tainted by the sins of the white man and of Babylon. To which the Brethren of the city retorted passionately that they had greater claims to having suffered. Look. Look at the bloated belly of the children. Look at the yellow of their eyes. Feel the scaly perversion of their skin—the skin so pure and black and beautiful in Zion, now a denizen of contempt. And the red-seamed agents of Babylon. Already, did they not experience the violence of their oppression? Did they not witness the agony of the poor slut Mary who was not even one of them, how they maimed and twisted her, then came back for her in the black van and took her off to the asylum? The city was the fountain-head of Babylon and they were the dogs who were soaked in its oppression.

At other times they spoke of lighter things. They would join together and mock the follies of Babylon. The Brethren of the city had no end of standard tales recalling the contempt they displayed, and the superiority, in their encounters with Babylon.

There was the case of Brother Zacharias the Second, who one day was strolling along the East Queen Street and accosted two stupid youths, one short and fat, the other long and meagre, sons of the brown lackeys; civil servants, no doubt, from the premature senility of their countenance. Brother Zacharias the Second demanded from them what was rightly his, a share of their salary which his sweat and that of his fellow sufferers had made possible. The short fat one, more out of fright, gave him half a crown. But the other was mean. A true son of Babylon. Only out of pride he grudgingly took a sixpence from his pocket and handed it to Brother Zacharias the Second. Brother Zacharias took one step backward, swelled his mighty chest and rolled his large black eyes at the gross indignity of the tall thin brown bastard.

'Hence! Thou withered fig-tree,' he admonished him. And you should have seen the two of them running.

Then there was the time when Brother Alawecious was walking down the King Street. He had just reached the intersection of King Street and Barry Street when a fat, red woman, all smothered over with packages, butted into him. Brother Alawecious held his peace and stared down at her. She moved away the parcel that blocked her vision and glanced up at Brother Alawecious. As soon as the seething fool realized he was one of the sons of Ras she flung away all her packages and screamed, 'My God!'

Upon which Brother Alawecious folded his arms with a calm dignity, drew himself up, and with divine condescension uttered down at the gaping, open-mouthed bourgeois:

'So, you recognize I.'

And of course there was the famous Miss Mollypols. One day, sun hot like hell, some Brothers were sitting by the sea mending their net. A little motor-car pull up on the roadside, and what you know? A meagre little woman with thick glasses and two round brown eyes behind them step out. She look to the right. She look to the left. Then she step forward. Not a thing she say. But God, you should see her face. She look like she just see the Holy Ghost. But she still coming forward till she was standing beside the Brethren. She look down at them, but don't say a thing. Every now and then she made as if to speak, but the words them dry up at her throat. All she could do is swallow. Finally Brother Salamanca ask her what business bring her here. She swallow again. She gape. Then at last she say in a voice like a half-dead bird:

'Good afternoon, gentlemen.'

The Brethren just keep looking at her and one of them said, 'Speak your piece, Sister.'

After she swallow some more time and clear her throat she say: 'Gentlemen, my name is Miss Susana Mollypols. I am the third Vice-President of the St. Michael's branch of the Blue Cross.' She nod her head to emphasize the importance of what she had just said, but nobody was taking her on, so she go on: 'Gentlemen, at the last meeting of the charities committee it was unanimously voted that the unfavourable conditions of West Kingston was a blot on the good name of our island country and that we had to do something about it. So we decided that we would have a charity ball. Not just a little charity ball, but a big, splendid charity ball; we plan to invite the Prime Minister and his wife, and his Excellency the Governor and his wife; if you're going to have a charity ball, have a big charity ball, that's what I always tell the committee. Well, they placed me in charge of the ball, but then it struck me that if we're going to have such a big ball for our unfortunate brothers down in West Kingston we should know something more about them, so that is why I'm here today. Of course, all my friends warned me against coming, but I knew I would be quite safe among you. So, here I am.' She finished her little speech, blow her breath, and stand up waiting. Nobody say a thing at first, then Brother Salamanca, who was the only one taking her on, just out of fun, say:

'Well, Sister, here you is, what now?'

'Well, you know, well . . .' she say, turning red all over, Brother, you ever see a brown woman turn red yet? 'Well, I've come to know about you, to . . . to study you, you know?'

'Oh, I see,' Brother Salamanca say, shaking his head smart-like. 'You come to study I.'

'Well, not just you, all of you, that is, if you don't mind.'

'But all of we is only one of I, for it is only through I that there is the other of we and is only through the other of we that I can know I, so if you study we you can only study I, you overstand or you understand? Is wisdom this you know. Sister?'

Poor Miss Mollypols, all the knowledge of Brother Salamanca just run over her head and confuse her. She start getting fidgety. Look like she want to run. Not a word she say.

'But, Sister, it look like you neither overstand or understand I, it seem like all you doing is just stand.'

All of a sudden Miss Mollypols start draw back. Fear start crawl like crab over her. Brother Salamanca get up.

'Keep standing, Sister. Don't fear the wisdom and power of the holy Ras.' But then Miss Mollypols start scream.

'Don't you come near to me. Don't you touch me. Don't. Don't.'

Then she take a left-about turn and make for that little motor-car. Brother, you never know them two little brown foot could move so fast. You never see motor-car speed up and tear out so quick. But hear the score now. Two weeks later the Brother them take up them Sunday newspaper and start read. Big headline.

'*My Sojourn Among the Rastafarian.*' The evening newspaper take it up big-big too, '*A Journey to the Underworld*', even the weekly newspaper have it up big-big in their woman's page, '*Spinster Risks Life for Knowledge*'. Miss Mollypols was a hero. When June come and they publish the Queen's Birthday Honours list, what you know? Miss Mollypols head the list among the women honoured. Not long after that the evening newspaper carry the life-story of Miss Mollypols, discounting the scandalous rumour that was going abroad that all her friends desert her, for, although admiring her courage, they all claim that it was a hell of a way to get a M.B.E.

And so their voices swelled with joy. They spoke against themselves. They laughed with the tinkling painlessness of bliss. It was their movements that so fascinated Brother Solomon as he stood by his window looking out at them—the dignity of it, the gracefulness of it all, the sheer waiting beauty of every turn, every little glide and start that made each instant joy. Oh, their movements and their bliss were the minds of the surface of evening streams beneath the nimble trembling of moon-drenched trees.

But they were above it all. They felt. They knew. Only the expectancy of the moment filled their souls.

21

AND the night was dark too. Hardly a star in the sky. Strange, though. There was no sign of rain. No thick, heavy black clouds. Just a vast dark dome.

And the drums were beating low-low. The drummer had not the heart to touch off the merry thrill of the kettle-drum. The songs they sung were those with the sad, unending notes. How their faces all bled with grief. The lips hardly moved and the white teeth did not glimmer. The dark faces hung down in a sidelong droop. The eyes now rarely shone with ecstasy, when they did it was only through the melting of their tears. All dressed in black. All parched with agony for the service that would be the last.

But why did he have to go? Was it the hands of God that drew him from them? If so, what was the sin so great they had committed? He was their life. He made them want to live. He made it possible for them to scrub the floors, to cook the food, to bear the everlasting insult that was their working life. Only he gave it meaning. Only with him could they continue. So why should God want to take away their Shepherd from them?

Or was it the work of Lucifer? In the pinnacle of good there is the working of evil. So Shepherd himself always said. And so it must be with him now. What else could be so cruel?

They looked at her. They always had their eyes on her. Shepherd said she was the chosen one. He should know. They would like not to hate her. For Shepherd's sake they would wish even to love her. But how could they? Things had begun to change from the time she had come. Now Shepherd wanted to go with her to backra land. Why should he want to leave his flock behind for one stray sheep? But she was more than a stray sheep. No. They must not think that. For Shepherd's sake they would try not to despise her.

The church was packed. All the Daughters of the First and Second Orders, the Armour-Bearers, the Water Mother and other dignitaries were present. Sammy, the garbage-man, had come when the missis told him that the Shepherd and the chosen one would be having their last service. The Elder Mother was dressed in full black. She stood steadfastly on the platform beside the front door, her folded arms just a foot from the switch for the electric light.

They were breaking the bread now. And they were eating. It was difficult to chew. Their sadness almost choked them. And then they drank the wine. One by one. The tears often dropping into the mug. They trembled with woe. The spirit did not take them. Nor Gabriel nor Miriam nor Michael. For their soul was a blunted stupor and the door was shut. Nor did they speak in the unknown tongues. For who could understand? The tongue must convey meaning. And what could they say with an empty soul?

It was his turn. He broke the bread. He ate. Then he took up the mug. Slowly he raised it to his head. It touched his lips.

Suddenly the lights went out.

There was a murmur, then a fearful silence. Dinah stood up on the platform beside the Shepherd. A shadow loomed by her. Then there was a wild, ghastly, gurgling scream. Something fell. Dinah remained petrified where she was, too overwhelmed by the suddenness of everything. Too shocked with the premonition of what had happened. Suddenly she felt a hand clasp her own. The handle of something was placed in her palm. She wanted to scream out, but was too frightened. Involuntarily her fingers folded around the thing in her palm.

Then the lights came on. There was a long heinous pause. Their eyes all gaped with terror at the sight on the platform. Shepherd was lying there. Blood all over his face. Blood down his neck. Blood all soaked through his chest and everywhere around him. And through the side of his neck a deep, dark, purple gush.

The Elder Mother was the first to speak.

'Look!' she cried, pointing to Dinah.

They turned their eyes on her. They burst out screaming. Then it was that Dinah realized what she held in her hand. It was a long butcher's knife. The blade was now completely red with his blood. The blood of the Shepherd was dropping from the blade. One by one. She stared at what she held, aghast. She wanted to let it go. She could not. She wanted to scream. She could not.

And they were coming. Their eyes were wild and frightening and they were fixed on her. And they were coming closer. In a semicircle. They were moving closer, engulfing her.

The knife dropped from her hand. The voice burst out loud and shrill. She brought her fingers to her lips and shrunk away from the red sight on the floor.

Now they were all around her. She could see their eyes. She could hear the panting of their breath. She shuddered under their slow, crab-like movement. Closing in. She sought the exit. But the Elder Mother was there. Christ Almighty. Large, monstrous, black and powerful. She rushed back into them.

Then they all burst out screaming again. They dashed in upon her. They ripped the clothes from her. They bashed her head against the floor. They ripped the hair in large chunks from her scalp. Fingernails clawed her. Teeth fastened down around her ear and ripped it half apart. More teeth upon her belly. Upon her back. Then deep into her breast they sunk. A head jerked sidewards and the breast ripped out from the base of her chest. They kicked her. They pinched her. They spat upon her. She begged. She winced and turned and screamed. But there was no mercy. There could be no mercy.

Suddenly a voice screamed, 'Police!' Some of them ran off. A male figure crashed his way through them. It was Sammy. He fought and kicked his way through until he finally reached her. Then he grabbed her up. He ran for the front door and kicked away the Elder Mother.

Outside into the night he ran with her. Out of the cacti. Then down through the narrow lanes. The life was still in her. He felt her struggling to get loose.

She had to get back. She knew she had to get back. There was no longer pain, for there was too much for her to feel. The life was almost gone. But she knew she had to be back there in the

Dungle. She knew she had to taste the filth again. She knew he would be there waiting for her.

With a mighty effort she struggled out of his arms. He was too tired to catch her. He stood amazed at her strength, all soaked with her blood.

'Dinah,' he shouted, 'don' be afraid o' me. I will tek care o' you. Dinah, is me. Yu don' remember me? Is me, Sammy, de garbage-man!' He started trotting after her. But she was soon lost in the dark, narrow little lanes. He suddenly became over-whelmed with despair. Everything burst inside of him. He was still panting. He was still trotting. Then he slipped upon the slime of the gutter and fell upon the asphalt. He burst into tears, hiding his face between the circle of his hands upon the cold solid tar. And he kept calling after her between his sobbing, knowing she was long gone, not really caring for her answer any more, for suddenly in the moment on the tar the realization that there never could be an answer crashed down upon him mercilessly. Yet his voice kept crying in the night repeatedly, purposelessly, 'Dinah, stop, Dinah, is me, is Sammy, de garbage-man, de garbage-man, de garbage . . . man. . . .'

22

THE knocking on his door grew louder and louder. 'Brother Solomon! Brother Solomon! Open up, dis is urgent!' He continued to lie on his back staring through the little window upon the vast emptiness of the sky. The knocking persisted and eventually his senses stirred him out of his reverie. He got up, walked slowly towards the door and opened it.

The three of them hurried in. Their faces were rigid with concern. Brother Ezeikel, tall, with his pointed beard, no longer possessed his serene look of confidence. His large red handker- chief kept moving from his pocket to his face, from which a seemingly endless stream of perspiration flowed. Brother John kept repeating 'Land of Midnight and t'under', as was his habit in the face of crisis, and Brother Simon could only walk from one end of the room to the other cursing beneath his breath, 'Sons of Babylon, those treacherous sons of Babylon.'

Brother Solomon stared at them, reading their thoughts. The faintest shadow of a smile crossed his face.

'Calm down, me Brother,' he urged. 'What is the problem?'

'What is de problem?' Brother Ezeikel repeated, with the handkerchief now permanently attached to his forehead. 'Yu don' hear 'bout de letter dat those two son of a bitches dat we sen' as delegates write back?'

'Ah hear dat a letter did arrive, but ah don' hear what it say yet.'

'It say dat de whole delegation was a flop. Dat de only person they manage to see in Ethiopia was some subordinate official in de public-relations department. Nobody in Ethiopia seem to tek dem seriously. Dat las' letter dat they write 'bout seeing de Emperor was jus' a pack a damn' lie.'

'An' to add insult to injury,' Brother John put in, 'they declare dat they not coming back. They staying in Ethiopia on our money. Fire an' brimstone shall consume those dogs. Those sons of Sodom, those, those——' He broke short. It was the first time that Brother John had ever found himself at a loss for words.

'Yu can't blame them,' Brother Solomon said with calm indulgence. 'Ah guess any of us would do the same.'

'Can't blame dem, yu say? Holy Emperor, yu realize de hell dat dem put we in now? How we goin' to explain to dem hundreds a people dat no ship not coming fo' dem? How we goin' to explain to dem dat it was all a big lie, dat they been tricked by those two stinking traitors we sen' as delegates?'

'Those people outside not tricked, Brother Ezeikel, an' even if they were it wasn't the delegates who responsible.'

'I don' know what yu mean dat dem not tricked. But if is not those worthless bastards den is who is responsible?'

'It is I, Brother, it is I.'

'You?' Brother Ezeikel gave a confused, suspicious glance at Brother Solomon, then looked at Brother Simon.

'What yu mean, you?' Brother Simon enquired, his heavy, black wrinkles coming together in a frown.

'I made up that letter. It wasn't the delegates that write it. I invent everything about the ship coming. It was necessary.'

The three men stared at one another in amazement, then all turned towards Brother Solomon.

'But, but how yu could do a crazy t'ing like dat. They will murder yu when they find out,' Brother John said.

'But you of all people,' Brother Simon's voice was pained with astonishment. 'They respec' yu, they worship yu, how yu could tek dem an' mek dem such a set a fools? How yu could conspire to make dem hate an' lose all de respec' they 'ave fo' yu like dat?'

' 'Ow yu could do it? 'Ow yu could do it?' was all Brother Ezeikel could repeat.

Brother Solomon was not listening to them. Instead he stared outside up at the sky. At length, in a voice which was not meant for them, he said: 'The sky is so empty tonight, Brother.

So empty. Never saw it so empty before. It never turn me round so much with nothing as tonight.'

The men glanced quickly at one another again. Then they looked uncertainly at Brother Solomon. He wasn't acting too right.

'But what de sky got to do wid all dis. Yu don' seem to realize dat we life in danger,' Brother Simon said.

'Yu mean his life,' Brother John quickly corrected him.

'Say something, Brother Solomon. These people waiting to go to heaven. What yu goin' to tell dem? Where is de heaven dat yu promise dem?'

'Speak not of heaven, Brother Ezeikel, but of hell; the thought of eternal bliss is a thousand times more frightening than all the brimstone you can give me. Man's soul was made for torture, Brother.'

'An' fo' peace too, Brother Solomon, for peace an' love; it is not wise to provoke the wrath an' hate of your brother man,' Brother Simon interjected.

'Ah yes, Brother, perhaps so. But the peace I know is not the peace that is an end. The only peace I know is the peace that come from overcoming misery. Whatever I do misery must always be present. The moment I conquer misery is the moment it conquers me. For I is man.'

'Listen, Brother Solomon, you don' seem to realize the urgency of the situation.'

Brother John was beginning to lose his self-control, but Brother Solomon, still half to himself, his eyes still lost on the vast blue void, interjected: 'What situation yu speak of, Brother? The only situation I know is life. The only other situation I can conceive of is death, an' in that I can see no urgency. This is one of the luxuries of poverty, Brother. There is no urgency. This we share with the very rich. Only the rotten rich or the desperately poor can truly contemplate the act of suicide.'

'Suicide!' Brother John exclaimed.

The three men rushed towards him.

'Now listen, Brother,' Brother Ezeikel said, holding him by the hand and looking around at his face, 'we don' know why yu did all dis. Ah guess yu 'ad yu reason. Ah know dat yu 'ave de wisdom of de 'oly Emperor in yu. Perhaps dis is your way to tes' we faith. Well, whatever it is, we will stan' by yu. Don' talk 'bout any suicide. But ah t'ink it wise if we get out ah de way till de disappointment cool down in dem. You don' need to talk 'bout any suicide. We will stan' by yu. Don't it, Brothers?'

There was an uncertain silence. Then Brother Simon said gingerly, 'Yes, but there mus' be a period of absence; we mus' leave now an' arrange for some kind of explanation.'

But Brother Solomon had drifted even farther from them. The dark-blue void still ensnared him.

'All the others are accidents, Brother, the result of an un-thinking moment. It is only the idle rich and the desperately poor who can sit down and contemplate the act of suicide and then decide to do it. Only we can see that suicide is the supreme reason. Only we have searched for the meaning and could not find it. The rich are those who've had all they want to have. They're few. You can neglect them. And in any case they have a way of hiding their knowledge even from themselves. It is the desperately poor that are many. It is only we who see the dreary circle going round and round.'

The three men were now completely confused as to what they should do. They were not quite certain whether Brother Solomon spoke under the influence of the Holy Emperor or whether he was beginning to go off his head. In either case, they realized that they couldn't leave him just like that. Brother Ezeikel tried once again to plead with him. 'Listen, Brother, you can't build up a man hopes an' then shatter them an' expec' them to listen to argument, even if it come from the divine. Those poor wretched people outside there been thinking of heaven fo' the past two weeks. I sugges' dat we arrange to tell them right now that the day of repatriation is put off. We can find some reason. But we mustn't delay any longer or hell goin' break loose tomorrow.'

They gathered closer around Brother Solomon, waiting for his reaction. Their faces brightened a little as his eyes moved from the sky. For the first time since they had arrived he seemed to be aware of their presence. He walked over closer to the window and looked out at the waiting cultists with their eyes all glued on the dark horizon. Then he turned towards the three men. A deep smile cut across his face.

'They are not just poor an' wretched people, Brothers. How you could say a thing as simple as that?'

'Then what else them is?' Brother John's voice broke in impatiently.

'They are gods. You can't see? Every wretched one of them is an archetype of the clown-man, playing their part upon the comic stage so well they are no longer conscious of playing. You can't see, Brothers? Every one of them is a living symbol full of meaning and revelation. Look! They have before them one hour, two hours, five, no twelve, before the ship come. Twelve hours of unreality. Twelve hours of happiness. Who else but the gods could enjoy such happiness? For the moment they are conquerors. For the moment they have cheated the dreary circle. And it's only the moment that counts.'

'Dis is crazy,' Brother Simon said. 'We not goin' to plead wid you much longer. Wisdom or no wisdom, dis is no time to meditate on life.'

'Life,' Brother Solomon repeated, and he had half retreated from them again. 'Life, you say, Brother. You speak of the long, comic repetition, don't it, Brother? But you don't fool yourself that it's only them that's tried; that have their hopes raised an' then shattered only to start again. No, Brother, no. They you see outside are just the gods that make plain by magnitude what ordinary mortals fear to face and run from. Everywhere, in everything, there is the comedy you see before you now, Brother. You eat to satisfy your hunger only that you can get hungry again, Brother. You roll upon your naked woman and satisfy your lust only that you can come again to her. You fool yourself into believing that deep down in you there is a hidden god, something real, something meaningful. You search and search. You're on the point of reaching, or you think you are. Then, crash! The mirage vanish and you're all alone in the wild and barren desert. This is the greatest comedy, Brother. At least you satisfy your hunger in your craving to be hungry again; at least there is some satisfaction as you fall off the belly of your woman, you have at least the knowledge that you believe you felt something. But with your inner striving, Brother, there is the complete comedy, for when the mirage vanish you have not just the agony of your own thirst still unquenched but the added agony of knowing that the mirage was always unreal. Hear me, Brother, to seek after God, to seek for some meaning, some essence, is unreality twice times over.'

'For God sake, Brother Solomon, how much you goin' tes' we patience? We 'ave to go. This is no time to philosophize. We worrying 'bout your neck, man.'

'But, Brother, what else you think philosophizing is except worrying 'bout our neck? Or perhaps, better, worrying about whether our neck is worth worrying about? Leave me with my happy gods, Brother. I'll be all right, don't worry. By looking and being with them perhaps I'll share a little of their joy. Perhaps I shall bow down and worship them, 'cause they're gods. They're gods, I tell you. Isn't it strange, Brother, how wretchedness and despair can make gods of men? Don't worry. They shall never have cause to belch their rage on me. Go now. Please. Keep running. You must keep running. The track is rough and round, but you must keep running. I must stop. I'm so tired.'

They lingered on in despair. He had fallen upon his back on the bed, his wide, black eyes fixed upon the frame of dark-blue nothingness. So they could only depart.

23

T̲HE life had almost completely gone. But still she kept
running. She staggered against the walls of the piazza.
She bounced against the lamp-posts. But on. She must.
Not even death could keep her back.

Her blood spattered the sidewalk. It smeared the glass
windows of the big department stores, it fell upon the large
chromed cars and on the donkey-carts.

They stopped and stared after her as she passed by them.
They pointed. They shouted and they laughed. But she could
only keep running. Past the roaring rhythm of the sound-
system dances; past the rum-bars; past the gambling houses;
past the whore houses. Across the Spanish Town Road. Down
the Industrial Terrace. She was almost there now. She heard
them where they crowded around the burst hydrant. Vaguely,
she could just recognize the little kerosine lamps in the
distance.

Nearer and nearer. Her senses were now almost gone. She
neither thought nor felt. She was only an impulse. Pulling.
Dragging.

At last. She struggled across the Marcus Garvey Drive. She
fell as she tried to move up the mound. She tried desperately to
pull herself up. She crawled. The breast was now almost
completely ripped off. It dragged on beside her as she made her
way up the mound. She was almost there. She knew he would
be waiting for her. . . .

He stood upon the chair facing the window. Then he
fastened the noose around his neck. He could see everything

now. The whole extent of the sky. Every one of them. He stared at their dark silhouettes, the peak of their beards all pointing to the sea. Their little bundles were by their sides. The olive oil that they would balm themselves with so as not to defile the holy land. The robes, the long flowing white robes they would begin to wear as soon as they landed.

Only Cyrus was not staring out at the sea. Brother Solomon looked down at him as he stood by his doorway, praying to the Holy Emperor to bring back his queen so he could take her home with him.

He took one last look around the little room. The candle. The incense. The table. The bed. Things. But they were so odd. They all seemed to stare up at him from some deep bottomless pit. They were so still. Yet in their stillness there was something laughable. It was so farcical. Why the dreariness? Why the silence? Were they trying to overawe him with their stillness? His eye fell upon the writing on the wall. The *Sic Vitae*. His mind ran through the last section of the sonnet:

> *The wind blows out, the bubble dies;*
> *The spring entombed in autumn lies;*
> *The dew dries up, the star is shot.*
> *The flight is past—and man forgot.*

How ridiculous, he thought. How stupid the person who wrote those lines must have been. Did not the fool see that even in the expression of his despair he was fooling himself that the whole thing could be taken seriously?

Then he looked back outside. She was there! She had just fallen at his feet and he was taking her up in his arms. Look! He was balming her down with the olive oil and putting her breast in place. All was happiness now. Everything was ready and perfect.

He looked up at the sky. He could hold himself back no longer. He burst out laughing. It was a deep, wild, soul-consuming laugh. It mocked the shanties and hovels in front of him. It derided the many mounds of filth. Far, far into the night it could be heard. Even the sea could not escape it. It reached out for the very sky, so vast, so dark, so stupid, it jeered and jeered and jeered.

He was convulsed. His eyes were wet and his throat swelled beneath the rope with his mocking spasm. He kicked the chair from beneath his feet. The rope tightened. The laughter gurgled up. His tongue pitched out and his eyes mocked the vast blue void with a wild, bulging, fantastic stare.

He finished wiping the blood from her body with the olive oil. His heart had been full and bitter at first. But then, on the morrow would not the holy ship be coming for them? Could not the spirit of the Holy Emperor bring her back to life. Babylon was wicked. He had never realized it could be so wicked. But, no matter what they did, there was nothing which the Holy Emperor could not repair. He made all things; he destroyed all things; and he could remake all things.

And so he kissed her gently on her lips. He said a short prayer for her. 'Tomorrow,' he whispered over her with all the deep fervour of his faith. 'Tomorrow we shall meet again in paradise.'